Praise for
AN UNLIKELY PROSPECT

"If only today's legacy publishers had Sandy Zimmer's steel in the face of lies and injustice."

—Gretchen Cherington, author of *The Butcher, the Embezzler, and the Fall Guy*

"Speaks with power and purpose on the perpetual struggle for women to be respected leaders in a male-dominated world. Masterful, believable, and riveting."

—Debra Thomas, author of *Luz*

"Sandy Zimmer faces an untenable challenge—to confront the powerful in favor of the vulnerable, when she has so little likelihood of winning, or cave to the establishment she desperately desires to lead. Zimmer's is the challenge we will all face one day, and she gives us hope we can do it."

—Ashley E. Sweeney, author of *The Irish Girl*

Praise for
POSTER GIRL

"Lively prose, enjoyably edgy dialogue, and a delightful, unconventional, feminist heroine add up to a captivating page turner."

—*Kirkus Reviews*

"Fans of Tracy Chevalier and Kate Atkinson will love being immersed in the detail-driven historical atmosphere, while hard boiled mystery fans will thoroughly enjoy being led by our whip-smart and street-savvy heroine through the maze of clues leading to a shocking final plot twist."

—*Chicago Book Review*, 5 stars

"Aficionados of historical fiction and the Jane Benjamin series will be delighted…The novel is an excellent read, with sympathetic characters and set in a place and time that leaps off the page."

-*San Francisco Review of Books*

Praise for
TOM BOY

"The heroine we need, the heroine we wish we were—determined, tough as hell, utterly loveable. This propulsive novel was a lot of danged fun!"

—Elizabeth Gonzalez James, author of *The Bullet Swallower*

"A spirited feminist noir that flips femme fatale and private dick archetypes on their heads."

—Anita Felicelli, author of *Chimerica*

"Combining the feminist can-do of Phryne Fisher and the snarky commentary of Veronica Mars, Jane Benjamin is a boatload of fun."

—Halley Sutton, author of *The Hurricane Blonde*

Praise for
COPY BOY

"Raymond Chandler for feminists."

—Sharma Shields, author of *The Cassandra*

"A rewarding historical novel with a ferocious, fascinating lead."

—*Forward Clarion Review*

"A stellar debut….Deftly plotted and expertly executed. Highly recommended."

—Sheldon Siegel, *New York Times* best-selling author of the Mike Daley/Rosie Fernandez novels

AN UNLIKELY PROSPECT

AN UNLIKELY PROSPECT

A World War II Novel

SHELLEY BLANTON-STROUD

SHE WRITES PRESS

Copyright © 2025 Shelley Blanton-Stroud

All rights reserved. No part of this publication may be reproduced, distributed, or transmitted in any form or by any means, including photocopying, recording, digital scanning, or other electronic or mechanical methods, without the prior written permission of the publisher, except in the case of brief quotations embodied in critical reviews and certain other noncommercial uses permitted by copyright law. For permission requests, please address She Writes Press.

Published 2025
Printed in the United States of America
Print ISBN: 978-1-64742-946-1
E-ISBN: 978-1-64742-947-8
Library of Congress Control Number: 2025907929

For information, address:
She Writes Press
1569 Solano Ave #546
Berkeley, CA 94707

Interior design by Stacey Aaronson

She Writes Press is a division of SparkPoint Studio, LLC.

Company and/or product names that are trade names, logos, trademarks, and/or registered trademarks of third parties are the property of their respective owners and are used in this book for purposes of identification and information only under the Fair Use Doctrine.

This is a work of fiction. Names, characters, places, and incidents either are the product of the author's imagination or are used fictitiously. Any resemblance to actual persons, living or dead, is entirely coincidental.

NO AI TRAINING: Without in any way limiting the author's [and publisher's] exclusive rights under copyright, any use of this publication to "train" generative artificial intelligence (AI) technologies to generate text is expressly prohibited. The author reserves all rights to license uses of this work for generative AI training and development of machine learning language models.

To Andy, my first and best reader.

"A good newspaper is a nation talking to itself."
—ARTHUR MILLER

"Power has no sex."
—KATHARINE GRAHAM

"The past is written on my body. I carry it every single day. The past sometimes feels like it might kill me. It is a very heavy burden."
—ROXANE GAY

CHAPTER ONE

Renee Taylor

From "Remarks on the Fiftieth Anniversary of V-J Day"

SAN FRANCISCO, CALIFORNIA
August 14, 1995

It was raucous. Air raid sirens. Car horns. Factory whistles. Church bells. All burst into clanging song when President Truman broadcast Japan's unconditional surrender. Minutes later, Market Street was a hullabaloo, everybody streaming out of buses, trains, department stores, insurance offices, and apartment buildings, onto the city's main street, where we romped and drained bottles, our hoarse cheers echoing through downtown's brick, stone, and asphalt canyons. In our factory clothes, we jitterbugged with crazy sailors who wouldn't be boarding Pacific-bound ships after all. These boys weren't going to die.

It was like a huge rubber band had been stretched too far, and then finally snapped back from the day almost four years before, when Japanese fighter planes and torpedo bombers surprise-attacked Pearl Harbor, dropping explosives that sank or damaged nearly every battleship in the Pacific Fleet, killing thousands of US sailors, soldiers, marines, airmen, and civilians, both men and women, wounding thousands more, forcing us to join the rest of the world in four years of bloody battle and total reinvention at work and at home, turning us into a country that could build the atomic bomb and then drop it on Hiroshima and Nagasaki. On their people.

But now all that was over. We could finally go back to normal life.
At least that's what we thought.
We were wrong.
Because you can never just walk back to some supposedly perfect point in the past. History doesn't move that way. It advances in multiple directions, each new unpredictable branch careening us down unmarked side streets and alleys, making it impossible for us to remember exactly where we started, much less how we might get back to that place that no longer exists, maybe never really did exist, except in our imagination.

CHAPTER TWO

Itty-Bitty Sandy

August 14, 1945

Yes, World War II had ended that day, but not for Sandy Zimmer.

She perched on her late husband Edward's high-back executive chair, the toes of her calf leather pumps barely grazing the floor beneath his grand piano–sized desk.

She'd spent countless hours in this office as Edward's secretary before they were married, listening to him go on about circulation numbers, ad revenue, and headline options. He'd always included her in his thinking about important tasks, mostly, she figured, because he liked being close to her. Or maybe he just liked thinking out loud, finding confidence in the sound of his voice with her as its audience.

The pages of a contract she was meant to sign lay before her, unread but smudged by a leaky pen—a mark of her passive aggression against the constant flow of decisions she was expected to rubber-stamp (but not influence) on behalf of Edward's flailing twice-daily newspaper, the *San Francisco Prospect*.

As his secretary, she used to watch him execute piles of planning documents. She'd nearly swooned at his decisiveness. Now, faced with minor versions of the same tasks, she felt inert, stuck between her desire to honor Edward and her own growing doubts about the *Prospect* and her ability to run it.

On the night before she dispatched Edward in a mahogany casket to a view plot at Cypress Lawn Memorial Park, Sandy learned he'd left her his ownership shares of the Zimmer Consortium of newspapers. She would be publisher and 35 percent owner. On the surface of things, anyway. She'd spent the past three years since he died trying, and failing, to fulfill this obligation.

Even as Edward's last mourner exited his high society funeral brunch, Wyatt Zimmer, Edward's father and *Prospect* board member, informed her they would need to sell the consortium's Cincinnati, Charleston, Springfield, and Dallas papers, everything but the *San Francisco Prospect*.

"We have no choice. We've got to streamline this company," he said. "Evaluate our holdings, divest every paper that's underperforming." Wyatt had spoken like a banker, though he wasn't a banker. He was the grandson and great-grandson of bankers who had made their fortunes off risk-taking 49ers swarming the city with gold-filled pockets. Just a few generations later, Wyatt was clean and polished, with less of his forebears' visible grit but all of their remaining money. Edward had told Sandy his father had never held a proper job. He just managed the family residuals.

Though Edward had appointed both Wyatt and his mother Olive to the *Prospect* board when he purchased the consortium, hoping in vain to win their approval, Wyatt constantly insulted Edward's business, the purchase of which he considered ill-advised, a vanity project. The newspaper world was too sordid, Wyatt said. He'd declined to invest his own inherited money into the *Prospect*, to Edward's everlasting humiliation. And where Wyatt led, Olive followed.

Yet Wyatt seemed to relish the role he'd commandeered at the *Prospect* after Edward's death—overseeing the paper's finances, managing relationships with advertisers and other commercial partners, cultivating connections with businesses, civic leaders, and influential community members. Sandy could tell he found this work tremendously gratifying as it elevated his role among the San Francisco upper crust. She had supported Wyatt in doing this work, first because it made him happy—and she wanted to make her father-in-law happy, wanted to be the one who accomplished that—

but also because she'd found herself so full of grief over Edward's passing and all that came with it that she could never have stepped in immediately to take charge of such business herself.

The *Prospect*'s board generally accepted Wyatt's maneuvers, since their alternative would have been to truly accept Sandy as the publisher, which they agreed in quiet conversations that Edward's will had firmly, legally, recklessly established—a twenty-nine-year-old woman publisher, who'd never held a single executive position anywhere. She was just a pretty secretary.

So, though Sandy was officially publisher, she had spent the past three years essentially reinhabiting her old secretarial role, this time on behalf of her father-in-law, who diligently went about the messy project of selling off pieces of Edward's consortium, everything but Edward's favorite, the *San Francisco Prospect*. Sandy was so busy helping Wyatt with this taking out of the trash that she scarcely had time to consider a publisher's other roles—guiding the paper's writers, ensuring the paper met its quality standards, fostering her preferred newsroom culture, or setting the paper's editorial vision.

The *Prospect*'s editor-in-chief, H. R. MacDonald, Mac, had worked hard to absorb a lot of this work on Sandy's behalf, not even consulting her about today's special edition headline—Peace! Japan Surrenders! War Is Over! But it was next to impossible for him to do so much of her work and his own job too, and the effort had created a tension between them. Mac resented the expanded workload without a new title, power, and paycheck to go along with it, and Sandy resented Mac for resenting her.

Things weren't prospering at the *Prospect*.

More readers and advertisers were jumping ship every day. This last of Edward's papers was sinking, imminently vulnerable to circling pirates, which Sandy had begun to suspect might be what Wyatt intended, and maybe what the rest of the board intended too, so long as the purchase price was high enough.

As Sandy brooded over all this, she felt Edward watching from dozens of framed photographs lining the walls around her, pictures in which he looked utterly at ease among famous men—mayors, athletes, industrialists, movie stars, presidents. With his wavy sable hair, angular jaw, and roguish Clark Gable charm, he'd made a dazzling figure in the newspaper world. When he died at forty-five of a heart attack, he'd left her behind, a young bride who hadn't even managed to deliver a baby, though she'd come close. Very close. Three times she'd conceived, and three times the pregnancy had failed. Edward said she shouldn't use that word, *failed*. It didn't apply here, he said. It wasn't her fault. She should relax and not think about it so much. Everything would work out the way it was supposed to work out.

She appreciated that kindness. It was part of why she loved him. But she didn't believe him. She had failed to deliver a baby. And now Edward was gone and she was alone.

Sandy's green eyes lingered on a particular photo of Edward at his desk, his crisp white shirtsleeves rolled up to the elbows as he pored over galley proofs. She'd spent many late nights by his side, watching him work tirelessly to keep the *Prospect* afloat. To be honest, often enough, she'd also jumped in to help, sometimes making a real difference. But it was always as a helper, never as any kind of leader, she thought.

Edward loomed large for everybody at the *Prospect*. Despite the challenges he'd faced, including his own parents' disapproval, he had planned to leave a lasting mark on the world. He'd imbued his paper with purpose. He loved those aspects of work that involved shaping its coverage, its editorial voice. Now Sandy found herself grappling with the legacy of this man who'd married her and then unceremoniously died, leaving her all alone with his paper and his parents.

The corner office was supposed to be Sandy's, but this wasn't really her chair, her desk, her office, or her newspaper. It was still 100 percent Edward's. Just ask anybody who mattered. Like the editors, the reporters, her in-laws, and the rest of the board. The day she'd first walked into this office as the *Prospect*'s new publisher, the newsroom silence had been deafening. She'd stood there, frozen, overwhelmed by the shift from secretarial desk, to matrimonial bed, to corner office.

She recalled an afternoon in this office a little over three years ago, Edward's hands warm and possessive on the small of her back. "One day, this will be all yours, Itty-Bitty," he'd said, flirtatious. Sandy had snorted adorably, knowing how absurd that was—she was no newspaper magnate—and suspecting the comment related to his appreciation for their morning connubial shenanigans.

Had he really believed she could do this, or had he simply been caught up in a moment, flush with love and optimism? Now Sandy found herself second-guessing their every conversation, wondering if she'd missed some crucial lesson he'd tried to teach her.

She'd tried to prepare herself for the world of work, graduating from the Katharine Gibbs Secretarial School in New York, where she'd honed diverse practical skills. As Edward's secretary—her first job after school—she'd excelled at anticipating his needs, occasionally bending pointless rules to get important things done expediently.

Once, when Edward had been about to lose a major advertiser due to a scheduling mix-up, Sandy had stayed late, rearranging appointments and smoothing ruffled feathers with a combination of charm and efficiency. By morning, she'd not only saved the account but also secured an increase in their ad buy. Edward had been thrilled, praising her quick thinking and persuasive skills. "You're a miracle worker, Bitty," he'd said, his eyes shining with relief.

But in her transition from Edward's charming, capable secretary, to his loyal wife, to the widowed publisher of a major newspaper, she'd found the skills that had served her so well before now seemed ridiculously inadequate. She didn't know the world of finance as Wyatt did, and she got no practice at the other parts of her job, since Mac's generous help took care of that for her. Sometimes she longed for the simpler days of taking dictation and managing Edward's calendar. Back then, success was clearly defined, achievement easily measured, hard work regularly rewarded. Now, every minor decision felt like a potential misstep, a possible betrayal of Edward's vision.

She'd never pictured anything like this for herself. How could she?

She hadn't known even one woman who'd worked inside an executive office. It felt like a tremendous success just to escape her father's dim, Bensonhurst, Brooklyn apartment. She'd nursed him there for years as he lay dying, protecting him from the worries that piled up with the bills and the doctors' reports. Bad news paperwork was stacked amidst tissues, ointments, and capsules, and the schedules of their consumption. All that devotion leading to loss, only to loss. This had been her life before coming to the *Prospect*.

Working for Edward, solving his problems, cleaning up his messes, elevating his public persona, had seemed the height of success and pleasure to her. Now, sitting in this corner office, she felt guilty to be dissatisfied with this supposedly exalted position, which ironically asked so little of her.

She resented the obligation to sign documents all day, every day, endorsing the infinite plans made by her board and editor. "Yessir, yessir, yessir." She was such an obliging yes-girl. Maybe she should leave a trained parrot in her office to squawk "Yes" all day. Would anyone notice the difference?

She looked out her window at the V-J Day celebration on the street, weirdly disconnected from it, a mute observer caged by amorphous expectations. She was one of only three female publishers in the country. And the only one who'd gained her position solely by dint of both marriage and death.

If she were honest, her marriage itself was mostly made possible by the easy beauty she inherited from her long-absent mother, whom she knew only from wedding pictures on her father's dresser. He'd looked so average, forgettable, though with a humble warmth in his smile, while her mother looked glamorously ambitious, something in the tilting up of her chin, the arch of one eyebrow. Though her father never spoke of his wife's leaving, Sandy assumed it was her mother's desire for more than their dim little life that drove her west. At least that's where Sandy imagined her mother had gone, as west was the obvious direction of desire when a person was unhappy in New York.

Like her mother, Sandy had a petite, curvy figure, rounded cheeks, a sweet, pink mouth, and bouncing brown curls. But unlike her mother, there was nothing harsh or provocative about the way she looked, only cheerful, soothing, affirming. She appeared, and was, a woman skilled at helping a man achieve what he wanted, helping him *feel* the way he wanted. Edward had loved her for that. And left her everything as a result, she thought. Maybe she should put "Professional Man-Pleaser" on her business card.

She glanced at her desk, those interminable stacks, agreements her board had hammered out, loans they'd arranged, needing only her compliantly looping signature.

She slumped in Edward's chair, enervated.

Then the desktop telephone rang. She answered, "This is Sandy."

"I've got Mrs. Cissy Patterson on the line from DC, Mrs. Zimmer," chirped the switchboard operator.

Sandy flushed at the name of the editor and publisher of the *Washington Times-Herald*, the most widely read daily in the nation's capital.

Sandy felt like a finch compared to this hawk of a woman born into journalistic influence. Her grandfather, Joseph Medill, was the owner and editor of the *Chicago Tribune*, and her brother, Joseph Medill Patterson, founded the *New York Daily News*. Her family was bona fide, unlike Sandy's.

Despite that, even Cissy had apparently faced resistance when she took charge of her paper. Yet she'd persevered and turned skeptics to stone with her damning glare. *Collier's* magazine claimed she was the most powerful woman in the country, and the most hated. Sandy suspected these things were of necessity linked.

Cissy's voice rasped, "Got your champagne chilling, Sandy? War's over, and you and the *Prospect* are still standing after all. You ready to say yes now, finally?"

Sandy frowned. "No, Cissy, I'm not selling. You know I wouldn't do that to Edward." Her heart pulsed with loyalty.

"Eddie's dead, Sandy."

Sandy winced, as much at "Eddie" as at the idea of selling the newspaper.

"You've held down the fort. I expect it's heavier work than you care for."

It *was* a heavy load. How had Cissy done it, running her paper, as a woman? Sandy's doubts tumbled like a rubber ball down an apartment stairwell. The board didn't take her seriously. They'd pat her hand and tell her not to worry her pretty little head about circulation numbers. The reporters looked right through her in meetings, and the advertisers would ask to speak to a *real* executive.

"I'm not selling the *Prospect*, Cissy. It was Edward's baby." She winced at her own wording. She paused before taking a risk. "I thought maybe . . . We're in the same boat, aren't we? Two women trying to make it in a man's world. How did you handle it when they assumed your male deputy was really in charge? Or when they mistook you for the society page editor at press conferences?"

Sandy's cheeks flushed with the admission of her struggles but also with the warmth of hope, believing in her ability to connect with important people. Cissy would sympathize, would offer sage advice, her secret to commanding respect. After all, wasn't there a sort of unspoken sisterhood among women breaking barriers?

Silence.

Then came Cissy's gruff laugh. "You want to know what my great newspaper family told me when I said I was taking over this paper? They shared the Medill family motto—'When they rape your grandma, put her on the front page.'"

Sandy gasped. "Cissy, that's awful. That's just not—"

Cissy interrupted, "If you think that's awful, don't keep the paper. I'm not a woman. I'm a publisher. Nobody can tell you how to turn from one into the other. It's in you to do it or it's not. Maybe it's not in you. Why don't you find yourself somebody nice to kiss out on the street? And call me back when you're ready to sell. I may be your best offer."

The line went dead. Sandy held the receiver, her mouth in the shape of an *O*.

She replaced the telephone handset and slumped back in Edward's humongous chair, dangling her legs like a girl in a swing.

CHAPTER THREE

The Bullpen

Sandy's door flew open before she heard the knock. It was Mac, his face ruddy with excitement, yellow hair mussy. His just-contained energy made Sandy think of a mountain lion, muscular, powerful, maybe dangerous.

"Finally!" he said, wiping wet golden-brown eyes with the back of his forearm. "Ho, jeez, I see it's got to you too."

Sandy realized her cheeks were wet after her call with Cissy.

Mac stood only a couple yards away, apparently unsure whether he ought to hug his sniffling publisher on the day World War II had ended.

Her relations had been so different with Edward, their easy camaraderie, even from the beginning, before they were *them*. With Mac, there was always a tension, a reminder of her uncertain position. She wondered if that was true of how he felt, or just her assumption. *So paranoid*, she thought. And also strange, since she'd always felt in control with men. They'd generally treated her as a lovely sort of helpmate because she'd made them feel that way. It didn't seem to work with Mac.

"Well, yes, it's got to me too," Sandy agreed. "I hadn't realized how much. All this waiting and worrying, for so long." She used a hankie to blow her nose, and then tucked it back into the waist of her pencil skirt. "So what's the plan? You must have a plan."

Mac snapped his fingers and then pointed at Sandy. "Yes, ma'am. Yes

I do. I've got a lot of guys on the street, for the quotes and pictures. I've got Wally over at the Presidio, trying to find out what the brass have to say—what'll happen with the military presence here, all that. Fleming's with him, for pictures of guys in uniform, Shawn's at City Hall, of course, with everybody else, trying to get comments from the mayor. And you know Jane—she's out there getting the mood on Market, stuff for her column."

Sandy could picture Jane's gossip column already—champagne, crying mothers, kissing couples, singing sailors, all mashed together in Jane's patented swingy, irreverent but sentimental way. Readers would eat it up.

Over Mac's shoulder she saw an unfamiliar face in the bullpen, bellowing to a crowd around him. He was a swarthy, stocky man, his head block-shaped. *Distinctive*, she thought. *Not in a good way*. "What about the new guy?"

"Lambert? Yeah, Derek Lambert. He's not new, he's old. Worked here for a long time before you arrived. Left in a huff for New York after he and Jane had a dustup—I lured him back."

She raised her brow at that. Was Mac trying to start something with Jane, bringing in someone she'd sparred with?

"Lambert's opinionated. Says we're boring but we shouldn't get too gossipy to fix it, like the *Tattler*. Says we need more rigorous reporting but we shouldn't be stuffy like the *Times*. Apparently we're doing nothing right."

"And yet you lured him back on purpose?"

"Yeah, I know. But he has ideas."

"What's his beat?"

"Special investigation kind of guy. Likes digging under rocks, sneaky stuff, that type. He was on the Grete Wright murder story, in '37."

"Before my time. He does look unpleasant."

"Yeah, he's kind of a rat."

"Just what we need."

"But sometimes rats do good work."

Sandy rolled her eyes. "If they're a fella, I suppose."

"Well your best friend's a rat."

"Jane? Don't be ridiculous. She's not a rat." But of course, Jane *was* difficult. Unpredictable. Troublemaking. Also brilliant. Loyal. Brave. Funny. Definitely not a rat.

"I'll introduce you." Mac opened her door and called, "Hey, Lambert!"

Lambert turned and answered, "You rang?"

"Come on in, meet the publisher."

Lambert leered from a distance and then sauntered over, smoke circling his head. "Good afternoon, Mrs. Zimmer. Auspicious day for our meeting." He shook her hand with a cigarette still pinched between two fingers, a little ash dropping onto her knuckle. He grinned widely and winked at her. *Winking at his publisher.*

From her secretarial days she knew about some reporters' wandering eyes and hands. Like most of the office girls, Sandy had been groped in supply closets, elevators, even at desks in the bullpen, until Edward's affection put an end to all that. She knew the signals that kind of guy gave off. This one seemed to see her as fair game, maybe big game. She wasn't going to like this guy.

But still she said, "Nice to meet you, Derek."

"Please call me Lambert, ma'am. Lamb-Bear. Everybody does."

"Mr. Lambert, then."

Mac intervened. "Listen, Lambert. I want to talk to you about coverage. Go wait in my office." And he waved the reporter out.

Sandy thought, *Why not talk about it here, with me?* But she didn't say that.

Mac turned his attention back to Sandy.

"So, great. Now you've met him. I gotta get going. Don't worry about things you don't need to worry about. I'm taking care of it."

Sandy decided to smile at the condescension.

"I think the biggest story since Pearl Harbor may fall on the list of things a publisher ought to worry about," she answered.

He looked at her kindly, as if she were a child.

Mac was a good pal to Jane, in spite of his saying she was a rat, and Edward had always counted on him. Sandy herself absolutely relied on him now—after all, he was doing most of her job. But she didn't like to be belittled.

He rubbed his head like he was wiping out annoying thoughts. "You're right. This coverage should be on your list. We'll go over what the reporters turn up, and I'll hear what you're thinking in the morning."

But would he hear her? She wasn't sure she believed that.

"Now why don't you have your girl call your driver to take you home? It's loony tunes out there. And you've got that dinner. It's important."

"Mm-hmm." Sandy nodded. "That dinner." This was the kind of thing everybody liked her to worry about. "You'll be there, right? You promised."

Mac checked his watch. "I'll get things finished up here and try to come by."

"Try?" she asked.

"I'll be there," he said with a rakish smile, and bolted out the door.

CHAPTER FOUR

Back-Seat View

Edward never drove the Lincoln Zephyr sedan. He only got behind the wheel of his red convertible Duesenberg, which was basically Edward as a car. But the Lincoln? It was like he'd chosen it knowing Sandy would soon ride alone in its voluminous leather back seat, driven by Tommy Fitzgerald, who was hired by Edward, not Sandy. She slipped submissively inside the door Tommy held open.

When he got behind the wheel, Sandy considered Tommy in the rearview mirror, the skin beneath his eyes shaded under a deep awning of bushy salt-and-pepper brows.

"Streets are right packed, ma'am," he warned.

She saw him tugging oddly at something in the front seat.

"It can't be that bad, can it? It's a celebration, after all."

He muttered something and then growled.

"Are you alright, Tommy? Have you got indigestion?"

"Sorry, ma'am. It's this guy." He held up the ugliest little brindle pug she'd ever seen, with a disconcerting lopsided underbite. The smash-faced dog snuffled at Sandy. "Caught him running in the street, darting between the crazies. Didn't seem safe. No tags, neither."

Sandy wasn't a dog person. She'd never had one, and other people's dogs had always seemed dirty and unpredictable. They apparently pooped a lot too. But still, she thought it was sweet that Tommy had scooped him up, though he looked embarrassed to have done so now.

"I'll figure something out for him. Not the pound." Tommy set the dog down and put the car in gear. As they pulled away from the curb, he added, "Let's get you home, where it's safe."

Tommy had always been solicitous of her—taking her arm as she stepped out over a wet or leafy curb, waiting until she got inside a building before turning away.

"I'm going to learn to drive this behemoth myself. Then I can brave city streets on my own." Her chin lifted as she said this, a gesture of challenge left over from adolescence.

"What would Mr. Zimmer say if he heard that?"

"I expect his hearing's not that good."

Tommy chortled.

She remembered warmly the time before her father had fallen ill, when it seemed like he took care of her, rather than her taking care of him. So she appreciated Tommy, though she sometimes resisted his ministrations, occasionally even seeming a little petulant. She knew that was wrong, and she worked hard not to let that get out of control.

They turned left on Mission. The rambunctious crowd celebrating victory on the sidewalks had taken over the street. Sandy saw Tommy's knuckles whiten, gripping the steering wheel, as he tried to drive through all the people. The scene reminded her of a painting owned by one of Edward's friends. Who was it? He'd had so many collector friends. It was called *Fifth Avenue, New York*. She'd admired it hanging in the man's dining room, where it inspired a rollicking dinner conversation. This scene on the street was like that.

She said, "They're pretty rowdy."

"I drove an ambulance in the last war, ma'am."

"That's right." Wanting to insult neither his skill nor his manhood by looking nervous, she leaned against the seat back, closed her eyes, and said, "Edward loved to drive, really loved it, don't you think?"

"Yes, ma'am. Too fast sometimes. I tried to talk to him about that."

That was true. Edward had a vast collection of speeding tickets, but couldn't be persuaded to slow down. He was just in a hurry, always hurtling toward something just out of reach.

Tommy had also taken a caretaking role with Edward, sometimes doing or saying things that Edward might have liked Wyatt to do or say. It was nice of him. But it wasn't the same as your own father acting that way. Edward was such a confident man, which is what most people saw—his charisma, his creativity. People found him inspiring, everyone, that is, but his parents. That was a wound that never quite healed, reminding Edward that maybe he wasn't in fact equal to his aspirations. He was always trying to prove himself. Tommy's concern certainly hadn't been a solution to that, but Sandy thought at least it was a balm.

Just as Tommy accelerated past a stoplight, two men in navy uniforms ran singing in front of the car, one slapping his hand against the hood, seemingly oblivious to the danger of being hit.

The pug rose up, his paws against the glass, snarling at the men through the passenger window.

Sandy steadied her voice. "Tommy, what's our route?"

"I've got it." He didn't add his usual "ma'am."

But had he thought the route out fully, the way she would have, if she were at the wheel?

She closed her eyes, seeing how to get home without crossing Market through the revelers, a puzzle to focus on, rather than on the wildness outside her window.

No, it was impossible.

Then she thought, *What's the narrowest spot on Market, the easiest to cross?* She saw the Thomas Guide in her head. Saw the Lincoln heading north on Ninth to cross the narrowest slip of Market and go left onto Hayes. Then right onto Van Ness and north until they reached Washington. Take a left, and finally home—safe, on Steiner Street. She could picture what to do.

She opened her eyes and leaned forward to advise Tommy of the best path and saw the sheen of sweat on his forehead.

"Ma'am?"

"I was going to suggest . . ."

Tommy turned right on Ninth, heading just where she was about to direct him. She was glad she hadn't said anything.

As they approached the crossing at Ninth and Market, they slowed into the line of other cars trying to escape downtown. The people on the street flowed toward something, some leveling. Where would they stop? Would they dance right into the bay and end the night by swimming?

Tommy nosed the Lincoln onto Market. In a tight voice, he said, "It'll be alright."

The crowd fairly writhed all around them. After all this time, so much bad news, so much death, unthinkable horrors—now, finally, they had cause to release.

There was something in the electricity of that release that surprised her—it was an emotional shock.

It had been so long since Sandy felt unreservedly happy. Of course there was Edward's death and all the complications at the *Prospect* to explain it. But also, like everyone else, she'd been depressed by the seemingly endless war, as if everything were sealed with a skin of gray. When she got home from the office at night, even her beautiful apartment, her four-course meals, seemed tasteless to her.

She knew that people had managed to have fun in these war years, especially the young. That was the point of the USO dances, to keep up morale. There were still bars and parties, and sometimes she went along. But even those small offerings of joy had seemed too distant to her. It was like everyone had stifled their emotions for years, and only now were able to release them.

She gripped the back of Tommy's seat, looking through the big window.

"Be careful, Tommy." She couldn't stop herself from saying it, though she knew that he was careful, that he was afraid, maybe as much as she was. "We don't want to hurt anybody." She couldn't keep it in.

Tommy didn't answer. Just kept inching them forward through the surging crowd.

In the middle of the street, a young woman with red hair and a yellow dress threw her arms around the neck of a man whose suit jacket and tie were missing, having shed the normal layers. They were locked in a passionate kiss. Sandy remembered Edward kissing her in that way sometimes, as if he couldn't get enough, as if he wanted to consume her. She sighed.

Tommy veered a little to the left and beeped the horn to encourage them out of the street.

The pug jumped over the front seat into the back and onto Sandy's lap, yipping and snarling at the couple through the glass. They turned and laughed at the dog, not caring.

Tommy rolled down his window. "Get out of the way! For your own safety!" he yelled, and pushed on the gas, jerking forward, as celebrants moved away around them. Finally they emerged on the other side of Market, turning left on Hayes, leaving the couple behind.

Sandy turned to look out the back window, but the crowd had swallowed them up.

Now, outside, the noise had dimmed, and the crowds diminished, as they moved toward home.

Tommy exhaled a breath he seemed to have been holding forever.

"Sorry about that, ma'am. Wasn't sure everything was going to be alright for a minute there. Them running in the street like that."

"Thank you, Tommy. That was . . . just . . ." Sandy's face was hot. She petted the pug's dirty fur, making her hand sticky. Her fingers rubbed his chest, and she could feel the beat of his heart. Her own heart rate slowed as she did this.

"They acted like they weren't afraid at all, in the street like that, even with cars passing."

In the rearview mirror, Tommy's eyes darted between Sandy in the back seat and ahead to the road. "Too much to drink, I guess."

"I suppose so," she agreed. "Certainly that."

"All those women," Tommy went on. "It's not safe for a lady on these streets. They should stay home, where it's safe. Any night. But especially tonight."

Stay home—Sandy's stomach cramped. She shut her eyes.

As they escaped downtown, Sandy's thoughts settled on the hilly, scenic route through Pacific Heights, such a contrast to what they'd just seen.

The car turned and faced the silhouette of her apartment building at 2500 Steiner, rising proudly twelve stories above its neighboring mansions, with a front yard of Alta Plaza Park. White masonry walls gleamed in the late afternoon sun, its mission-style red-tiled crown contrasting against the sky. This was the first apartment building constructed in Pacific Heights, with the very highest penthouse in the city—Edward's penthouse. Her penthouse now.

Tommy parked the car and raced around to open her door.

She considered the pug, how warm he felt on her lap, how petting his plump belly felt good.

"I'll just take the dog in and get it some water," she said.

Tommy tipped his hat, sweat dripping down his cheek, and took the dog as she exited the car with her purse on her shoulder. She reclaimed the pug, carrying him under her arm, with her hand under his chin.

Under the building's dollar-green entry awning, the doorman swung the front doors open, looking with shock at the pug. "Mrs. Zimmer, may I keep him for you, in the below-ground quarters, until you take him home?"

The apartment building had a no-dog policy.

She did pause to consider his offer.

"No thank you, Mr. Olson. This is my dog now. This is his home."

CHAPTER FIVE

Sophisticated Lady

The sun threw its last slants of gold through a vast wall of windows into crystal goblets set on the table, bending light, casting rainbows on silky jade-papered walls and the large mirrors adorning them. The penthouse dining room was a testament to Edward's modern taste: a sleek, elongated table of high-gloss macassar ebony, surrounded by streamlined chairs upholstered in emerald velvet. A modern chandelier hung above, tiers of chrome and glass throwing light as well. Sometimes Sandy felt like she was living on a movie set.

She'd inherited so much from Edward. Everything, really: the cars, the apartment, the staff, the newspaper, her job, his family, their expectations. His parents, Wyatt and Olive, would be dining at this table this very night. *Ugh*. She wanted to please them but always seemed to fail—a constant source of stress.

"I should be grateful," she muttered. "I'm lucky, alive, much more than safe. By any sane accounting, I'm thriving." Yet the nagging feeling persisted. That the everything she had wasn't the everything she wanted. "Because I'm churlish," she added.

She put down the squirmy pug and he scrabbled off, his claws scratching the hardwood floors, back toward the penthouse foyer, his stocky body a chaos of motion.

As if on cue, the voice of Dumont, the butler, echoed from the foyer. "There is an *animal* urinating on the entry rug!"

Sandy suppressed a guilty smile as the pug barreled back into the dining room, unrepentant, skidding to a stop at Sandy's feet, his bulging eyes signaling disdain. He'd run right back to her, as if she were home base.

"Oh, you ugly gargoyle." Sandy reached down to scratch behind his wrinkled ears. "It's a small thing, Dumont," she called back, scooping up the pug despite his grumpy protests. They'd have to stash him somewhere before the guests arrived.

Head housekeeper, Mrs. Connelly, bustled into the dining room with a binder of dinner instructions. Her red hair was neatly pinned back, and despite being in her forties, she moved like a much younger woman. "Oh! Mrs. Zimmer, what is that?" She pointed at the dog.

"Tommy saved him from the street," Sandy explained.

"He's an awful ugly fella. Now it looks like it's you who . . ."

"We'll figure something out. I think his name is Wilford." That had come to her immediately. He looked like a Wilford.

Mrs. Connelly summoned a junior maid hired for the night's party. "Find a good place for the dog tonight." The girl giggled and took Wilford from Sandy, heading down the hall.

"Perfect night for your dinner, ma'am. Not a brighter view to be had," she said, her eyes approving Coit Tower, the Golden Gate, and the bay in between.

"Only the best for Edward," Sandy agreed, with just a hint of derision.

Mrs. Connelly caught the tone and looked surprised, as if her employer was a little off tonight.

The room filled with staff hired for the party, to collect their to-do lists from Mrs. Connelly's binder.

Sandy considered the wine glasses and called out to Dumont, "Charles Jones will pour too full a glass for himself and the others nearby. He always makes a ruckus and usually stains somebody's taffeta when he does. Monitor his end of the table, please, and go ahead and pour for the guests on either side of him before Charles does."

Mr. Dumont, a tall, distinguished man with graying hair and a vaguely European accent, cleared his throat. "If I may, Mrs. Zimmer." His voice was like an old clock tolling. "That may be why Mr. Edward always preferred to keep the wine on the sideboard, and for us to do all the pouring. He thought it was more . . . refined that way."

Irritation scratched in her throat. "I'd like the bottles on the table, please, as I've said many times before."

Dumont's lips thinned. "As you wish, madam," he replied, his tone conveying his sense of her foolishness.

Noting the tension, Mrs. Connelly said, "I think that's wonderful, Mrs. Zimmer. It gives the table a more convivial atmosphere." She shot Dumont a look that said, *Let it go.*

Sandy remembered a time just a few months before Edward died, of him adjusting her necklace before a charity gala, his fingers rough against her skin. "There," he'd said, "much better. Pearls suit you best, Bitty. Leave diamonds to the showier women." She'd smiled and accepted his judgment, as always. But she remembered how that had annoyed her. It wasn't as if she aimed at being showy. It was just that everybody, especially Edward, had ideas about what she should do and how she should do it. He'd been more instructive than usual in the time before his heart attack, sometimes acting impatient when she didn't seem to catch on quickly enough to what he wanted. She'd shown extra sensitivity then, waiting before responding to him, so she would be more likely to do or say the right thing. She didn't want to upset Edward. Now she thought his mood may have been a sign of his heart attack approaching. Had she been patient enough?

As she headed down the hall to her quarters to change, her thoughts returned to the newsroom. The *Prospect* faced trouble, and tonight was a chance to gather information from the board members, and maybe even do a little persuading.

Opening the door to her dressing room, which might have become a nursery, had there been a baby, Sandy stopped short. Hanging on the clothes valet was an ice-green Dior gown Edward had bought her just before the war, delicate and demure as Edward's view of her.

Mrs. Connelly appeared behind her in the doorway. "I laid it out, Mrs. Zimmer," she said, then hesitated. "Though . . . if you'd prefer something else, I'd be happy to help you choose."

Sandy stared at the dress, remembering Edward's appreciation of it. "You're loveliest like this, Bitty," he'd murmured, his eyes soft in the dim light of their bedroom. "You're like the morning." He'd kissed her then, tender, trying not to muss her hair or smudge her pale lipstick.

Sandy had felt cherished in such moments, like a piece of ceramic art. Edward adored her, yes, but always as his vision of her—a reflection of his own tastes. Was she really so delicate?

"Thank you, Mrs. Connelly. But I think . . . I think I'll choose something else tonight."

"Of course, Mrs. Zimmer. What did you have in mind?"

Sandy turned to her closet, pushing past the rows of Edward-approved gowns until she found what she was looking for—a deep turquoise silk gown she'd bought on a whim and hidden away years ago, before the war, never daring to wear it, fearful it was wrong.

Mrs. Connelly gasped softly. "It'll bring out your eyes."

Sandy slipped on the dress, its silk cool against her skin. The neckline dipped just a little lower than Edward might have liked. And the slit showed a hint more of her leg than her in-laws would consider strictly proper.

Was it too much?

No. This was a minor thing, just a dress she'd chosen herself. It wasn't about Edward or his parents. This was about her, Sandy Zimmer. She wanted to be seen.

She replaced her pearl earrings with a simple pair of diamonds and matching bracelet. As she applied a deeper shade of lipstick than usual, Sandy steeled herself for the evening. Tonight's dinner table would be a chessboard of influence. Experience had taught her that when she looked especially beautiful, men dropped their guard and she could sneak by them to accomplish something they might not expect. That had always worked when she was a secretary.

Sandy centered herself in the full-length mirror. The woman staring back looked confident, bold. Ready to take on the world, or at least Pacific Heights.

She walked down the hall to the strains of Duke Ellington—Edward's favorite—on the record player. Dumont knew the man who'd hired him.

Then she smiled. The song was "Sophisticated Lady."

As she reached the foyer, she saw Dumont's eyes widen at her appearance, a flicker of disapproval quickly masked. Mrs. Connelly, on the other hand, beamed with admiration.

"Are we ready?" Sandy asked.

"I have placed the wine on the table, as you requested, Mrs. Zimmer," Dumont said, doubtful.

"Thanks, Dumont," Sandy said. "Let's have a wonderful evening, shall we?"

Mrs. Connelly gave her an encouraging nod, while Dumont twisted his mouth. Sandy felt a tiny surge of power. Sometimes the smallest things made the difference.

CHAPTER SIX

Bubbly

The living room where her guests gathered would have sparkled without light bulbs or candles, relying only on the twinkling of boat lights on the bay visible through her wraparound windows. In fact, the room's lamps were kept intentionally low, so as not to compete with the view. Just enough glow indoors to flatter the faces of her well-tended guests.

"I sure wish you'd warned us about the glamour factor tonight," said Nina Warren, admiring Sandy's gown. "I might have bought something new." The governor's wife smiled warmly, between deep dimples. Sandy wondered how she always seemed so pleasant, a woman raising six children in the governor's mansion, who regularly orchestrated official dinners and teas for dignitaries, and even cooked weekly meals for needy families. Sandy considered Nina a bright spot at any event and was always relieved to sit at her table. Besides, she looked plenty glamorous in her black velvet gown.

"Don't be silly, Nina, you're always elegant without trying too hard. That's an art. And I'm so pleased you're the first to arrive." *Fifteen minutes early*, she thought, kissing Nina's cheek.

Governor Warren said, "Sorry to show up early, though I see you're already dressed. Lipstick on and everything." He gave her a wink. "We expected to hit a lot of traffic coming from The Mark, but our driver managed to avoid most of it. We circled the block for fifteen minutes and decided to come up before we ran out of gas."

This was predictable. The governor could hardly keep himself from getting anywhere early. Inviting the Warrens to dinner led savvy hostesses like Sandy to carefully calculate their start times.

Nina rolled her eyes at her husband and said, "The man was born in a barn. Literally. I told him we should just park and wait until the proper time, but you know he doesn't care to wait." The governor laughed. He was a man at ease with jokes at his own expense, at least from Nina.

In spite of their warmth, Sandy felt a bit unnerved, her hands jittery. As she poured champagne for Nina and the governor, the bottle clinked against the glass. She quickly steadied herself, hoping they hadn't noticed. Maybe she should have stuck with Dumont's suggestion and foregone her own pouring as unnecessary intimacy.

The governor gazed out the windows. "You can see half the city from up here. Edward sure set you up well, eh?"

Sandy's cheeks flushed. "That he did."

Nina squeezed Sandy's waist in a supportive gesture and then chimed in, "Everything's so exciting, isn't it? The god-awful war finally over. Unconditional surrender. I love those two words, coming from the other side, of course. And what do you think about the United Nations settling here? Wouldn't it be wonderful for the city? All those diplomats and their families coming to town? A new age for San Francisco."

"California too," the governor added. "Nina thinks she'll be able to buy a better sort of dress when that happens. She'll drive over from Sacramento twice a month just to shop, I'll bet." He smiled at his wife. "But a whole lot comes with it, headquartering something like that. Turns a place international. You've got to be ready for it. Got to have a whole lot of infrastructure, more than just buildings. You need the right people managing everything."

Sandy caught the reflection of her gown in the glass, shimmering defiantly, making her feel a little too showy for serious conversation.

"Still, it would be quite a coup, I think," she said.

Wyatt had recently been named chair of the Commission to Recruit the UN Headquarters to San Francisco, and Sandy felt oddly protective of him on this topic, worried her father-in-law was vulnerable to feelings of failure because he wanted it so much.

The governor just raised his brows in a *we'll see* kind of way.

The elevator dinged and Mrs. Connelly delivered to the living room industrialist board member Adam Lowe, who looked like some kind of trophy, his gold, wavy hair shining where the lamplight hit it, his tailored black suit fitting his wide shoulders and trim waist. Adam arrived with his thinly dour wife Marian—dark hair, dark eyes, dark dress, making Sandy think of a wealthy witch. She suspected Adam's philandering gave Marian plenty of reason to look so bitter, especially since her inheritance had likely given him his start.

The next elevator expelled banker board member and zealous wine pourer Charles Jones, who looked as usual chock-full of butter and bourbon. He wasn't truly fat, he just seemed fat to Sandy, the way his skin tended to grow pink and moist as he ate and drank. He was the sort of man people might call Baby-Face. Though he was at least forty years old, his sycophantic attitude toward Board Chair Wyatt made him seem like a freshman in thrall to the fraternity president. He brought with him a very young woman, Una Tyler, whose dress Charles had likely purchased. Sandy thought it looked quite expensive but ill fitting, probably in fact purchased this very morning for the dinner. Una didn't appear to enjoy wearing it, the way she kept tugging at her ruffly georgette sleeves. Sandy thought this girl could potentially be quite beautiful in the way a twenty-one-year-old can be after she finally discovers who she actually is. Sandy was fairly sure these two would not be more than a two-date couple.

Next came Sandy's in-laws, board members Wyatt and Olive. Though he was only average height, Wyatt had such an upright posture and trim build, maintained through regular golf and tennis, that he seemed much bigger. His square jaw and steel eyes, salt-and-pepper, neatly groomed goatee, all announced the rigor with which he tended his standing. It mattered quite a bit to Wyatt what the right people thought of him.

His wife Olive looked his opposite, with a delicate, heart-shaped face, smudged features, and expressive, gray eyes. Her silvery blonde hair was coiffed in a loose, classic style, and her fair skin was nurtured by a meticulous routine of beauty products that couldn't hide all the wrinkles. Still, she carried herself with refined, submissive grace. Lovely, as usual.

Thirty minutes in, Mac hadn't arrived.

Sandy's guests clustered in the living room, in male and female groupings, champagne lubricating their conversation, she hoped. The men all knew each other well, and seemed quite happy to be talking about President Truman's announcement, all in agreement that Japan's surrender was going to open up a world of economic opportunities, which is what interested them most about the end of war.

Of course, good friends Nina and Olive had paired up in whispered conversation. Sandy approached them first because they were the easiest.

"Sandy, dear," Olive purred. "You've outdone yourself again. This 1934 Bollinger is perfect with the blinis. I always love the saltiness of the caviar, don't you, Nina?"

Nina licked a little crème fraîche off her finger, nodding happily.

Olive continued, "Edward would be so proud of you, Sandy." Her hand brushed the antique brooch at her crepey décolletage. "You know, Wyatt and I have been talking. There's a lovely house for sale right on Broadway, just a few doors down from us—you would love it. We really need to get you in there. All our friends have their children living in the neighborhood." She blinked her doe eyes with longing.

Nina asked, "This penthouse is in your neighborhood, isn't it?"

"Well, Wyatt says it's in the neighborhood, but not really *in* the neighborhood, you know, not exactly built on our bedrock."

Wyatt and Olive had bought Edward a place on Broderick, around the corner from them, on their bedrock, which he'd lived in for a year before he traded it in favor of this penthouse. His had been an extended adolescence, they said, when he made decisions like that. Sandy felt the strain in her cheeks, not knowing how to answer any of it. She did understand Edward's wanting to be independent, but worried he shouldn't have expected to use the house they gave him to do so. Still, though the penthouse wasn't exactly her, she didn't want to live a few doors down from Wyatt and Olive. She thought there might be some better place out there, that seemed more like her. *What neighborhood, though?* She had no idea.

"Thank you for thinking of me, Olive," she said, and pivoted toward the next pair.

Neither Marian nor Una looked eager to speak to the other. Clutching her champagne glass, Marian glared in the direction of her husband, Adam, who seemed to be having a fabulous time. Was that his third glass of champagne already? Sandy had given up on her plan to fill everyone's glasses herself and she'd just left the bottles in the silver urn behind the couch, where the men were helping themselves.

Una looked deeply uncomfortable with Marian. But honestly there was probably no one at the dinner she might enjoy, least of all her date, Charles. Sandy pictured him pompously correcting her every move, the way she held her fork, sat at the table, walked through the room. Sandy picked up one of the champagne bottles and headed to the two unhappy women.

"More bubbles?" she asked.

Marian answered with a look like she smelled something bad. Una desperately thrust her glass toward Sandy. *Oh dear*, Sandy thought.

"Marian, how are the boys?" Sandy asked.

"Oh, they're off at school. We only had them two weeks after summer camp, but they were both eager to get back for football practice before the semester starts." She sighed. Sandy felt for her. That must be disappointing. But she also expected the boys were eager to get away from their mother. She knew that wasn't nice of her to think, but it was the truth.

"I know you must miss them, and they must miss you too. But it's good you've got them in a school they love."

"Well, a lot of parents don't take care to get their children in just the right place. They don't put in the work to arrange for their children's trajectory."

Sandy thought of her own absent mother and of the years she spent caring for her father after his early retirement from the post office because of cancer.

"Well, at least this gives you and Adam private time together. Have you been enjoying that?"

Marian's face went white. Una raised her brows and looked at Sandy, intrigued.

"You know how busy Adam is, with his business dealings, and of course working so hard to bail out your *Prospect*. I know it's one thing for you to devote yourself there, but quite another for someone with a spouse and children to take on that challenge."

I hate her, Sandy thought, smiling, her face brittle from the effort.

"Well, if he weren't busy bailing out the *Prospect*, I'm sure he would find something else to keep him occupied, tennis perhaps?"

Marian flinched at Sandy's not-so-veiled reference to one of Adam's recent tennis playing paramours.

Sandy turned to Una, who extended her glass in a second desperate plea for champagne.

From across the room, Mrs. Connelly gave Sandy a sign with one raised brow, and Sandy announced, "Shall we all move to the dining room?"

As the party set itself in motion, she excused herself, slipping into the powder room. She gripped the edge of the sink, staring at her reflection. "Come on, dummy! You can do better."

CHAPTER SEVEN

Job Makes the Man

"Quite a time for San Francisco, wouldn't you say, Governor?" Even with a nothing sort of comment, Wyatt's pronouncements could fill a room, his great, square jaw chewing up anything soft around him. The shadows cast by the table's candlelight exaggerated the effect, projecting his nose out like a pointing finger, Sandy thought. Or maybe it was the wine.

At the head of the table, the governor set down his Sancerre and answered, "There's more at play here than civic pride. Stakes are high. The State Department's keeping a close eye on you all. Things like the ruckus outside tonight can make a difference in the big picture. I hope City Hall's on top of these antics." Something about his high, broad forehead always made Sandy assume his ideas were also high and broad and so she too wondered if the city was on top of things.

Adam jumped in. "Good God, the possibilities are endless if we get the UN. We can reshape the entire waterfront, build something great." His eyes shone with the fire that propelled him from working-class roots to captain of industry, along with the fuel of Marian's seed money. He was a very good salesman, even for his most outlandish ideas.

Charles chuckled, doubling his pink chin. "And remunerative. As your banker, I'm aware you're always thinking about the bottom line. But what about the practicalities? It's not just where all these diplomats will live. It's how we'll handle security concerns."

Sandy opened her mouth to share her own thoughts—that it might be good if the recruitment committee had a wider variety of members, to see a wider variety of problems and possibilities—but then she closed it, thinking what she might say would be received badly, feeling the familiar pain that came with constantly biting her tongue.

Through the dining room windows, the clamor from the streets below grew louder. Sandy noticed the governor's eyes drifting to the window. Then he leaned back in his chair, swirling his wine glass. He looked around the table and said, "Hard to predict. There's a whole lot of change right now. The question for all of us is whether we choose to change with the times. I've had to do so several times over. Being Alameda County DA was different than being state attorney general. And they're both worlds different from being governor. And none of that approaches the change required by my moving from Bakersfield to Berkeley in the beginning. In my experience? You have to see and do things differently at such junctures or you'll go nowhere. It takes a certain amount of courage."

Sandy recalled the governor's agreeing to Japanese American internment when he was attorney general, and wondered how he felt about his "courage" at that juncture, now, though she didn't ask. She would never have asked. That would have been rude.

The governor looked straight at Sandy. "In my experience, the job makes the man."

The table fell awkwardly silent.

"Or the woman," Nina added, gently squeezing her husband's arm.

Sandy's cheeks were hot. *What's he implying, looking at me that way? That I haven't changed? That I have? That I ought to change more? Ought to be more courageous? That I ought to be a man? Why would he do this to me at this table?* It felt like an attack. Her palms were wet.

Wyatt cleared his throat. "With all due respect, Governor, I'm not sure that exactly applies here. Sandy's background typing and filing for Edward hardly prepared her for the role he asked her to take on. She's done so bravely of course, quite bravely. But was it reasonable or fair of Edward to ask this of her? Anyone might have calculated the unlikelihood of her success in a role she'd had precisely zero training for."

The unlikelihood of my success? Sandy had heard him hint such things before, in the boardroom, but here? At her dinner table? Were the two of them colluding to humiliate her? How should she answer this?

Adam jumped in. "I've found that unexpected decisions can lead to the greatest innovations. I had no plans to build dams and highways and Liberty ships. And now I'm thinking about hospitals and insurance. The point is, I didn't have real experience at any of it before I did it. Sometimes you've got to jump in. Sink or swim."

Adam had thrown her a lifesaver. *Get yourself in it! Start swimming!* she thought. But no words came.

Charles took the opening. "I think what Wyatt suggests is that some roles require more . . . specific preparation. Running a newspaper isn't like hosting a dinner party, after all."

Oh my God! Charles is awful! As if hosting dinners was her dream! How dare he talk about her like that. She'd known she wasn't anybody's first choice to take over for Edward, but to insult her this way! What a windbag.

Now Olive stepped in. "This soup is just delectable. My compliments. Absolutely brilliant."

Sandy's cheeks burned.

She looked at Mac's empty seat at the table. *He would have backed me up. Who am I kidding? No, he wouldn't.*

Perhaps because of an under-table kick from Nina, the governor now saw the need to defuse the situation he'd created and changed the subject. "What is the paper's take on the United Nations, Sandy?"

Sandy sipped her Sancerre, swallowed, and took a breath, buying time. *Turn it around.* "Actually," she said in a steady voice, "I agree with my father-in-law that San Francisco has a strong chance of winning the headquarters battle, given the success of the spring conference here. Everyone loved us, the food, the views, the architecture, the style."

Wyatt nodded vigorously and said, "All the numbers pencil out, they all recognize that. Even the flying or sailing distance for members arriving from Pacific nations. They all were impressed by that."

"Sally Stanford may also have played a role," Sandy added.

Everyone laughed. It was funny but also accurate that Sally Stanford's Pine Street *parlor* provided amorous dignitaries compelling reason to visit.

She'd broken the tension, for the rest of them, at least.

The men went on to discuss less weighty topics—sports, movies, local business gossip—and Sandy struggled to slip herself back into the conversation. But every time she seemed about to speak, she stopped herself. Her noisy gown felt like flimsy armor to protect her from her guests.

Conversation volleyed, and the sounds from outside grew more insistent, cheers mixed with what sounded like breaking glass. Sandy saw the governor exchange a worried glance with Nina.

As Dumont served the halibut, the elevator door opened and Jane Benjamin threw herself into the room like a grenade.

"Sorry for the surprise, y'all," she drawled, her accent more pronounced than usual. Sandy knew it was tactical—Jane regularly deployed her native "y'all" but not "ain't," which wasn't so stylishly effective. She'd learned how best to use her tomato-picking history in rooms where no one else had the residue of dirt under their nails. "Been chasing leads all day, even found some. Thought I'd come drop 'em on your doorstep, Madam Publisher!"

Wyatt and Charles gaped at the *Prospect*'s gossip columnist and resident troublemaker as if she'd actually dumped a rat at their feet. She did in fact grin like a feral cat.

Sandy felt both agitated and relieved at her friend's arrival. Jane always made messes for Sandy to clean up, but she thought she needed another ally in the room, wondering if it was stupid to put Adam in that category with her.

"Jane, sweetheart," Sandy said. "Take Mac's seat. Looks like he's stuck in the newsroom." She heard a little gasp from the dull Marian Lowe, who knew how things were supposed to work, and last-minute guests were not on that list of possibilities, especially interloping gossip girls.

"So he didn't make it?" Jane asked, her face dimming a little. She'd clearly come to see her editor, who'd apparently been too busy to keep his promise to attend or even send a message.

Jane sauntered over, leaning down to give Sandy a hug, long past the hugging hello hour of the evening. Dumont could scarcely hide his disdain as he worked to deliver an extra plate on the fly. Jane plopped down in Mac's spot before Dumont had finished.

"What are these leads you've fetched us, Miss Benjamin?" Charles belched, as he tended to do when he'd been drinking too much.

Jane looked to Sandy for permission. Sandy shrugged.

Jane speared a piece of her swiftly arrived fish, then waved it as she spoke. "Well, people are on the streets everywhere, here, Sacramento, Los Angeles, all over the country. Apparently all over the world."

"Obviously," Charles said.

"But something's off here."

"Off?" Sandy asked.

"The guys on the street are way past drunk, mainly sailors who have yet to ship out. So relieved they won't have to fight—who can blame 'em? Nobody's stopped the shops from selling booze to any kid with a buck. Then those kids are turning around, breaking windows, stuff like that. One guy's actually dead from somebody else throwing a trash can full of water out of an apartment window onto his head."

"Dear Lord," Olive whispered.

Jane looked at Sandy. "I don't think that's the extent of it."

"What then?"

"The city police and military police aren't exactly Johnny-on-the-spot. Nobody's telling those boys to head back to their boats."

"I think you mean ships," said Charles, who was correction oriented.

Sandy thought of Police Chief Dullea. No surprise he wasn't taking all necessary action. He'd been running so low on officers because of the war that he'd enlisted an auxiliary core of 2,500 men and women. He gave them a crash course in police work and firearms. Not exactly the gold standard for a city police force.

Nina said, "It's terrible, such unruliness when there ought to be pure gratitude."

Sandy noticed Una shift uncomfortably in her seat. The young woman had been quiet all evening, but now she looked jittery.

"Like I said," Jane interrupted. "That won't be the extent of it."

Charles spoke up, "What are you implying?"

"I haven't seen anything that goes too far yet. Mostly *boys will be boys*," Jane said, mimicking what at least half the people at the table must be thinking. Then she looked around at each of them. "But I know when a payday party's about to turn into a bar fight. I'm saying, lots of folks are gonna get their heads bashed. And the rest, which you can imagine. Like I told Mac today, good turns bad real quick with too much booze."

Charles jumped in. "Is this coming from your gossip sources?" He said this with more distaste than alarm. "Please do not spread loose talk. There's no reason to..."

Jane set down her fork. "I've heard things and seen things today because I'm on the street and not sitting up here all night, slurping down *Sawn-sayr*, sir." She grinned at Sandy. "Did I pronounce that right?"

Sandy's fingers trembled. This was not good. She could picture their headline: DOWNTOWN WILD IN V-J DAY ROMP! Or maybe V-J DAY CELEBRATIONS GIVE POLICE A HANGOVER. She asked, "Are you saying you've witnessed something beyond the pale, Jane, because if you have..."

"I'm not saying I witnessed anything yet. I'm saying it's going to happen, the out-of-control stuff, because the police and the military don't have a handle on it. The way they said it was in 1906, during the old earthquake and fire, right? Five hundred people shot dead by military who should have been spraying water on the flames instead?"

The governor rose. "Where's your telephone?" Dumont guided him out the door.

Wyatt, Charles, and Adam followed the governor.

At Sandy's direction, Mrs. Connelly led the ladies to the drawing room, though they'd consumed only half their meal. Sandy resigned herself to following the women, rather than the men making the calls. Nina, Olive, and Marian clustered, whispering on the sofa, in a social coup for Marian. Una stood on the balcony just outside the window, smoking a cigarette. Jane and Sandy huddled near the fire.

"You're not going to just let them handle this?" Jane accused. "Why are you in this room with the seconds instead of across the hall with the firsts? If you're gonna hole up in your penthouse, at least hole up in the right room."

"Jane," Sandy moaned.

"Come on. You're the publisher, Sandy. Call Mac. Tell him what to do."

"Don't you think Mac knows what to do?"

"Those guys across the hall are gonna tell him to hold back. They're gonna say, 'Keep it quiet.' You know they are. They don't want to report bad news, just parrot what's good."

"Why do you have to think the worst . . ."

"Because I've seen it over and over and over again, Sandy. They're gonna want to quiet this down because they don't want the city to look bad. And they don't want the military to look bad. Or war. Or men."

"Not everything's a conspiracy, Jane."

"Yeah, but some things are. And they're gearing up for it. Just call Mac, will you? Say you want reporters investigating all this. All of it. Not tamping it down. Get on the telephone, Sandy. Get in your office and make your call."

"Jane, I'm not some, some, Cissy Patterson. I'm not even you. I do things my way."

"Cissy's a bully," Jane said, fixing Sandy with a fierce look. "And yeah, I'm perfect. But you're Sandy Abbott Zimmer, publisher. It's time you acted like it instead of whimpering around the edge of everything. Where's the girl I used to know, the girl who always gets crackin'?"

As usual, Jane's instincts were right. She'd turned herself from the best girl-dressed-as-a-copy-boy the paper ever had into a well-loved, highly syndicated columnist and on-the-side reporter. She was right that

Sandy used to be a cracking girl. But that was when the stakes were lower than they were now. That was when she lived to support Edward, not when the decisions were all her own. Jane deflated Sandy more than pumping her up by reminding her who she used to be.

Una approached. "Please let Charles know I had to leave."

"I can have my driver get you home," said Sandy. "It's not safe."

Una nodded. "Thank you."

"Dumont, please call Tommy. Have him get Miss Tyler home."

Within the hour all the guests were gone, the remnants of the dinner party scattered around Sandy as her staff cleaned. She walked to the window, looking down at the street. Faint crowd sounds drifted up.

There was a profound disconnect between her carefully curated world and the world outside her windows. She was the publisher of a major newspaper, yet she felt as removed from the real story as she had been when she was just Edward's wife.

Call Mac, Jane had said.

The job makes the man, the governor had said.

She stared at the credenza telephone.

Wyatt's disapproving scowl flashed before her eyes, followed by Olive's look of disappointment. She could almost hear the whispers at the next charity gala: *There's Sandy Zimmer. Can you believe what she's done to Edward's paper?*

She thought of her husband, of the faith he'd placed in her. What would he think of her now, hesitating in the face of what might be a real story?

The diamonds at her throat squeezed like a choker.

CHAPTER EIGHT

Tipping Point

The silk of her gown felt clammy and confining. *What am I, a mermaid?* Sandy thought, cringing. How childish to think a dress could prove anything. The men at dinner wore interchangeable dark suits, their authority coming from inside. Or sometimes not inside, sometimes from wealth or connections, she knew. But not from their clothes. Or maybe, yes. She had no idea—*dimwit!* Why had she expected anything to be different for her because she rebelled and wore a turquoise dress?

A car horn blared, followed by screeching tires and the crunch of metal on metal. Sandy rushed to the window. Two cars were crumpled in front of her building, steam hissing from under the back car's hood. Men spilled out, angry shouts carried up on the night air. A punch was thrown, the solid thud of fist meeting flesh audible even from her perch. Another man joined the fray—the accident turning into a fight.

Was this what the end of war looked like? Not parades and ticker tape, but broken glass and bloody knuckles?

Sandy yanked the curtains closed and unzipped her dress, letting it fall to the floor. She kicked it aside, distancing herself from the woman who'd put it on hours ago, and then slipped into her pajamas. Wyatt's words haunted her—*Typing and filing for Edward hardly prepared her for the role.*

Her bare feet pressed into the carpet as she paced. Seven steps to the window, pivot, seven steps back. She was always circling, never moving forward.

Olive's voice joined the chorus in her head. *Edward would be so proud.* Sandy's hand grazed her stomach. The achy emptiness of her womb was duller now. A failure to please him, a failure no one else knew about but many probably suspected.

She drew back the curtain. The fight had dissipated—just the dented fender, a discarded hat, a smear of something dark on the sidewalk remained. Jane's words, *One guy's actually dead.* So stupid, so preventable.

Sandy's fingers twitched, a typist's muscle memory. She should be doing something. She twisted her wedding ring, the gold warm from her skin. For years, she'd deferred to others. Why? To avoid Wyatt's and Olive's sneers at her working-class roots? Was it fear of the responsibility Edward entrusted to her? All those employees and their families to think of, the obligations.

Maybe she could use the *Prospect* to support the UN bid. A series of editorials highlighting San Francisco's suitability? That would please Wyatt, maybe help strengthen her position, making it more possible to do what she should. But she felt a twinge of unease. The paper should be objective about these things. Wasn't that boosterism what the other local papers would be doing?

Jane's voice cut through it all. *You're the publisher. Call Mac. Tell him what to do.* But was that really her? It sounded more like Jane, all relentless drive. Sandy had always been the one who smoothed things over, made things better for Edward. Could she be anything else?

Her gaze fell on his photo on her nightstand, his smile frozen in time. He must have seen something in her, some potential. What was it he used to say, tracing the blue vein in her wrist? *I see the ink.*

She wasn't like Cissy Patterson, crude and unkind, in it for ad dollars. And not like Olive, sweetly submitting to Wyatt.

Sandy opened her notebook and wrote.

1. Do nothing.
2. Call Mac.
3. Go to office.

She tapped her pen in a nervous rhythm. What was she worried about? Getting the story? Board approval? Jane's respect? Her own job? She crumpled the paper in her fist, then smoothed it out again. So simple, so complicated.

A police siren wailed outside, growing louder. Sandy returned to the window. A patrol car pulled up, lights painting the street red. George, the doorman, emerged, gesturing wildly at the officers. His face creased with concern. This was his city too. Everybody's city.

Sandy's reflection stared back.

"Okay, enough," she said. She looked at the telephone, hesitated for a heartbeat, then grasped the receiver. "Operator? The *Prospect* editor-in-chief, Mac MacDonald, please."

"*Prospect* newsroom, Marie Johnson speaking."

"Marie? It's Sandy Zimmer. I need Mac."

"He left an hour ago, Mrs. Zimmer. Should I try his home?"

Sandy's free hand clenched. "No, that's . . . that's alright." She replaced the receiver, her mind racing. The easiest path blocked.

She threw open Edward's old closet, now housing her long unused clothes. A cotton blouse and skirt would do. No time for stockings—she slipped bare feet into loafers, leather soft against her skin. She pulled on an old peacoat—summer in San Francisco—and put a pen and moleskin in her purse.

In her desk drawer, her fingers found an old set of keys. Tommy was taking Una home. She'd drive herself.

She paused at the door. She didn't know exactly what to do when she got to the office, but she'd figure it out. That's what Edward would have done. What a publisher would do.

The elevator descended, numbers lighting up as she passed. 10 . . . 9 . . . 8 . . . With each floor, she felt herself shedding an old self. 7 . . . 6 . . . 5 . . . The socialite, the grieving widow, the secretary. 4 . . . 3 . . . 2 . . . The student, the caregiver, the good girl. Who would she be when she reached the ground floor? *The job makes the woman.* She'd find out what kind.

The elevator dinged, and the doors slid open to the Steiner garage, where her old '35 Ford waited, a relic from pre-Edward life.

The key turned with a birdlike *skree*. The engine sputtered, reluctant, before shrieking to life.

Sandy pulled out of the garage and onto the street. Even in Pacific Heights, red, white, and blue streamers clung to lampposts like patriotic ivy. Cheers, car horns, and music ahead almost drowned out her doubt.

The old car whined as Sandy navigated Washington Street's hills, its gears grinding in protest, the transmission as rusty as Sandy's own instincts.

Finally Market Street loomed ahead, a river of people overflowing its banks. Bodies pressed against her car, rocking it like waves against a ship. Hands slapped the hood and roof.

She was scared but she gripped the wheel tighter, cracked leather still familiar under her fingers.

She inched forward. Sweat beaded on her forehead.

A narrow gap appeared in the crowd, revealing a place to park. Should she stop? Sandy guided the car into that opening, alive with the precariousness of this choice. The mob closed in, sealing off retreat. She was nowhere near her office, but this was where everything was happening.

She turned off the ignition. Her heart kept time with the percussion of the street. Terrified at what was outside, she grabbed her purse and opened the car door.

The racket of celebration nearly knocked Sandy back into the driver's seat. She steadied herself against the car's doorframe, pushing her shoulders back before stepping onto Market.

The pavement thrummed. Bodies pressed in from all sides, surging, swelling, receding. Flags waved—a patriotic canopy fluttering in the cool night air. The scent of alcohol mixed with sweat and the acrid tang of gunpowder from impromptu fireworks.

A cheer went up from somewhere to her left. Sandy turned, watching as a group hoisted a young sailor onto their shoulders, like he was the winning quarterback. Rather than a football, he brandished a bottle, sloshing amber liquid as he pumped his fist in the air. "We won!" he bellowed, his voice cracking with emotion. "We showed them Krauts and Japs!" Tears flowed down his cheeks, and Sandy's.

The crowd around him roared in response. Sandy found herself elated in spite of her apprehension. This was history unfolding before her eyes, raw and unfiltered. She pictured the headline: SAILORS ROMP—AND NOBODY CARES!

She took a tentative step forward, then another. The crowd made room for her, allowing her to move down the sidewalk, part of the rest of them. Her eyes darted from face to face, drinking in the emotions on display. Joy, relief, exhaustion—and something else, something wilder, exuding from their skin.

A trio of young women danced by, arms linked, singing "God Bless America." Their laughter was infectious, and the mirth rose in Sandy's own chest too.

Then a group of sailors barreled past, hotly boisterous. One clipped Sandy's side, sending her stumbling into a store window. She caught herself, her palms pressed against the glass.

"Watch it, lady!" the sailor called over his shoulder.

Sandy straightened, buttoning her coat.

She continued down Market, perceiving a frenetic edge. Someone tall rushed by, hitting her head with his elbow.

People climbed lampposts, jumping down, climbing up again. A man in a business suit, tie askew, held court atop a newspaper stand, conducting an invisible orchestra with exaggerated sweeps of his arms. "Extra! Extra!" another crowed. "War's over! Peace at last!"

A cheer went up. Sandy overheard snippets as she passed.

"—showed 'em, didn't we? Dropped the big one—"

"—when the boys come home—"

"—gonna be out of a job now, mark my words—"

The last comment caught her. The war had brought prosperity to San Francisco, but what would peace bring? This was something that had to be reported.

A loud crack split the air, sharp and sudden. Sandy whirled, her heart pounding. A store window had given way under pressure of a crowd, spiderweb fractures racing across its surface. Everything seemed to pause until the glass fell.

Then came frenzy.

Hands reached through the opening, grabbing merchandise. Three men dragged a mannequin to the sidewalk, its limbs contorted. Someone let out a whoop of triumph, hoisting the lifeless figure overhead.

Where does this go in the paper? On the front page, above or below the fold? Does every page of the paper cover an element of this night? Property damage? Shifting mood of the people? Absence of police? She looked for photographers but couldn't see any. She had to remember all of it. She pressed on, through the thickening crowd.

In the intersection ahead, a streetcar sat motionless, surrounded by bodies like ants on discarded meat. Sandy's breath caught in her throat as she realized what was happening.

"Tip it!" shouted a middle-aged woman, her cheeks bright red, eyes glassy. "We run this town tonight!"

The crowd surged, pressing against the streetcar's sides. Metal groaned in protest as dozens of hands pushed and pulled. The conductor's face was visible through the window, a mask of terror as his vehicle began to rock. Thin as a rail, elderly too, there was nothing for him to do.

No! That's a person! He would get hurt. Any of them could get hurt.

She had to do something.

"Stop!" she cried, but her voice was lost in the roar. Sandy pushed forward, elbowing her way through the press, but she was so small and surrounded by bigger bodies. "You can't do this!"

One burly man fixed her with a hard stare. "Says who, lady?"

"Someone will get hurt!"

The man barked a laugh that sent flecks of spittle flying. "None of us gets hurt tonight!"

Too many of them think this.

He turned back to the streetcar, adding his strength to the effort.

Sandy watched, helpless, as the vehicle began to tilt, slowly at first, then all at once.

"No!" The word tore from her throat. But it was too late.

With a jarring crash, the streetcar toppled onto its side. Glass shattered, spraying into the crowd. The conductor cried out through the din, no words, just fear. But he was alive, crawling out of his streetcar.

She stood frozen, unable to process the scene before her. *Where are the police?*

The crowd's motion shifted, surging toward the Civic Center.

She glanced back at the overturned streetcar, overtaken by people picking through the wreckage for souvenirs. The conductor stood, dazed and bleeding from a cut on his forehead. Sandy's first instinct was to go to him, to offer help. But she couldn't, not now. Instead, she followed the crowd to see what would come next.

CHAPTER NINE

―・―

Renee Taylor
Transcript from Reporter D. Lambert's Notebook

It wasn't like me to go out into the street like that. I just wasn't the type. More likely at home with a book. But Tasha pushed me to come with her. I didn't want to make her go without a friend, and the other welder girls had already rushed off the dock together. Only Tasha waited for me to get back from my errand to the headquarters building. Just before I got there, the noise started up—the horns and blasts announcing war was over—everybody was running, even out of headquarters.

I found Tasha at the dock. We dropped our helmets right there—who cared? —and caught the next bus from the shipyard, still in our work clothes, me in pants, her in coveralls.

On the bus over the Bay Bridge, we borrowed a brush from a girl behind us and fixed our hair, and put on red lipstick Tasha kept in her pocket. Tasha was always ready in case somebody was going to take a picture.

On the bus, they were all passing a bottle—something awful—and we joined in. I didn't like it, that hot, stinging feeling in my throat. But I thought, Why not, just tonight?

Everybody was singing, all of us, "Over there, over there . . ." We were girls, old men, white, Black, Oriental. All of us overjoyed. We wanted to be with the people who felt like we did.

War was over. We were going to be alright. Our boys were going to be alright.

CHAPTER TEN

Random Accident

The euphoria had given way to something primal. Revelers danced on top of overturned cars, their silhouettes backlit by bonfires.

A trio of police officers huddled near a streetlamp, their faces exhausted. One spoke into a radio transmitter while the others scanned the crowd with wary eyes.

Sandy stood near, listening carefully, catching bits and pieces.

"—can't keep up with the calls—"

"—where's the damn backup—"

"—never seen anything like this—"

An ambulance wailed just ahead, its siren a mournful counterpoint to the cheers. Sandy watched it weave through the crowd, red lights painting revelers' faces in a ghastly glow. It was the third ambulance she'd seen in the past hour.

As she rounded the corner onto Powell Street, the atmosphere shifted. The jubilant roar of Market Street faded, replaced by a more subdued buzz. A crowd had gathered at the intersection, forming an audience around a stopped ambulance. Flashing lights cast long shadows, turning viewers into specters.

Sandy quickened her pace, elbowing her way through the throng. The crowd parted reluctantly, some too engrossed in the unfolding drama to notice her, others shooting her resentful glares.

She broke through to the front, to a crime scene.

On the ground was a woman's body. Sandy didn't want to look at her face. She focused on her hand, chubby white fingers reaching for something just out of grasp, pink nail polish. A pool of blood spread below her, making a red creek flow on the concrete.

Sandy swallowed what tried to come up.

She'd only ever seen her father dead before. But that was different, very still and cold, no blood. Just her own sobs to make things messy.

Nearby, two ambulance attendants worked over a young man stretched out on a gurney. Sandy got near. His face was bloody, blond hair matted with it. One attendant pressed something to his head.

"Stay with us, son," he urged. "Can you tell me your name?"

The man's lips moved. "Morris. Seaman First Class John Morris." His eyes, wide with shock and pain, darted wildly before rolling back in his head.

"Get him in now!" the attendant shouted.

Sandy's gaze shifted to two police officers on the side of the road. She moved closer to them, until she was arm's length away. They yelled to each other over crowd noises.

"—blue Ford—"

"—driver never slowed—"

"—three sheets to the wind—"

A man with grease-stained coveralls pushed his way to the front of the crowd. "That's Jack and Stella!" he cried, his voice cracking. "They got married today at City Hall!"

The news rippled through the onlookers, turning shock into outrage.

"Newlyweds?" a woman gasped. "Oh, the poor things!"

"Goddamn drunk!" another man yelled. "Oughta string 'em up when they catch 'em."

The mood of the crowd shifted. Sandy felt a hot knot of fury in her chest. This wasn't just property damage. People were dying out here. *Where are the reporters? The photographers?* Shouldn't she be able to see them, even in this crowd? If she could get to a telephone . . .

"Find the bastard that did this!" someone shouted. "Police ain't doing shit!"

A murmur of agreement swept through the crowd. Sandy saw several men begin to peel away, fury on their faces.

One of the police officers, a sergeant by his stripes, stepped forward. "Folks, calm down," he said, hands raised. "This was a random accident. We're doing everything we can to—"

"Random accident?" the man in coveralls roared. "That girl's lying there dead on her wedding night! Ain't nothing random about some soused bastard plowing into 'em! It's predictable!"

The crowd's anger, briefly frozen by shock, had thawed and was now boiling into rage. Sandy saw several men square off against the outnumbered police.

"If you won't find 'em, we will!" someone shouted.

"Let's go hunting!" another voice chimed in.

The police formed a ragged line, hands on their billy clubs. Sandy could see the fear in their eyes, the realization that they were hopelessly outmatched.

She had to do something.

"Wait!" she called out, surprised by the sound of authority in her own voice. "Everyone, please, listen to me!"

Heads turned.

"This won't help Jack and Stella!"

She gestured toward the ambulance, where attendants were now loading the gurney inside. "That young man needs our prayers right now, not vengeance. And his wife—" Sandy's voice caught, but she pressed on. "She deserves justice, not a lynch mob in her name."

The crowd's energy wavered.

"The police will find whoever did this," Sandy said, meeting the sergeant's eyes. She saw gratitude there, and a flicker of something else. Doubt?

A long moment of silence followed. Sandy waited, aware how easily the mob could turn.

Finally, the man in coveralls spoke. "She's right," he said, his voice thick with emotion. "Jack wouldn't want no one else hurt on account of him. Not even the son of a bitch that killed Stella."

The tension bled out of the crowd like air from a punctured tire. Men unclenched fists, stepping back, releasing the tension from their limbs. Several people bowed their heads as an old man said a prayer: "Wash her in the blood of the spotless lamb that she may rest in your eternal peace. Amen."

Something in that bothered Sandy, as if there was something wrong with Stella, as if she needed cleansing. She shut down that thought.

The ambulance doors slammed shut. The siren wailed back to life as it pulled away, carrying Jack toward an uncertain fate.

The sergeant approached Sandy, mopping his brow with a handkerchief. "That could have gone real bad, real fast."

Sandy felt her adrenaline ebb. "Will you find the one who did this?"

The sergeant's face tightened. "I don't know. With all this . . ." He trailed off, gesturing at the disarray beyond this little bubble of tragedy.

"They deserve better."

Sandy noted the red in his eyes, the slump of his shoulders.

As the crowd began to disperse, she found herself standing alone, watching as a van arrived to claim Stella's body. In the distance, firecrackers popped and people cheered, oblivious to the tragedy that had unfolded here.

Sandy closed her eyes, trying to reconcile the two faces of this night—jubilation and devastation, victory and loss. Her jaw clenched.

As Stella's sheet-covered form was lifted into the coroner's van, Sandy turned and walked back toward Market Street. No photographers had caught this. Would it run in the paper with no pictures? Should she leave the street to get to a telephone?

I don't know what to do.

CHAPTER ELEVEN

Renee Taylor
Transcript from Reporter D. Lambert's Notebook

When we climbed off the bus, we just followed the crowd. It seemed like it naturally knew where to go, like salmon, you know? Swimming upstream? In the dark, all those people on the street almost felt comforting to me. We weren't alone. It wasn't like I was walking by myself at night down a city street. We were all together.

Then our side street broke onto Market. Tasha grabbed my hand, and we ran straight into the middle of the road. Imagine our feelings. We felt so daring. We laughed so hard. Tasha was crying with all that happiness. I just laughed. So, so happy.

Then this guy yelled, "Hey there, girls!" It was somebody I used to know from my neighborhood, from high school. He used to like me in ninth grade, I remembered. "We've got two bottles!" he said. He was wearing a sailor's uniform.

So Tasha nodded at me and we ran over to the sidewalk where his crew was, because I knew that guy and he'd invited us. I remembered him as nice, safe. He played trumpet in the band, was good at math. So we drank with him and his friends, all of them sailors. We couldn't hear much of what they said, but we laughed at everything.

There was another little band of guys who took up playing "Don't Fence Me In" on the street—trumpet, saxophone, bongos—seemed like everything but piano and drums.

This shorter red-haired guy took my hand and asked, "May I have this dance?" He said it so sweet and formal that I kind of curtsied and gave him my hand to dance.

He swung me around and I was glad he wrapped his arm around my waist because, honestly, I wasn't used to drinking, not as much as I had that night. And definitely not spirits, just some wine sometimes, for special occasions. So I was clumsy. I was glad I was still in my work boots. No way could I have danced, dizzy, without breaking a heel in my nice shoes twirling on that street.

The red-haired boy kept on spinning me and spinning me. It was like I was in some kind of time machine, because, when he finally stopped, I was standing still, but the world—the sky, the buildings, the people—were all whizzing around my head, until they finally slowed and I saw Tasha with the boy who'd liked me in ninth grade. He was kissing her so hard, his arms wrapped around her waist, bending her backward. It looked so unnatural. Her arms were waving, not hugging him back, like she was crying for help with her arms.

I wanted to run to her, but I was wobbly and slow. But I got there and I pushed at that boy's head. I hadn't meant to shove his head, but I was so off-balance.

"Hey!" he yelled. "Who do you think you are?"

CHAPTER TWELVE

Soldier Down

Civilians in workers' uniforms—"Earl's Auto" stitched on chest pockets—stumbled past, chanting something Sandy didn't understand. One, a lanky guy with a shock of straw-colored hair, caught her eye and grinned.

"Gawgeous!" he slurred. "How 'bout a kiss?"

Sandy sidestepped his grasp, her heart pounding. The guy's friends laughed, pulling him along. "Plenty fish in the sea—pick a live one!"

Their laughter faded into the din as Sandy pushed on. She found herself scanning the crowd for police. The couple she saw looked overwhelmed.

As she followed the crowd toward the Civic Center, a commotion caught her attention. About a half dozen sailors had formed a tight circle, facing inward. Sandy felt a chill of recognition. She'd seen groups like this before, kids in high school, surrounding a fight.

A young woman in the uniform of the Women's Army Corps broke her way through the circle. The corporal chevron on her sleeve shone in the streetlight as she breached the circle of sailors.

Sandy got closer, the scene coming into sharper focus.

The sailors had hemmed in a young woman with strawberry-blonde hair against the side of a stopped car. The woman looked terrified, her eyes darting frantically from one leering face to another.

"C'mon, girly," one of the men bullied. "You owe us."

"Please!" she cried. "Let me go."

The WAC corporal's voice cleaved through the noise. "Step away! Now!"

The men turned, startled by her intrusion. Sandy saw a flicker of uncertainty cross several faces, quickly replaced by contempt when they seemed to have processed her limited height and girth, and the soft skin of a girl scarcely out of her teens.

"Ho, ho," drawled the apparent ringleader, a wiry man with a day's growth of stubble on his chin. "Army's sent us a snack."

Oh God!

The corporal didn't flinch. She wedged herself between the men and their intended victim. She crouched slightly, knees bent, arms out. "I said step back. This woman is leaving. Get out of her way!"

Sandy pushed even closer. The corporal's eyes never left the men as she gave directions to the woman behind her. Sandy saw her point down the street.

The woman's eyes were huge.

The ringleader loomed over the corporal. "You got a nerve. Need to learn your place."

The corporal's hand went to the stick hanging from her belt. "This *is* my place."

Sandy glanced around, looking for backup, but no help was coming. She thought she would gag. What could she do?

The corporal screamed, "Run!"

The young woman with the ponytail bolted, pushing past the startled men. A couple of them reached to grab her, but the corporal was there, stick out, creating space.

"Bitch!" the ringleader roared. He lunged forward, his meaty hands grasping for the corporal's throat, as two more men ran after the escaping woman.

The corporal brought her stick down in an arc, landing on her attacker's forearm with a sickening crack. He howled, stumbling back.

One of the other men shouted, "Get her!" And the scene broke open. Her stick was a blur as she fended off attackers. But she was outnumbered.

Do something, call for help, intervene. But her feet were rooted, her voice silent. She wasn't strong enough.

More people gathered, drawn by the commotion. Some cheered the fight, while others looked on, helpless, in horror. Sandy heard a woman's voice: "They're going to kill her!"

The corporal was flagging now, her movements failing to hit. She fumbled for the walkie-talkie at her belt and brought it to her mouth, yelling, "This is Corporal Martinez, requesting immediate backup near Seventh and Market. Multiple hostile—"

Sandy repeated to herself, *Corporal Martinez.*

The corporal's words cut off as a fist connected with her jaw. The transmitter clattered to the ground, lost in the scuffle of feet.

"There's nobody to call!" one of the men yelled.

Martinez spat blood, her eyes defiant. "My abuela hits harder, *pendejos!*"

Enraged, they rushed her.

Martinez ducked and weaved, her smaller size an advantage in close quarters. Her stick found vulnerable spots—knees, groins, solar plexuses. Men stumbled, cursing.

But then Sandy saw it. Someone on the periphery, his face twisted in rage, raised a broken bottle. Time slowed as he held it high, over the back of Martinez's head.

"Look out!" Sandy screamed, finding her voice.

Martinez half turned at the warning. The bottle came down in a vicious sweep, missing her head but catching her shoulder. She staggered, momentarily stunned.

It was all the opening her attackers needed.

A punch caught Martinez in the stomach, doubling her over. Another connected with her temple. She went down hard, her head hitting the pavement with a thud.

"Stop!" Sandy cried, pushing forward. "You're killing her!"

Her voice was lost in the uproar. The crowd had grown, some still cheering, others trying to intervene. Sandy saw a flash of blue—was it a police officer, finally?—but no, just a man, unable to push through.

Then, as suddenly as it had all begun, the ringleaders peeled off in response to Martinez's apparent unconsciousness. The crowd regenerated, new arrivers curious, unaware of what had happened. But the woman Martinez was trying to save was gone and her attackers were too.

Corporal Martinez lay still on the pavement.

Sandy rushed forward, her heart in her throat. She knelt beside the fallen WAC, gently turning her over. Martinez's face was pulpy, blood flowing from a cut above her eye into dark wavy hair pulled out of its bun. But it was her stillness that terrified Sandy most.

"Corporal? Corporal Martinez, can you hear me?"

No response. Sandy pressed unsure fingers to her neck, searching for a pulse. She'd done this with her father. For a moment, she felt nothing. Then—there it was. Faint, but present.

"She's alive!" Sandy called out. "Someone get an ambulance!"

But as she looked around, she saw only confused, frightened faces. In the distance, sirens wailed, but whether they were coming closer or moving away, she couldn't tell.

She couldn't leave Martinez here, not like this. Gritting her teeth, she hooked her arms under the unconscious woman's shoulders and began to drag her toward the relative safety of a nearby doorway. Martinez was small, but compact, her body heavy with muscle. Sandy's weak arms struggled. Finally, she laid Martinez alongside a wall, out of the main flow of foot traffic.

"Hold on," Sandy murmured, though she knew Martinez couldn't hear her. "I'm going to get you help. Just hold on."

She looked around frantically, trying to get her bearings. The streets were chaotic, revelers oblivious. No help seemed to be coming. Sandy's mind swirled, weighing her options.

She couldn't leave Martinez alone and vulnerable, but she needed immediate medical attention. Sandy pressed her handkerchief against the corporal's wound, her other hand reaching for Martinez's wrist to check her pulse again.

It was still there, weaker. Time. It was all about time.

Sandy stood, her legs shaky.

"I'll be right back," she promised the unconscious woman. "Hold on, Corporal."

With one last glance at Martinez's battered face, Sandy turned and scanned the street. There had to be help somewhere nearby. *Let her live. Let me find help in time.*

CHAPTER THIRTEEN

Renee Taylor
Transcript from Reporter D. Lambert's Notebook

The boys were all around us now. Everything was still spinning. So were the guys, maybe six or seven of them, sailors. But they were so blurry it seemed like a hundred. That same guy who'd been kissing Tasha was behind her now, with his arms wrapped around her, one around her belly, the other around her shoulders. He was slobbering all over her neck and laughing about it.

Tasha was sobbing.

"Stop it!" I yelled, but he didn't.

They all just laughed. Then that guy from ninth grade lifted Tasha up off the ground, her feet kicking, arms waving, trying to stop him.

I don't know how I decided, but I just raced up and kicked him between his legs. I kicked as hard as I could, wobbly as I was.

He fell and so did Tasha. Then the other guys were mad and I yelled, "Run!" Tasha got up and ran, and no one ran after her. They stayed there, in a circle, with me in the middle. I'd gotten Tasha out.

I understood I was going to get hurt. The anger in the eyes of those boys. The anger! And that one guy moaning on the street, grabbing his crotch where I'd kicked him. Maybe I shouldn't have kicked him so hard. They were like a pack of wolves or something. Except the red-haired boy, he looked worried. He held his arms out to the sides, like he could keep them away from me.

I said this prayer, Dear God, save me from these boys.

Then I heard somebody else yell, "Get out of her way!"

It was this woman in a WAC uniform.

I started crying. Maybe she and the red-haired boy could help me.

But then the group of guys turned on her. They weren't afraid of her. They started punching her, but she fought back, swinging her stick at them. I wanted to help her, but I just couldn't. Everything was so blurry.

They were all around her now and I heard her voice: "Run!"

I saw room in front of me, so I did. I ran.

CHAPTER FOURTEEN

Breaking Glass

City Hall's dirty, dark dome loomed against a misty night sky. Sandy glanced down at her hands, stained with Corporal Martinez's blood.

"Telephone," she told herself. She circled the building.

Every door she tried was locked. She rattled handles, pushed against unyielding wood and metal, more desperate with each failure. She considered running to the *Prospect* office, using the telephone there. But no—that would take too long. She didn't have that kind of time.

Her gaze fell on a pile of concrete debris near her feet, from a knocked-over planter. She picked up a large piece, testing its weight.

"I'm sorry," she whispered, apologizing to the building, to herself, or to the rules.

Sandy stared at a ground-floor window. She raised the chunk of concrete, hesitated, and then threw it. The sound of shattering glass crackled across the plaza. Sandy winced, expecting alarms to blare, police to come running. That was what she wanted. But there was no reaction on a night when so much was breaking.

Carefully, she cleared shards from the windowsill. But as she prepared to hoist herself through, she saw the narrow window's opening was too small. She'd underestimated her own size. She'd never fit without seriously injuring herself.

"Damn it!" Sandy slammed her palm against the wall in frustration. She was wasting time.

Her eyes scanned the building's facade, settling on a larger window about seven feet off the ground. It was a risk—she'd have to find a way up, and the fall inside would be worse. But she was out of options.

Sandy dragged a bench beneath the window, her muscles protesting the effort. She climbed atop it, wobbling, and steadied herself with a hand on the wall. The new chunk of concrete felt heavier as she raised it above her head.

The window exploded inward in a shower of glass. Sandy used her sleeve to clear the frame as best she could.

"Ridiculous," she muttered, and hauled herself up.

For a moment, she teetered, her legs kicking in empty air. Then gravity took hold and she tumbled through the window, landing hard on the floor below. Pain shot through her side, and she felt a warm trickle on her palm where a piece of glass had cut it.

But she was in. She was in.

Sandy stood, her shoes crunching on glass. The space was dark, lit only by the glow of streetlights filtering through windows. She fumbled for a light switch, but nothing happened when she flicked it.

"Hello?" she called out, her voice small and lost in a government office. "Is anyone here? I need help!"

Only her echo responded.

Sandy moved to a door, relieved to find it unlocked. She stepped out into a long, dark corridor. Paintings of California scenes, mountains, meadows, the ocean, pastoral and peaceful.

"Please," she called again, louder this time. "A woman needs help!" Her words rebounded off marble floors and vaulted ceilings. Sandy had never felt so unheard.

She tried door after door. Locked. Locked. Locked. Her frustration mounted.

Where are the night watchmen? The cleaning staff? Has everyone abandoned their posts?

"Is anyone here?" she shouted. Couldn't someone—anyone—hear her? "Please! I need help!"

Sandy's voice cracked on the last word. She leaned against the wall, exhausted. What was she doing here? Breaking into City Hall, screaming like a madwoman. If Edward could see her . . .

Sandy pushed off the wall, determined to search every inch of this godforsaken building if she had to.

As she rounded a corner, a faint sound stopped her in her tracks. A low, rhythmic ticking. Sandy followed it to a massive grandfather clock, its face gleaming in a beam of moonlight from a high window. On that wall was a light switch. When she flipped it, lights came on.

The clock read 3:15.

How long had it been since she'd left Corporal Martinez? Twenty minutes? Thirty? Time was slippery, hard to grasp.

Sandy's eyes strained in the gloom. She passed doors opening onto conference rooms, long tables stretching into darkness. Empty secretarial pools, typewriters sitting silent.

And then—there it was. An office door, ajar.

Sandy's heart leapt as she pushed it open. A large desk dominated the room, and there sat a telephone.

She ran for it, fumbling with the receiver. For a horrible moment, she feared no one would pick up.

Then the operator came on.

"How can I help you?"

"Thank God. I need an ambulance."

"I'll put you through."

The voice that picked up was female, harried.

"Yes, hello!" Sandy said. "I need an ambulance right away. There's a woman, she's been attacked. She's unconscious, possibly dying."

"Miss, please calm down," the dispatcher said. "Where is the victim located?"

Sandy gave the cross streets where she'd left the corporal. How long ago had it been now?

"I'm sorry, miss, but we're completely overwhelmed tonight," the dispatcher said, her voice exhausted. "I can't guarantee when we'll have an ambulance available."

"You don't understand," Sandy insisted, gripping the handset so tightly her knuckles looked like white pebbles. "This woman is a corporal in the Women's Army Corps. She was protecting someone when she was attacked by a mob. She needs help now."

"I understand, miss, but—"

"No, I don't think you do," Sandy cut her off. "Are you telling me that on the night we're celebrating an end to war, we're going to let an American soldier, a woman, die in this San Francisco street?"

When the dispatcher spoke again, her tone had changed. "Ma'am, I assure you we're doing everything we can. But surely you've seen what's happening out there tonight. We have reports of fires, accidents, assaults—"

"I've seen it," Sandy said. "This woman saved another woman, and now she needs saving. Please. There has to be something you can do."

The dispatcher said, "I'll try. I'll really try. But I can't make any promises about how long it will take."

Sandy closed her eyes, fighting back tears. "Thank you," she said. "I appreciate anything you can do."

The line went dead. Sandy replaced the receiver with a shaking hand. It wasn't the assurance she'd wanted, but it was something. Now she had to get back, and Martinez had to hold on long enough for help to arrive.

As she turned to leave, her eye caught something on the desk. A nameplate, its brass surface reflecting light.

ASSISTANT TO MAYOR ROGER LAPHAM

She'd broken into the mayor's office. Under any other circumstances, Sandy might have laughed at the absurdity. Instead, she felt a surge of anger. Where was he now? Where was any semblance of authority or order?

"Some victory," she muttered, making her way back to the broken window. She moved a desk to the wall and used it to climb back in the window.

Sandy lowered herself as far as she could, then dropped the last few feet, landing awkwardly on the plaza below. Pain shot through her ankle, but she ignored it.

She limped back toward Corporal Martinez. What if the ambulance didn't come in time? What if she was already . . . No.

Sounds of celebration seemed more distant now, or maybe it was just Sandy's focus narrowing to a single point: *Get to the corporal.*

Everything else faded away.

CHAPTER FIFTEEN

Renee Taylor
Transcript from Reporter D. Lambert's Notebook

I ran away from those guys, as fast as I could. I couldn't see straight. I stumbled. I heard them getting closer to me and then one of them grabbed me and pulled me off the street into an alley, and he pushed my face up against this brick wall and he said, "Crazy bitch!"

The other one pulled him off me and he said, "Me first."

I don't remember after that. Maybe I blacked out.

This isn't me just deciding not to say what happened out loud. I can't bring it up. I know I was glad Tasha had run away and no one followed her. I really hoped that WAC was okay. But everything else? It's just like it's all walled off. The door's locked.

CHAPTER SIXTEEN

Helpers

Sandy made it back to that small patch of sidewalk to Corporal Martinez. Her breathing was shallow, her face bloody and swelling. Sandy held her hand, whispering words she doubted Martinez could hear.

Distant cheers confused and angered her. She hated the celebrants.

"Come on," she muttered, glancing up and down the street for what felt like the hundredth time. "Where are you?"

Making it worse, she saw tomorrow's *Tattler* headline in her head: GOOD GIRLS STAY HOME: NOT OUT IN THE STREET! Maybe even the *Prospect* or the *Bay City Times* would blame the strawberry-blonde girl. It made her sick.

A siren rose through the noise. An ambulance turned the corner, its red lights lifting her hope.

It screeched to a halt beside them. Its rear doors flew open and a man jumped out. He was older, maybe in his fifties, with rusty grayish hair and lines etched deep around his eyes. She wanted to hug him. She hadn't believed anyone would come.

"What have we got?" he asked, kneeling beside Martinez.

"She was attacked," Sandy said, trying not to fall apart. "A group of sailors beat her up. She hit her head when she fell."

He shook his head in disgust as he checked the corporal's vital signs. "I'm Mike," he said. "Let's get her loaded up."

Together with the driver, he arranged Martinez onto a stretcher and lifted her into the ambulance. Mike climbed in and Sandy followed.

"I'm coming with you," she said. This ambulance was the first good thing she'd seen all night.

Mike raised an eyebrow but didn't object. From the front seat, the driver called out, "We ain't running a taxi service here!"

"Can it, Joe," Mike shot back. "Get moving."

As the ambulance lurched into motion, Sandy settled herself on a small stool, careful not to get in Mike's way. The interior was cramped, filled with equipment she couldn't name. The smell of antiseptic mingled with something metallic—blood, she realized with a shudder.

"I'm Sandy Zimmer," she said, watching as Mike checked Martinez's pupils. "I'm with the *Prospect*."

Joe's derisive harrumph was audible even over the siren. "Ain't that grand."

"I'm here for her." But she wondered if that was completely true.

"Joe's been working eighteen hours," Mike said.

Sandy understood. "It's awful out there."

The radio crackled. A dispatcher's voice, tight with stress, rattled off codes and addresses. His voice calm and professional, Mike said, "That's our third call to a location within a half mile of this in the last hour. Never seen anything like it."

Sandy slumped, thinking of the overturned streetcar, the broken windows, the tragic newlyweds. "People have lost their damned minds."

Mike smiled at her swearing. "Some have." He pressed a bandage on Martinez's head, gentle despite the ambulance's jarring progress.

The corporal's eyelids fluttered but didn't open.

"Corporal Martinez?" Sandy leaned forward. "Can you hear me?"

Her eyes settled, closed. Mike frowned, checking her pulse again.

"How is she?"

Mike's face was grave. "Not great. Head injury's serious. We need to get her to the hospital fast." He leaned toward the front of the ambulance. "Come on, Joe—get us to Central!"

"I'm going as fast as I can!" Joe called back. "People won't get out of the dang way!"

Mike said, "It's close, you won't believe how close, but it's been taking us forever to get there with all this clogging up the street."

Joe hunched over the wheel, navigating through oblivious crowds. He was young, his skin marked with acne.

The ambulance swerved suddenly, throwing Sandy against the wall. Equipment clattered around them as Mike struggled to keep his balance.

"Sorry!" Joe shouted. "Some idiot ran right in front of us!"

Sandy's heart was racing. She looked down at Martinez, so still and vulnerable on the stretcher. What if they didn't make it in time? What if, after everything, she died here in this ambulance?

As if sensing her thoughts, Mike spoke up. "WAC, right?"

"A corporal. She was protecting someone when they attacked her."

"A hero, then."

"She is," Sandy agreed. If—when—Martinez woke up, Sandy would tell her that.

Joe said into the radio, "Dispatch, this is Unit 7. We're a couple minutes out from Central Emergency Hospital. Patient is critical. Request priority clearance."

"Copy that, Unit 7," the dispatcher responded. "Be advised, Central's at capacity. They're setting up overflow in the hallways."

Sandy's stomach dropped. "What does that mean?" she asked Mike.

He sighed. "It'll be crazy. But I know the folks there. They'll take care of your friend."

The word struck Sandy. They'd never even spoken.

"She's not my friend. I don't know her. But it feels . . . I don't know why it feels this way."

"Helping somebody makes you want to keep helping 'em."

Martinez's body went rigid. Then her back arched off the stretcher, her arms flailing.

"She's seizing!" Mike shouted.

The next few minutes were a blur. Sandy pressed herself into the corner, trying to stay out of the way as Mike worked to stabilize Martinez. Sandy thought she might be having a heart attack herself—she could barely get air to her lungs. What if Martinez died right before they got her to the hospital? What if all this was wasted effort?

When they screeched up the alley near Polk and Grove outside Central Emergency Hospital, Sandy felt like hours had passed in the back of that ambulance. Yet they were almost spitting distance from the windows she broke at City Hall.

The rear doors flew open, and a team of nurses swarmed the gurney.

"Female, early twenties, severe head trauma," Mike rattled off as they unloaded Corporal Martinez. "BP's dropping, she had a seizure en route."

Sandy stumbled after them, her foot tender from her fall at City Hall.

The hospital entrance was controlled chaos. Nurses and orderlies rushed back and forth, white uniforms glowing against the dark night. Moans and cries from every direction.

As the team wheeled Martinez through the hospital doors, Sandy tried to follow. A nurse yelled, "Family only beyond this point!"

"But I—" Sandy began, then stopped. What was she?

"She's with me, Vada," Mike told the nurse. "She saved this woman."

Sandy's mouth dropped open. She hadn't saved her.

Vada hesitated. "Well stay out of the way. We're swamped."

As they followed the stretcher down a crowded hallway, Sandy felt the adrenaline that had been fueling her begin to ebb, replaced by a wave of exhaustion, and she stumbled.

Mike caught her elbow, steadying her. "You alright?"

Sandy closed her eyes momentarily, and Mike reached for her hand. "Let's take care of that cut." He opened his bag. "How'd that happen?"

Sandy looked down, surprised to see blood oozing from the cut she'd forgotten. "I broke into City Hall, looking for a telephone. I cut myself on the window."

The simple explanation sufficed.

Mike didn't press for details.

He led her to a quieter corner, sat her on a gurney, and began choosing supplies from his bag—disinfectant, pads, bandage wrappings, scissors.

"You don't have to do this," Sandy said. "You should be..."

Mike shook his head, his eyes squinting at his work. "Can't let the publisher get infected."

He knows who I am.

As he cleaned her cut, his touch gentle despite stinging chemicals and gloved hands, Sandy's tears welled up. The events of the night—the violence, the fear, the desperate race to get help—it was all too much.

Mike paused in his work. "Hey now, it's alright. No stitches needed. You're young and healthy. That won't even leave a scar."

Sandy shook her head, wiping at her eyes with her free hand. "It's just . . . everything. This whole night has been terrible. So many people hurt, so much destruction. And for what?"

Mike snorted agreement as he trimmed the bandage. "Yep. Seen a lot of ugly tonight. But I've seen some good too."

"Where?" Sandy asked.

"Young publisher breaks into City Hall to save a woman she's never met?"

Sandy rolled her eyes. "It's what anyone would do."

He shook his head. "Nope. People talk a big game about what's right to do. But they don't commit. You did. That's beautiful."

He saw her, what she had to offer.

They sat in silence, the frenzy of the emergency room telescoping away. Some of the tension left her shoulders. It seemed like, for the first time in hours, she could breathe.

"You're gonna be fine," Mike said, resting his hand on her shoulder. "I gotta get back out there. And you better go see about your friend."

CHAPTER SEVENTEEN

Eye of the Storm

Every chair in the waiting room was filled with the injured or ill. People lined the walls, some slumped on the floor, others leaned heavily on friends or family members, the smell of blood filling the air all around them. A harried nurse rushed past, her arms full of supply boxes.

"Nobody but patients," she called over her shoulder. Sandy thought it seemed like the nurses spent most of their time trying to chase her away.

She worked her way to the admissions desk to find out about Martinez's condition, but the line stretched halfway across the room, full of people with visible injuries far worse than her own. She scanned the crowd—*Where are the reporters?*

She pulled her moleskin out of her purse and jotted down notes to share with Mac, or whatever reporter he assigned, noting a man with a bloodied face, holding a cloth to his neck; a woman cradling what looked like it might be a broken arm; two sailors supporting a third one between them, all three reeking of alcohol.

"I said you can't stand there," a voice snapped.

Sandy looked up to see the same nurse glaring at her. She'd been blocking the path to the exam rooms.

"I'm sorry, I'm just waiting to find out about a patient—Corporal Martinez. She was brought in with a head injury."

"I can't give out patient information."

Sandy opened her mouth to argue, but something caught her eye beyond the nurse. A woman in a white doctor's coat moved through the crowded hallway. Unlike the frantic energy of those around her, she moved with a steady purpose, her jaw set, eyes ahead. *A woman doctor.*

"Excuse me," Sandy said, pushing past the nurse. "Doctor! I need to speak with you!"

The woman didn't even break stride. "Unless you're bleeding out, take a number," she called over her shoulder.

Sandy limped after her, dodging patients and staff.

"Please, I'm Sandy Zimmer. It's important. I need information—"

The doctor whirled to face her, her dark eyes flashing behind wire-rimmed glasses. "I don't care if you're the Queen of England. We're in the middle of fifteen different crises here." Then she strode away, leaving Sandy open-mouthed in her wake. She really couldn't disagree. The woman had urgent work to do.

"You the Red Cross volunteer?" a gruff voice behind Sandy asked. Sandy turned to see an older nurse glowering. "Then make yourself useful."

"What can I do?"

The nurse thrust a pile of supplies into her arms. "Fine. Take these to Room 3. And try not to trip over anybody."

Sandy was glad of the task. She cautiously walked the crowded hallway, balancing a loose collection of bandages, antiseptics, surgical instruments, syringes, rubber gloves, and clipboards, listening.

"—so many head injuries—"

"—running low on sutures—"

"—another rape victim in 5—"

Rape victim. She'd expected, intellectually, that such crimes were happening. But hearing it stated so matter-of-factly was different.

She made her way to the Room 3 storage area. As she entered, she saw the same doctor bent over a patient, on a gurney, her back to the door, the space having become a makeshift treatment room.

"I'm sorry," Sandy said hesitantly. "I have supplies."

The doctor turned, her eyes narrowing at the interruption. "Just—for crying out loud—set them on that table and get out," she said, immediately turning back to her patient.

Sandy did as instructed, but as she placed the stack down, a clipboard slid off the pile, clattering to the floor. She scrambled to pick it up, her face hot with humiliation.

"I'm sorry, I didn't mean to—"

"It's fine," the doctor cut her off, not unkindly but with impatience.

Sandy placed her hand over her heart and then quickly left the room, embarrassed.

As a presumed Red Cross volunteer, she found herself directed from task to task by various staff members. Fetch clean sheets for Bed 7. Hold pressure on this man's arm wound in the waiting area. Comfort the crying child in the corner while her mother gets stitches.

Sandy threw herself into each task, no matter how menial, all the while watching for the doctor. There was something about her—a strength, a surety—that drew Sandy.

An hour passed in a blur of activity. Sandy's feet ached, and her cut hand throbbed beneath its bandage.

She was getting an elderly man to a chair in the corner when she spotted the doctor again, this time writing on a clipboard. Sandy settled him and then approached the doctor cautiously.

"Excuse me," she said. "I know you're busy, but I was hoping—"

"Mrs. Zimmer, was it?" the doctor cut her off. "I do admire your persistence—and your help—but please . . ."

"I understand. I just . . . I need to know about a patient. Corporal Martinez. She's a WAC we brought in here with a head injury. Please, any information at all."

The doctor sighed, the stress lines in her forehead softening almost imperceptibly. "I can't discuss her with non-family members. You understand."

"Of course," Sandy said, deflated. She did understand, but still. "I'm sorry to bother you, Dr. . . ."

"Bayer," the woman said. "Leona Bayer."

Sandy's eyes widened. "Dr. Bayer! I read your essay about maternal morbidity in *Ladies' Health*. It's an honor to meet you."

Dr. Bayer's head tilted. "Well you and my aunt Hilda, that makes two readers now."

"Oh, it was fascinating. I like to read about issues affecting women in our city. I'm the publisher of the *Prospect*."

"Really?" said Dr. Bayer, looking at Sandy more thoroughly. She opened her mouth to speak, but was interrupted by a shout from down the hall.

"Dr. Bayer! We need you in Room 4!"

She dropped her clipboard in a box on the wall.

"Maybe we can speak later."

Sandy watched her go, both frustrated and energized. She'd made a connection, however brief. She wanted Dr. Bayer's insight. It was a start.

The next few hours passed in a haze. Sandy continued to help where she could, all while trying to piece together the larger picture of what was happening in the hospital—and by extension, the city.

She overheard fragments of conversations, each more disturbing than the last. Stabbings on Market Street. A woman thrown from a moving vehicle. A man with severe burns, reportedly from celebratory fireworks gone wrong.

And through it all, Dr. Bayer and the nurses kept tending the citizens.

It was nearing dawn when Sandy finally got her chance. She was restocking linens in the storeroom when Dr. Bayer entered, closing the door behind her.

"Oh Lord, you again," the doctor said. She lit a cigarette.

Sandy straightened, wincing at the ache in her back. "Like the common cold. No cure for my questions."

The doctor removed her glasses to rub the bridge of her nose. "I suppose I owe you a minute, given you've been helping all night."

Sandy took her notebook out of her pocket. "Thank you. What are you seeing here tonight?"

Dr. Bayer's eyes hardened. "I'm seeing the aftermath of a drunken bacchanal. I'm seeing what happens when people abandon their humanity. When there appear to be painfully few authorities ready to control it."

She began ticking points off on her fingers. "We've had nine deaths so far. Stabbings, beatings, vehicular incidents. More will likely follow—some of our current patients are touch and go."

Sandy scribbled, trying to make her notes passably readable for whoever she gave them to. "And . . . other types of assaults?"

Dr. Bayer's jaw tightened. "If you're asking about rape, yes. We've treated six victims so far. Three are still here. The others left, refusing to file reports or even their names. We can't reach them to follow up."

"Worse than I thought," Sandy muttered.

"It always is," Dr. Bayer said. "There are many more cases we'll never see. They'll go home without seeking treatment, in pain, humiliated, traumatized, distrusting the hospital and the police." She took a drag of her cigarette. "But what concerns me most is how unprepared we are for all of it. This hospital is underfunded and understaffed on a good day. Tonight? We're barely keeping our heads above water."

This is the story—not just the violence itself, but the failures that allowed it to spiral out of control. Sandy had to reach Mac.

"What's your interest in the WAC?" Dr. Bayer asked.

Just say what happened.

"I was on the street when she was beat up. I watched it. I didn't stop it, didn't feel I could. I did find a telephone and called the ambulance. I rode here with her. I want to make sure she's alright. And I know she's part of an important story."

Dr. Bayer picked an ashtray up off the counter and stubbed out her cigarette. "Okay. I'll make sure we let you know when she wakes up."

A young nurse poked her head in. "We've got more casualties on the way. Some kind of brawl near the Embarcadero."

Dr. Bayer smoothed the loose hair off her forehead. "That it, Mrs. Zimmer?"

"No. I also need a telephone."

CHAPTER EIGHTEEN

Long Row to Hoe

Sandy leaned against the wall of the hospital corridor, her eyes closed for a brief moment. The chaos eddied around her, but for the first time since she'd arrived, she felt a thread of control. She'd left a switchboard message for Mac to get at least one reporter to the hospital.

When she opened her eyes, a familiar figure caught her attention. Jane strode through the emergency room doors, her long gait unmistakable even amidst the bustle of nurses and orderlies. Sandy felt a surge of relief at the sight of her friend.

Jane's eyes scanned the room. When they landed on Sandy, her smile broke open. Sandy pushed off the wall and made her way over, weaving through the crowd.

Jane gripped Sandy's shoulders, looking her up and down, at her bandaged hand and blouse stained with Martinez's blood. "So how's the other guy look?"

"Mac sent you?"

"No. I haven't talked to Mac. I just got all I needed on the street and headed here. What happened to you?"

"You were obviously right about conditions out there. I went to see for myself and got caught up in it. There's a WAC who was beat up by a bunch of sailors. I rode over in the ambulance with her."

Jane nodded, approving. "I expect you're the only publisher who had a night like that. You know that's not in your job description, right?"

"Well, where are all the reporters? Isn't it in their job description to be here?"

"Good question," Jane said. "Maybe you and Mac need to start cleaning up your bullpen. Is there anywhere quiet to talk?"

Sandy led Jane to a less crowded corner of the hall, away from the main flow of traffic. Jane's hand absently adjusted her beret, a head covering Jane had never liked as it seemed silly to her, but which she'd adopted as a gesture to a gossip columnist's required femininity. She met the minimal requirements. The beret, lipstick, a silk blouse over pants, and sensible shoes, all impressively stained by the night.

In their private corner, Jane said, "So talk. What have you seen?"

"Well, let's see, what should the headlines be? SAILORS, GIRLS, AND ALCOHOL—BAD CHEMISTRY?"

"Yep," Jane agreed. "That'll be the *Tattler*. What about the *Commerce Journal*?"

"Probably RETAILERS SWEEP BROKEN GLASS AND COUNT RECEIPTS."

"The *Bay City Times*?"

"Definitely no color—V-J DAY CELEBRATIONS LEAD TO PROPERTY DAMAGE. Nothing nasty."

"Good party trick. What did you actually see?"

Sandy sighed. "The riot spread beyond Market. There are injuries coming from all over downtown now."

"See any patterns?"

"Most of them are what you'd expect—broken bones, lacerations. But nine people killed, that we know of." Sandy hesitated, the flood of information slowing her. "But also, there have been at least six rapes reported at this one hospital."

Jane leaned in, her eyes sharp.

"Dr. Bayer told me they're treating three women who say they were raped. Three others were obviously raped too, but they left right after treatment."

Jane's eyes widened. "God's teeth, that's what I was scared of."

"What we're all scared of."

Jane pulled out a pack of Lucky's and offered one to Sandy.

"No thanks, not now."

Jane lit up and said, "No other paper will cover it. You know that, right?"

"Rapes aren't for a newspaper like ours, a paper that wants credibility."

"They're for what our paper should be," Jane said, her voice low and intense. "The truth. We could be the only ones who really report it."

Sandy thought of Cissy Patterson's family motto—"When they rape your grandma, put her on the front page." She'd been horrified to hear that. *Not in our paper. It's too sensational.*

She answered, "These women have been through hell. We can't just barge in and start pushing questions. They're even afraid of the doctors. They need help, privacy, dignity."

"Yeah, sure, I know that," Jane said, impatient. "But this is a news story, Zimmer, and you run a newspaper. We need to act fast. If we wait too long, we might lose our chance to get the story before the victims disappear. Besides, in addition to *privacy*, they might also need *justice*."

"Please, Jane." She didn't want her friend's aggression right now. "These women need time to recover, physically and emotionally. And we don't need to inflame the city with grotesque violence on the front page. We don't want to be tawdry."

"Zimmer, if we wait, they won't tell us or anyone anything about it. Nobody will get in trouble."

That's what Sandy would do if she were them, go home to heal in private. Keep it to herself. "Then they'll leave. Their choice."

Jane started pacing, her energy jerking her every which way. "I get it, I do. But think about it. If we don't tell their stories, who will? The men running the other papers won't. Or if they do, they'll do it all sensational-like."

"I know, that's what I'm—"

"No," Jane interrupted, her voice intense. "You're in a unique position here. You were the first one at the hospital. You're a woman. You can say yes to this. We don't have to be tawdry."

She knew what Jane meant, of course. But she resisted. "We can't just walk in there and interrogate rape victims, Jane. I mean, the police aren't even here. It's not right. Besides, I'm not a reporter. And strictly speaking, neither are you. We can't send a gossip columnist in to interview a rape victim."

Jane winced, insulted. "Okay. We have to start somewhere. Have you called Mac, asking for a reporter?"

Sandy nodded.

"Until he gets here, what about the nurses? Let's at least talk to them. Get the straight dope without bothering the patients directly."

"Alright, we could get more preliminary information before the reporter gets here."

"Attagirl," Jane said, triumphant.

Sandy sighed, seeming worried.

"What?"

"I'm just thinking about a reporter interviewing rape victims."

"A *man* interviewing rape victims."

"Right. Okay, so you draft questions, sensitive ones. We'll make sure they do it carefully."

Sandy saw by the set of Jane's jaw that she considered all this planning to be foot dragging. Jane was the type who operated on instinct. *Not this time*, Sandy thought. *Not today.*

Despite her doubts, Sandy felt a rising thrill at the idea of developing this story.

Jane was right. Investigation was clearly necessary. What they might do with what they discovered, well that was another question, which they could ask themselves later. But still, it was filling her head right now. Was it possible to get the truth out there, tell what happened, without being crude and sensational? Without exposing the victims to public attack to match the physical attack? She pictured TRAGIC DEATHS AND SEXUAL ASSAULTS CAUSED BY CELEBRATION. Emphasis on the tragedy.

One thing at a time.

"Okay, okay, okay. Let me see what I can find out from the nurses. You work on the questions. Meet here in an hour?"

"Forty-five minutes," Jane said, turning to go. "We've got a long dang row to hoe."

CHAPTER NINETEEN

Do No Harm

"What do the nurses say?" Jane asked.

Sandy glanced around, making sure they weren't likely to be overheard. "It's not good. Like we figured, they say these probably weren't isolated incidents. They've heard other cases haven't been reported. They say women don't usually even go to the hospital. They go home and tend to themselves with their mothers or sisters."

"Or all alone," Jane said. "I knew this wasn't just six cases."

Sandy bit her lip. "They say the three remaining women are shell-shocked. The last thing they need is to feel like they're being exploited for a story. We can't do that."

"I get it, I get it," Jane said.

"Well, hello, Mrs. Zimmer, Jane Benjamin." A gravelly voice emerged from a cloud of cigarette smoke.

"Oh God no, not him!" said Jane. She whipped her head around to Sandy. "Not him!"

Lambert approached, an antagonistic smirk plastered on his face. "I understand you're in need of a reporter?"

"Over my dead body!" Jane threw her shoulders back, looking like she was about to throw a punch.

Sandy stepped between them, putting a hand on each one's shoulder.

Lambert continued, "What can I say? For a big story, the editor-in-chief trusts me over a bush-league gossip monger."

"You dirty pygmy..."

"What is it with you two?" Sandy interrupted.

"He's a cheating double-crosser. He stole my byline on a massive murder story I worked by myself."

Judging by the vermilion shade of Jane's cheeks, she hadn't healed in the years since that incident.

"That's rich. It took half the bullpen and a squad of lawyers to fix everything she botched. She nearly burned the building down!"

"Biggest story of the year was mine and you stole it because you're a drunk failure too vain to hustle your own facts."

"I gave you exactly what you wanted—your name on a syndicated gossip column that currently pays for your questionable personal life. The best result you could hope for, you tomato-picking, cross-dressing, Hedda Hopper poser."

Sandy threw her arm in front of Jane, halting what would surely have been a punch to Lambert's face. "Stop. Put this down. You're both wasting time. We need to get ready to do this story our way—carefully and ethically."

"Our way?" Jane repeated. "That's not *his* way."

Nurses rushed past, orderlies wheeled patients to and fro, but the general level of frenzy had abated somewhat, as compared to the tornado spinning between the three of them.

"Listen. Jane, we *need* a reporter. Lambert, okay, you are on this. Stop antagonizing. We have three women currently in the hospital who appear to have been raped. I've got notes for you. You have to follow our directions. Jane's worked up some questions that..."

"Follow *her* directions?"

"That's what I said."

"Good God." He rolled his eyes so far back she could see only white.

"Go ahead, Jane."

"Alright," Jane said, her nostrils flaring. "Okay, ease in slow, ask where they were when they heard the war was over, their initial reactions. What led them downtown."

"Why that?" Sandy asked.

Jane gave an exhausted sigh. "Because that's what everybody's going to wonder—why'd they come down there?"

Sandy frowned, remembering Tommy, her driver, who thought girls should stay home where it was safe. She felt a pang, realizing how she'd at least partly agreed with him. She saw a *Tattler* headline: ASKING FOR IT.

Jane said, "We can't ignore topics readers will be wondering about." She flipped to the next page. "Then ask about the crowds, the noise, the general stuff. They can describe the scene without just diving right into the attack."

"Yes, yes," Sandy said.

"Jesus," said Lambert, who did not relish being lectured by Jane.

"Finally," Jane continued, "their personal experiences. But here's what you do—you ask them just to recreate what happened, everything they sensed. This ought to get more of the real memories. But it'll give them control over the story, let them shape it."

She looked at Lambert, intense. "Only use open-ended questions, no leading statements. And don't say 'attack,' 'assault,' 'rape,' 'victim,' anything like that. Let them choose those words, if they're the right words."

"I didn't just roll off the potato truck, like some people."

Sandy glared at him. "Have you ever interviewed a rape victim?"

Lambert didn't answer.

"I'm going in with you," she said.

"You're not a reporter."

"I'm the publisher. And I'm a woman. That's the way it's going to be. Understood?"

Jane grinned, flaring her nostrils in support.

Sandy knocked and waited for a response before opening the door to Room 12. A brunette with a nasty cut above her left eye sat on the bed. She was wearing a hospital gown.

"Good morning," Lambert said, dipping his head deferentially. "I'm

Derek Lambert, and this is Sandy Zimmer." He looked at the clipboard hanging on the end of the bed and saw the patient's name. "We're from the *Prospect* newspaper, Anita. We'd like to talk with you about your experiences last night. If you're willing."

Anita eyed them warily but didn't answer. Sandy lifted her chin toward Lambert, signaling *Go*.

"Okay." He jumped in. "First, why were you out on the street last night?" he asked.

Sandy winced. That wasn't right. It was very wrong. Why did he lean into that question that way, so abruptly?

Anita's eyes narrowed. "What does that have to do with anything?"

He looked flustered. "We just need to establish where you were when the celebration began. Were you already downtown? Why were you there?"

Idiot!

Sandy instinctively stood, wanting to step between Lambert and the victim.

Anita's voice rose sharply. "You mean what was I looking for? You think I was asking for what he did to me? You going to blame *me* for what happened?"

Lambert's face darkened. "No, ma'am, I didn't mean—"

"Get out," she spat. "Both of you. I'm not some whore for you to shame!"

Sandy tried to fix it. "No, that's not..."

With a shocking burst of energy, Anita swung her legs off the bed and stood, swaying slightly. She grabbed a muddy coat from a nearby chair and, with shaking hands, began to pull it on over her hospital gown. Her eyes bored into Lambert and Sandy. "Go!" she shouted, her voice breaking.

Sandy felt like she'd been struck. She watched Anita struggle to gather her things. They were driving a woman who desperately needed care away from the hospital that could give it to her.

"Please, wait," Sandy pleaded.

"I said *out*!"

They backed out of the room, Sandy's face burning with shame. They moved quickly down the hall, around the corner. She knew what Anita expected and she wasn't wrong.

Lambert looked ashen.

"I'm, I'm sorry," he whispered, his voice barely audible. "That was terrible. I'm so sorry."

"It was worse than terrible! You were arrogant and cruel!"

This was an awful fix. He'd ruined it. But she needed a reporter and he's what she had.

Lambert looked down, shaking his head.

"I need you to do better. We are in a crush. You have to *listen*. Okay? We both went in there thinking we knew how to handle this. We were wrong. But we are going to do better."

Lambert looked shocked. She was giving him another chance.

Sandy paced in a little circle. "So we've lost Anita. She needed treatment, and now she's heading off somewhere, alone and traumatized. That's our fault. Now we need to get it right." Sandy rubbed her forehead. "We need to figure out how to do this without making things worse."

Sandy thought about her own experiences of loss and trauma, about the loss of her mother, about tending to her father through so many medical emergencies. And of course, losing Edward.

"These women are going to need a slow approach. They aren't going to know how to make sense of what just happened to them. We can't even be sure they'll recall what happened last night. We can't rush in a few hours later demanding explanations and justifications. And we must say absolutely nothing that sounds like judgment. Good God. They've been raped once. Don't do it again."

Lambert flinched, wounded, but then leaned in. "How?"

"They are victims, not criminals. We have to promise that we're on their schedule. That we're asking their permission. That they're in control. And that we'll respect their wishes about sharing their story or not. They absolutely must be given permission to decide."

Lambert nodded.

She continued, "I'm introducing us, setting the tone. Then you step in, follow my lead. Understood?"

"Got it."

"And for God's sake, don't make any assumptions about their choices. They are absolutely not to blame for what was done to them. Absolutely not."

CHAPTER TWENTY

A Fragile Trust

She's a victim, not a source.

Sandy knocked gently.

"Come in," a hoarse voice answered.

Sandy entered, her steps careful, measured, Lambert at her heels.

A young woman, maybe twenty, sat upright on the bed, her hands folded on her lap, strawberry-blonde hair in a ponytail, the whites of her blue eyes red. A bruise bloomed across her left cheekbone, and there was an ugly cut on her bottom lip.

I know her.

It was the girl the WAC had risked her life to protect. Sandy had very nearly forgotten this girl in thinking about the corporal. Now here she was, the victim. *We can't mess this up.*

"I'm Sandy Zimmer. This is Derek Lambert. We're from the *San Francisco Prospect.*"

The girl's eyebrows lowered. She said, hesitantly, "I'm Renee."

"May we sit?" Sandy asked.

Renee nodded and Sandy and Lambert pulled up chairs beside the bed, close but not too close.

"We'd like to talk with you about what happened last night, if that's okay."

Renee's fingers twisted the bedsheet. "Why?"

Tell the truth, Sandy thought.

"I saw you running from those men last night. I didn't know how to help you. I feel bad about that."

Renee's expression looked unfocused. She didn't say anything.

"You were gone so fast. So I tried to help the corporal. She was fighting those men and they beat her up. I was able to get her here, to the hospital. And now I find you here, the person she was trying to protect." Sandy took a deep breath. "I'm sorry I couldn't help you last night."

Renee shook her head, like she was trying to break some thought loose. "Is she alright?"

At this moment, she felt for someone else.

"They're working on her. I can let you know when I hear."

Renee nodded.

"Renee, I'm the publisher. Mr. Lambert is a reporter. He works for me. I'd like him to ask you some questions. I will stay right here while he does."

Renee looked back and forth between them.

Lambert cleared his throat. "Renee, can you tell us where you work?"

She looked at Sandy and then back again at Lambert. "I work at Lowe Shipyards," she said. "Or I did. I don't know if I do now. Everything's changed."

That was right. Everything had changed.

"How long have you been working there?"

"Since '42," Renee said. "I started as a welder's assistant. Now I'm lead welder on my shift. I guess that doesn't matter, does it?"

Sandy nodded, thinking of Jane's columns promoting those jobs for women. She'd written that the job required a special kind of resilience.

"What brought you to the shipyards?"

Renee's eyes took on a faraway look. "My brother joined the navy right after Pearl Harbor. I wanted to do my part too. Building ships . . . it felt like I was helping to bring him home."

Sandy leaned forward slightly, asking, "Has he made it home yet?"

"Just last month."

Sandy nodded. Lambert took a deep breath.

Renee continued to describe her work and her brother Carl, her voice growing stronger. Sandy and Lambert listened, asking questions about Renee's work and about Carl's recovery at Letterman's Hospital. Renee's shoulders started to drop, and the wariness went from her eyes.

She fell silent, though her face moved through several changes, as if she was thinking about what she was willing to say and what she was not.

"About last night, I just can't say much," Renee began hesitantly. "My memory . . . it's foggy . . . I just don't want . . . Look, okay, I was downtown with my friend Tasha. We were happy the war was over. Everybody was." Her voice caught. "Then . . . everything went wrong."

Sandy pressed her spine into her wooden chair, willing herself not to look eager, and spoke up again. "You don't have to say anything you don't want to say, Renee."

Lambert looked at Sandy doubtfully—*You sure about that?*

"It's all mixed up in my head." Renee took a shaky breath. "There was that woman . . . the soldier?"

"Corporal Martinez," said Lambert.

"She tried to stop the sailors from pestering me . . ." She trailed off, her eyes filling. "But there were too many of them, they started fighting her. She was helping me and then she said to run and I did. I don't know what happened to her. What happened to her? And when I ran off, then . . ." She shuddered, unable to continue. Her face went white.

Sandy worried something bad might be happening to Renee right now. "Would you like me to get a nurse? Have the doctors here been able to help you?"

Renee shrugged. "No, don't get the nurse. I guess they helped. They did some tests, gave me pills to calm me. I don't know what happens now."

"What do you mean?" asked Lambert.

Renee's fingers twisted the sheets again. "I don't know what I'm supposed to do after this. Do I go back to work? Is welding over? Am I too damaged to work? Anyway, how would I face my coworkers? My mom? My brother?" She choked back a sob. "What if . . ."—her voice dropped to a whisper—"what if I'm pregnant?"

Sandy wanted to vomit. A pregnancy. She'd wanted a child more than anything. And here was Renee terrified of that possibility. The headline in her head was Victim Raises Rapist's Baby.

Lambert said, "You don't have to face this alone. There are people here who want to help you. We will do our part."

Sandy was surprised at the tenderness of his gruff voice, the puffiness under his eyes.

Renee looked up, doubtful.

"Dr. Bayer and her team can help you with . . . with all of your concerns. Will you let them continue treating you?" he asked.

Sandy thought, *Does he mean abortion? They can't. Rape's not legal grounds for that, unless she's dying.*

Renee hesitated, then answered slowly. "I guess. Maybe."

"That's good, Renee. That's good. Is there anyone you'd like us to contact for you? Your mother or brother?"

Renee shook her head. "Not yet. I can't . . . I can't face them right now."

"I understand," Sandy said. She chose her next words carefully. "Renee, if you decide you want to share your story about what happened last night, the *Prospect* will listen. Mr. Lambert and I will listen. But that's your choice. Only yours."

Renee met Lambert's eyes directly for the first time. "Why are you doing this?"

"Because I believe you," he said slowly, "and because I want to bring down the bastards who did this."

Sandy's heart skipped. That wasn't right to say. This would not be the story of his own anger. But it wasn't wrong either.

"I'm tired," Renee said.

Sandy nodded, and she and Lambert stood to leave.

He paused at her bedside. "Is it okay if I come back to see you?"

"Maybe, we'll see," Renee said, looking back and forth between them.

They'd done better. Not perfect, but better. And now they had to do it again with another victim.

CHAPTER TWENTY-ONE

She's Awake

Sandy stepped into the alley at the hospital's entrance, the cool air a relief after the stuffy corridors inside. A coffee cart stood nearby, its owner pouring Folgers for hospital workers and visitors. The contrast between the quiet alley and the bustling hospital made Sandy feel like she'd taken a peculiar jump in time.

She fumbled in her purse for change. "One coffee, please. Black."

As the woman poured her a cup, Sandy leaned against the brick wall, closing her eyes for a moment. Their conversation with Renee replayed in her mind. She felt drained but relieved that they were making progress. And she was surprised at the way Lambert had adapted. Maybe he wasn't entirely the ogre Jane said he was, though the third victim, Nancy, hadn't opened up to him at all. To be fair, she might not have opened up to anybody.

"Here you go," the woman said, handing her the steaming mug. "Black as the mood inside."

Sandy wrapped her hands around the warmth. She took a sip, bitter liquid promising clarity. She lifted the mug for her second taste.

"Zimmer!"

Sandy turned, startled, as Jane came barreling down the alley. Before Sandy could react, Jane collided with her, splashing hot coffee across her blouse and sending the cup skittering on the asphalt, breaking into chunks.

"Oh, cripes! I'm sorry!" Jane exclaimed, grabbing napkins from the cart for Sandy's blouse.

Sandy used them to dab at the spreading stain. "It's fine. I'm fine, Jane." She bent to pick up the broken mug, which she handed to the vendor with an apology, and a dime to cover the cost of replacing it.

"So I got my stupid column done, called it in," Jane said.

"Good, good." She knew how it stung her friend not to be the reporter in the room with the victims. But Lambert was right. They couldn't put a gossip columnist on this. They needed real credibility. The problem was that someone like Jane deserved to be a straight news reporter, officially on the big stories. Then again, with syndication, the gossip column paid well enough, and Jane was lucky to get that gig.

"How'd the louse do?"

"You know, ultimately, he was fine. He got it. I was a little shocked. I really stepped back in the third interview and just watched him. She didn't open up, but he's established something with the second victim. We have to follow up. And, of course, a woman needs to be in the room with him, for obvious reasons. He exudes a very male energy."

"I think it's a troll energy. Either you or I need to be in there with him, or we send in somebody off the switchboard."

"Yep." *Something else that needs fixing—too few women on staff.*

"Mrs. Zimmer! Miss Benjamin!"

They turned to see nurse Vada hurrying toward them, her face flushed with exertion.

"What?" Sandy asked, a knot forming in her stomach.

Vada huffed, "Corporal Martinez is awake."

In an instant Jane and Sandy were running back into the hospital. Corporal Martinez was awake!

They reached her room, pausing outside the door. Sandy chanted again in her head, *She's a victim, not a source.*

"Ready?" she asked Jane.

Jane nodded, her usual brashness stifled.

They entered the room quietly. The corporal lay in bed, her skin wan against white sheets. Her dark, wavy hair was loose around her shoulders, a far cry from the neat bun Sandy had seen in the street. Bandages were wrapped around her head, and her brown eyes blinked slowly, as if she was trying to focus.

Her gaze moved around the room, her brow furrowed. She opened her mouth to speak, then closed it again, struggling to say something. Her hands clutched at the sheets, then released, a couple times over.

"Corporal Martinez," Sandy said softly. "I'm Sandy Zimmer, and this is Jane Benjamin. We're from the *Prospect* newspaper. How are you feeling?"

A flicker of uncertainty crossed her face. "I've been better," she said, her voice scratchy. "My name's Gloria. You can call me Gloria."

"Do you remember what happened last night, Gloria?" Jane asked, her tone more direct than Sandy's. Sandy shot her a warning glance, but Jane pressed on. "Anything at all?"

Sandy moved closer to Gloria, careful not to loom over the bed. "We know you've been through a terrible ordeal. I saw you go down last night at the Civic Center."

Gloria's brow wrinkled as she tried to focus on Sandy's face.

"Saw me go down?"

"She got the ambulance," Jane said. "She stayed with you."

Gloria closed her eyes and then opened them. "Thank you."

Sandy said, "We'd like to talk to you about what happened, if you're comfortable. You're in control here."

Gloria's eyebrows rose slightly at that. She studied Sandy for a moment. "You're with the paper, not the police? Not the military?"

"That's correct," Sandy said. Jane's face registered their shared opinion—police should be here. Military should be here. The implications were troubling. Were the authorities turning a blind eye, or were they simply overwhelmed? Either way, it wasn't good.

"So you're the only ones taking information?"

"So far."

Gloria paused for a moment. "I'm not sure what I should . . . I mean . . ." Her eyes darkened. "The military, they'll want to handle this."

"The beginning might be a good place to start," Jane said, though that was not always so. "I'm not sure what the military wants."

Sandy pulled up a chair, gesturing for Jane to do the same. "Why don't you start by telling us what you remember from last night? Take your time."

Gloria absently patted her gown where the breast pocket of her uniform should be, checking for something that wasn't there. Sandy noticed the gesture, wondering what it meant.

"I was on patrol," Gloria began. "I'm military police, supposed to be keeping control, but it was . . . crazy. People everywhere, dancing, singing. Just wild. I'd never seen anything like it."

She pushed a stray lock of hair behind her ear.

"At first, it was mainly that everybody was drinking," Gloria continued. "The merchants were all out on Market Street selling alcohol. Even the ones whose business had nothing to do with that—I mean sofa salesmen were selling big bottles to the guys. So everybody was just having fun for a while, I guess. But as the night went on, things got ugly. Fights broke out, people smashed windows. I called it in several times, but . . ." She trailed off, shaking her head.

"But what?" Jane prompted gently.

Gloria's eyes hardened. "Nobody came. No backup. It was like they'd just decided to let the city burn."

Jane tensed. "Are you saying that was a decision somebody made?"

"How would I know that, ma'am?"

Sandy leaned forward. "What did you do when you saw all this?"

"My job," Gloria said simply. "I tried to maintain order where I could. Break up fights, stop people from destroying property. But I was just one person. I couldn't even see anybody else doing that."

She fell silent for a moment. When she spoke again, her voice was quieter. "Then I saw this group of sailors, surrounding a woman. They were laughing. An awful kind of laugh. You know what I mean. I'll bet you've heard it."

They both nodded. They had. Every girl had heard that bully laughter on the streets, even on the school ground.

"I could see she was terrified."

Sandy's heart quickened. She was describing Renee.

"What did you do?"

"Told the men to back off. I told her to run."

"Did she?" Jane asked.

Gloria said, "She tried to. I don't know how far she got. A couple of them ran after her." She trailed off.

Sandy waited, resisting the urge to push. After a moment, Gloria continued.

"So they turned on me, kind of wrestling me back. I used my stick, but there were too many of them. The last thing I remember is falling, then . . . nothing."

The room fell silent as Sandy and Jane absorbed Gloria's story. Sandy's mind worked to fit this piece into the puzzle.

She leaned forward, her voice low but intense.

"Gloria, the woman you saved . . . she's here. We've spoken to her. Her name is Renee. She works at the shipyards." She paused, watching Gloria react, releasing pent-up air. "And we've spoken to another woman who was also attacked last night. She works at the shipyards too. There may be some connection."

Gloria grimaced. "Of course there's a connection. It was all the alcohol, and all the guys, and just all that . . ."

"Energy?" Sandy added.

"I expect they'd all been scared for some time, waiting to be shipped off to the Pacific. Then all of a sudden, they were off the hook. No way were there only two girls," Gloria said.

Jane answered, "There were six women in this hospital who'd been attacked, but four of them left without sharing details."

"But you know it's not just six," Gloria replied. "On a night like that, there were a whole lot more girls hurt. They just found some way to get home. It's not like they're all going to come here or to the police or anything."

"I know," Sandy said. But she also knew that the number didn't matter if no one talked. "What you did was incredibly brave."

Gloria shook her head, wincing. "I did my job. Wish I could have done it better. Maybe a man could have . . ."

Sandy leaned forward, meeting Gloria's eyes. "You *did* your job, Gloria, valiantly."

Gloria's eyes blinked. "How is she, the one who ran away?"

"She's hurt," Jane said honestly. "But she's alive and talking."

Gloria's shoulders relaxed slightly. She rubbed her forehead.

"Can I ask you something else?" Sandy said.

"Go ahead."

"Earlier, you reached for your pocket. Were you looking for something in particular?"

Gloria's hand lightly, briefly, returned to the phantom pocket. "Just a good luck thing, an old carved bird my grandmother gave me when I joined the WACs. A Cooper's hawk. It's supposed to represent strength and focus." She laughed. "It tells you something that I lost it. Maybe that's why I'm here."

"One more question," Sandy said. "What do you want to see happen now? With the men who did this, with the way things have been handled?"

Gloria lifted her chin slightly. "They need to answer for it," she said firmly. "What happened last night—people need to own up."

Jane leaned in, her voice low. "I swear we'll try. Will you go on the record with your story?"

Gloria studied them both for a long moment. "What do you think would happen to me if I go on the record? To my position in the WACs?"

The question hung in the air. Sandy exchanged a glance with Jane. They didn't know.

"This job is everything to me. You don't know how hard I worked to get here, to prove myself. It means a lot to my whole family. I'll bet I've already put myself at risk by doing what I did with those sailors. Going in the paper? I don't know . . ."

"We'll look into it," Sandy said. "We won't publish anything about your story without your consent."

Sandy could see the doubt in Gloria's eyes. She reached out, gently gripping Gloria's hand. "We understand, Corporal."

Sandy thought, what would the papers say? ANGRY WAC ACCUSES SAILORS ANONYMOUSLY.

This was growing more complex by the minute.

"What do you think?" Sandy asked Jane as they walked down the corridor.

"We've hit a gold vein, but just nicked the surface."

Sandy answered, "She's got good reason not to talk."

Jane added, "I guess you've noticed nobody else is even asking questions."

"I've noticed," she answered.

CHAPTER TWENTY-TWO

Good Luck

That afternoon, Sandy settled into the back seat of Edward's Lincoln, the hum of the engine a low, comforting murmur as Tommy navigated through midday streets from home to the office after a shower, breakfast, and a change of clothes. The city, still reeling from last night's upheaval, bore fresh scars of celebration. Streets were clearer now, but evidence of turmoil remained—overturned trash cans, blankets of confetti, and broken glass. Most people had gone home, but not everyone. Small clusters of revelers loitered, unwilling to let the festivities die. Or unable to find their way home or back to their bunks.

She glanced at Tommy's eyes in the rearview mirror. He was focused on the road ahead. She reached forward and dropped the keys to her old car into the front seat and told him where he'd find it so he could arrange to get it back to the garage.

Her mind returned to Gloria. She'd taken bold steps in a world that didn't want her to. Sandy wanted to borrow even a portion of that courage.

The exhaustion was creeping in, not just physical but emotional. It had been a long night and morning. Yet amid this fatigue, determination flickered.

This story could redefine the *Prospect*. Were they ready for the scrutiny and potential backlash?

She drummed her fingers on the leather seat, looking out the window at the department stores and office buildings, windows broken, wares dragged to the street.

Gloria, Dr. Bayer, and the shipyard women had carved their paths in male-dominated fields. They'd faced their own struggles, found work-arounds, made sacrifices.

She rubbed her temples, trying to clear her head.

This story was a chance to prove the *Prospect* could be more than it had been, and to show that she was more than just Edward's placeholder.

Tommy glanced back at her, worried. "You okay, Mrs. Zimmer?"

She managed a small smile. "Just thinking."

The car hit a pothole, aggravating her headache.

She'd been given this role for a reason. She would embrace it. The *Prospect* needed to lead, not follow. And she needed to be the one to guide it. It would be rigorous, and daring, and she needed to be thoughtful.

She could picture Wyatt's disapproving scowl, Olive's look of disappointment. The board might get rid of her if the story didn't pan out as expected. The stakes were high, almost impossible.

"I need your help," she said, breaking her silence.

"Of course, ma'am. What do you need?"

"I know someone who lost a lucky charm," she said.

Tommy shook his head. "That's a shame."

"It was a small wooden carving of a bird, a Cooper's hawk. She seemed quite upset about losing it."

"You want me to find something similar for her, ma'am?"

"Yes, please," Sandy replied. "She needs a little luck right now."

"I'll find something that fits the description."

"It might be hard to find something like that, Tommy."

"I know a guy who carves wood."

It wouldn't match what Gloria had lost, but it would be something. Sometimes the best thing wasn't an option.

CHAPTER TWENTY-THREE

Swift Justice

Sandy pushed through the heavy doors of the *Prospect* building, the oily, chemical scent of ink hitting her nostrils, even far from the mechanical end of the business. Her heels clicked against the marble floor as she made her way to the elevator, each aching step a reminder of the long night.

"Good afternoon, Mrs. Zimmer," called the receptionist.

Sandy waved and decided not to take the elevator. She didn't feel like the usual pleasantries, even with the elderly elevator attendant. Steeling herself for conflict, she walked up the spine, the spiral staircase at the core of the building, pulling her way along on the wrought-iron rail to the second-floor newsroom.

Typewriters clacked, phones rang, the air buzzed with frantic energy. Reporters huddled in small groups, comparing notes and shouting across the room to check details. Copy editors hunched over desks, their pencils scratching over pages of copy. Sandy paused, readapting herself to the office.

Mac spotted her from across the room and made his way over, barking. "What happened at the hospital? I've been trying to reach you all day."

Sandy held up her hand. "Thanks for sending Lambert."

"Really? Oh good. I was a little worried. I know he can be gruff, but..."

"No, no he was fine, really."

He looked her up and down, staring at her bandaged hand. "What happened? Lambert said he's investigating something about a woman being attacked. It was a gawdawful mess out there. Deaths, property damage, overturned cars, smashed windows, looting. We've got reports of fires in North Beach, a fight at the Palace Hotel. The police were completely overwhelmed."

"I know. I told you I was out there."

"What do you mean by 'out there'?"

"I mean I went out on the streets last night to see for myself. I wound up at the hospital."

Mac's forehead creased as he looked again at her hand. "Did you get stitches? What happened, Sandy? Do you think that was a good idea?" He sounded angry in the same way that her father had when he was worried about her.

"No stitches. And actually, yes. It was a very good idea to see what was happening. Frankly, I was shocked not to run into any of our reporters or photographers on the street."

He stiffened. "It's a city. You wouldn't expect to see someone in the exact place you happened to be."

"Well, I saw Jane. Never mind, I'm sorry. What about the editorial meeting? I'm not too late, am I?"

Mac looked at her with surprise. "You don't go to those."

"I'm going today, Mac."

She scanned the room again, noting the feverish activity. Everyone was chasing a story. But not necessarily the one she wanted them pursuing.

"You wanna give me some idea what you're . . ."

"A number of women were raped out there last night. I'm upset, Mac. And I want to talk about how to cover that."

Red creeped down from Mac's face to his neck. "Well, sure, yeah, we have to figure that out. But Sandy, this type of thing goes through me. I mean, last night I was glad to send Lambert over because you asked for a reporter."

Her anger flared. "Okay, so about that. Did you choose Lambert because you thought he might put me off?"

"Sandy, I already told you he's a strong reporter. That's why I brought him back." A vein in Mac's forehead visibly pulsed.

"Okay, fine. He was great. It's just that I want to make sure the women's stories are part of the plan for our coverage. I don't want what's happened to them to get swept under the rug."

"And you don't trust me to understand? Sure, fine. We'll talk about it." Mac turned on his heels and marched off toward the conference room.

Her headline? SHE USED TO BE SO NICE.

She took a deep breath and followed him, trying to keep up, her short legs working overtime.

As the two of them rushed through the newsroom, the din of typewriters, ringing telephones, and chatter washed over her. Sandy noticed reactions as they passed—some reporters glanced up with barely concealed surprise; others pointedly kept their heads down, avoiding eye contact. A few exchanged looks of confusion or irritation at this departure from the norm—should they stop behaving as usual in her presence? Sandy rarely cruised through the bullpen. Since Edward's death, she'd mainly skirted the edges of the room, going from the elevator to her office, to Mac's, as some kind of peripheral person.

Together they entered the buzzing conference room. Chatter waned at their arrival. Sandy took a seat at the head of the table, acutely aware of the silence that followed. Mac awkwardly retrieved another chair for himself, so Sandy rose to give him hers and he gestured—*No, sit*—so she did, embarrassed to have taken his place. *Would Cissy have moved or just assumed the seat?* Most of the writers and editors in the room were people she didn't have much interaction with, but there was Jane and there was Lambert.

Mac started off by reviewing what had gone in the morning paper—Japan's surrender, what Truman had to say about the boys coming home, the developing UN headquarters race, and news about the chaos of celebrations, including generalities about property damage and some fatal accidents—all pretty compatible with what the other papers wrote.

"Okay, so what have we got coming up?"

It got real noisy real quick—guys shouting out what their reporting had turned up.

"We got the newlyweds, wife dead, husband hanging on after a drunk mowed 'em down."

"And that old guy, killed when somebody threw a trash can full of water out the window that landed on his head." There was some grim laughter at that.

Lots of details yelled back and forth, guys trying to shape stories according to this angle or that—about thousands of frenzied, drunken revelers, 90 percent of them navy enlistees who went on a spree of vandalism, looting, assault, robbery. Nine people dead so far, almost a thousand injured, gross damage to businesses, public buildings, streetcars, cars, traffic lights, signs, barber poles, and marquees.

"Nobody's ever seen anything like it in this city."

"And the rapes," Sandy said.

"Yeah, the rapes!" Jane added. "At least six of them. But a whole lot more than six."

Mac asked, "What do we know for sure? I assume the deaths and all that are clear. What do we know for sure about the rapes? Is anybody willing to talk to the police and reporters?"

Sandy breathed in through her nose. "I expect you know that women who've been raped don't often choose to come forward because questioning by the police and reporters can feel like a whole new assault."

"That's tragic, I know," Mac said. "But we can't put it in the paper if nobody's talking."

"They'll talk," Jane said. "We just have to take it slowly."

Sandy nodded.

"Are you proposing that Jane, our gossip columnist, should report on this?" Mac asked, incredulous.

Sandy looked over at Lambert, a question in her eyes.

"I'm on it," he said.

"And you think *you'll* persuade rape victims to talk? I mean, no offense, but you're no Prince Charming."

Sandy winced. "The victims don't want *Prince Charming*."

Lambert looked at Sandy and Jane. "Give me a couple days. I can't go at it fast like with the other stories. Let me take a crack at it."

The ancient news editor, Jorge, sitting next to Mac, cleared his throat in a phlegmy rumble, his tiny spectacles perched on a massive nose. "May I clarify things? I assume Lambert might struggle to persuade any lady anywhere to talk to him about anything. But you think he might get a lady who's been raped to share the bloody details with him?"

"Go to hell, Jorge!" Lambert interrupted.

"Alright, then," Jorge continued. "Let's say you're able to work this previously unheard-of magic. You get these ladies to tell all to you. Are you all, also, saying that we would want to put it in our paper? We want to put *rape stories* in our paper?"

"Yes, we do!" Sandy answered.

Everybody else jumped in.

"It's dicey!"

"We're not going to get them to talk."

"It's not our brand."

"We can't ignore the news because we're squeamish," Sandy said.

Mac said, "Okay, Sandy's right. She wants us to investigate this. We've got to try."

Sandy exhaled.

"But we can't afford to move reporters from other stories. I mean we have deaths to report, all of that. So Lambert, if you're willing to do this, go ahead and take a few days on it. Meantime, let's plan the rest of it."

"Thank you, Mac," said Sandy. "All I'm asking is for Lambert to do the reporting, and if the story is good, we put it in."

Old Jorge blew his nose with a blast, folded up his handkerchief and put it back in his pocket, wet.

"God I hate guys like Jorge—they've always got a million reasons why you can't do what you know you ought to. It's like he has to personally protect everything from changing, ever." Jane crossed her ankles, her shoes up on Sandy's desk.

"Come on, Jane." Sandy slapped her friend's feet.

Lambert's face was dark red. Now he was all in favor of reporting the rapes. "If we want actual readers, we gotta turn up the lights. We're last place in readership. We gotta do this story and do it right."

Sandy felt herself warming to this guy. Apparently when he was in, he was in. She remembered Edward talking about some reporter, saying he was the kind of guy you want in your foxhole. She wondered if that described Lambert. She'd never been in a foxhole.

Her secretary, Ruby, knocked and opened the door. "Mrs. Zimmer! Telephone call for you. Says it's urgent."

Sandy waited for Lambert and Jane to exit, still bickering, and closed the door behind them. She centered herself before picking up the receiver. "This is Sandy Zimmer."

"Hello, Mrs. Zimmer. This is Una Tyler." Charles's date from last night.

"Una? Please call me Sandy. How can I help you?"

"I'm sorry to bother you, but I thought you should know. I work at the DA's office. Something's happening here."

Sandy looked into the bullpen at Mac and then reached for a notepad. "Go on. What's happening?"

Una's voice lowered. "District Attorney Brown is planning to announce an investigation into the riot. He's talking about convening a grand jury, fast."

Sandy's pen scratched across the paper. "How soon?"

"Immediately, from what I've overheard. He wants to move quickly, calm the city, show them justice will be swift."

DA TO THE RESCUE—WHAT WILL HE RUN FOR NEXT?

Sandy leaned back in her chair. A grand jury investigation would definitively announce he was taking the riot-related crimes seriously. And it could complicate things for the *Prospect*'s investigation into the assaults. But there was something else in Una's tone that gave Sandy pause. "I'm wondering why you're calling me? Surely the DA's office will make an official announcement soon."

"I'm not sure I trust Mr. Brown to handle this properly."

"Go on."

"It's . . . Well, you know he's ambitious. Very ambitious. I've worked here long enough to understand what that might mean. Every case, every public statement—it's all calculated to advance his career."

Sandy recalled Pat Brown raiding Mrs. Inez Burns's high society abortion clinic, though half the men in government and law enforcement had sent women there themselves. He'd raided it for the headlines, she'd thought when it happened. "He's more concerned with his image than with justice?"

"Please don't write that down. That's not it," Una said carefully. "Mr. Brown does care about justice. But he also sees every high-profile case as a potential stepping stone. The riot . . . it's big news. He'll want to make a splash, show how decisively he can act."

"You're worried he might gloss over important details?" Sandy probed.

"Something like that," Una replied, and exhaled dramatically. "So much happened last night. So much that people aren't talking about. I'm afraid he'll focus on the obvious—the property damage, the looting—and miss the other things. The ones that are harder to fix."

Gloria, Renee, and the other women at the hospital. All the system-wide failures that had allowed the night's events to spiral out of control.

"Have you spoken to Mr. Brown directly?"

Una's laugh was bitter. "I'm a secretary, Mrs. Zimmer. You remember how that works, don't you?"

"I do." That was true.

"Mr. Brown barely knows I exist, let alone cares for my opinion. But you're the publisher. You have influence."

Sandy thought of how humiliated she'd been at dinner over the conversation on whether she ought to be a publisher at all. Una had heard that. And yet she was talking about her influence. She'd underestimated Una last night. She would try not to make that kind of mistake again. "Not as much influence as you might think. But I'm working on that. Thank you for calling. It was the right thing to do."

"I couldn't not call. Not about this."

Sandy did the math. A hasty grand jury investigation could potentially hinder their own efforts to uncover the truth about the assaults, maybe somehow shut it down early. But it could also provide a way to bring the issues to light in a formal, legal setting, if Brown brought charges.

"Will you go on record with any of this? Mr. Brown's ambitions, his approach to cases? Specific examples?"

"I need this job . . . I don't have anybody else. I mean it's not like Charles Jones and I . . ."

"I understand," Sandy said quickly. She knew the compromises required for survival. "Okay, let's keep this conversation between us. But if you decide you're ready and willing to speak more openly, and you have information to share, please let me know."

"I'll think about it."

As Sandy hung up the telephone, she leaned back in her chair, her mind whirling. The grand jury announcement would break soon. They had to act quickly if she wanted the *Prospect* to stay ahead of it. How to proceed?

She paced her office. The *Prospect* had a responsibility to report the truth, but with care and sensitivity to the victims.

She stuck her head out the door. "Jane!"

Sandy waved her in. "We need to talk strategy."

Sandy quickly filled her in on the conversation with Una, watching Jane's face shift from curious to concerned.

"Awful fast for a grand jury, isn't it?" Jane mused. "That complicates things."

"It does," Sandy agreed. "Do we publish the little we know now, or wait to see how the official investigation unfolds?"

Jane drummed her fingers on the arm of the chair. "We don't wait too long—we don't want to be scooped. Not just by other papers, but by the DA's office itself. But if we publish too soon..."

"We push the women before they're ready."

They sat in silence for a moment, the question hanging heavy in the air.

Finally, Sandy spoke. "We approach this strategically. It's not just about getting the story out there; it's about how we position the *Prospect* in relation to the investigation. That has to take victims into account."

Jane leaned forward. "Look at you, smarty pants."

"Write a story," Sandy began. "We need to frame this as a larger story about systemic failures. But we can't offer details the women haven't agreed to share yet."

She stood, pacing as she outlined her thoughts. "We can start with the lack of police presence. Touch on the unchecked alcohol sales. Paint a picture of a city caught unprepared for the scale of the celebrations."

Jane scribbled notes. "Got it. Set the stage."

"But here's the crucial part: We're the paper willing to ask hard questions. Make it clear our investigation is ongoing. We're digging deeper than the surface-level chaos."

She paused, considering her next words carefully. "And Jane? We need to be prepared for pushback. Not just from the authorities, but from our board, maybe even our readers. This story... it's going to ruffle feathers."

Jane's eyes gleamed. "That's my girl! So, what's our angle on Brown and the grand jury?"

Sandy tapped her fingers on the desk, thinking. "We'll report it straight. But make it clear that we'll be watching the process closely. We'll say, 'The *Prospect* will continue to investigate,' and 'Sources suggest there may be more to the story.' We want to signal we're not just accepting the official narrative."

"Got it." Jane nodded. "So Lambert's on the rapes. I report the rest, right? Even if my name isn't on it?"

"We shouldn't do that anymore. We'll figure it out." Sandy hesitated, then decided to trust her instincts. "Reach out to Dr. Bayer. See if she'd be willing to provide a statement about the injuries she treated, without violating patient confidentiality. We need her official voice, somebody authoritative to talk."

Jane jotted this down, a small smile playing on her lips. "You're getting very bossy, boss." She paused, her expression turning serious. "But I'm not completely sure anybody will see a woman doctor as authoritative."

Sandy sighed.

Jane continued, "Plus, what about Mac? Shouldn't he be in here?"

Sandy hesitated, uncertainty crossing her face. Jane was right. And it was rare for Jane to be cautious, Sandy impulsive. Mac should absolutely be in on this discussion. But something held her back, maybe his management of her, or maybe a fresh confidence in her own judgment. She said, "Sure, but for now, get started. We need to move quickly and quietly, and I don't want to get bogged down in some lengthy editorial discussion."

Jane snorted. "I hate to be a wet blanket since that's usually your job, but Mac's not going to like it."

"I'll work it out with Mac. Trust me."

Jane's eyebrows shot up, amusement on her face. "Putting your lady wiles to work?"

Sandy felt a flush creep up her neck. It was true that she had a history of persuading men to see her point of view, or if not that, at least comply with something she wanted, by appealing to their vanity, somehow making herself seem smaller and them larger. And Jane had long made fun of her for that, even though it often worked.

But she didn't feel like deploying that tactic here. It didn't sit right. Besides, she'd noticed that a charm offensive of that type just didn't reliably work on Mac. It was like he had no time for it. Or maybe his ego didn't need much shoring up.

Whatever the reason, she'd need to try something new. She needed to test her publisher wiles instead. For a change.

CHAPTER TWENTY-FOUR

Power Play

DRAFT: EMERGENCY DOCTOR SADDENED BY V-J DAY ASSAULTS

By J. Hopper, reporter

Central Emergency Hospital's woman doctor, Leona Bayer, hadn't seen anything quite like it before—at least six female patients who appear to have been attacked in the V-J Day celebrations. As is often true in such cases, the alleged victims were all unwilling to reveal their identities.

"Predictably, our patients hesitated to report the crimes or even to seek care. We have no idea how many other women went home injured at downtown's celebration without receiving any medical treatment. . . ."

Sandy pored over Jane's draft, words swimming before her eyes. She'd been right to trust her. The article walked a delicate line, hinting at the issues without exposing too much. Her byline read J. Hopper, her birth name, rather than Jane Benjamin, the pen name she used for her gossip column. This was what she did when she committed straight reporting. Gossip paid the bulk of Jane's salary; news fed her brain.

A commotion in the newsroom roused her. She moved to her office door just as Mac's voice boomed over the din, "Turn that up! DA's making an announcement."

Sandy rushed into the bullpen, toward the radio, where reporters clustered. The tinny voice of the announcer crackled through the speaker:

" . . . and now, KSFO brings you District Attorney Edmund G. 'Pat' Brown with an important announcement regarding the events of the last twenty-four hours."

The room fell silent as Brown's voice filled the air. "Citizens of San Francisco, in light of the disturbances that occurred during last night's victory celebrations, I am asking the grand jury to investigate some incidents police officers have reported."

Sandy wondered if police had mentioned any rapes if the victims didn't officially talk. Would the police report hospital notifications?

"We will not allow the joy of peace to be marred by a single episode of lawlessness and destruction. The grand jury will work swiftly and effectively to bring anyone responsible to justice . . ."

Mac sprang into action. "Johnson, get down to the courthouse. See what you can find out about the grand jury. Who's on it? How it works, all that. Peterson, get me reactions from city officials. Matthews, talk to some business owners affected by the riot, the looting and all. I want perspectives from all over the city."

Reporters scrambled, grabbing notepads and rushing for the door. Sandy caught Mac's eye and motioned him over.

"We need to talk," she said quietly.

He followed her into her office. As soon as the door closed behind them, he burst out, "A grand jury, this fast. Kind of surprised at Brown."

Sandy took a deep breath. She would tell him straight. "Jane's working on a story about what the doctor said, about the rapes."

Mac's excitement faltered, replaced by confusion. "What story?"

"I only just a few hours ago found out about the grand jury, from a source in the DA's office. I wanted to make sure we got a jump on it."

Mac's eyes narrowed. "And you didn't talk to me? You went *around* me? I'm the editor-in-chief. Do you not understand how this works? Reporting goes *through* me!"

Sandy felt her resolve waver. "I know, Mac. I'm sorry. But we have to get ahead of the grand jury."

"Oh. You and Jane have figured this out, the two of you?"

She ignored his sarcasm because she knew she'd been wrong to go around him.

"Christ, Sandy." Mac ran a hand through his hair. "You keep shutting me out of my work!"

"Well you keep doing that to me too!"

He looked both furious and confused.

"Listen, Mac, I know. It won't happen again. But let's be clear. I am the publisher. I will not be blocked out of this either. I need to know I can trust you to recognize that."

"Trust goes two ways," he said.

"It does. Okay. You can trust me. Can I trust you?"

"Alright. Okay."

It didn't *feel* like they trusted each other, but they said it, so that was something. She sighed.

Mac said, "So I've got a lot of questions. I didn't raise them all in the meeting because I didn't want to put you on the ropes. But putting *rapes* on the front page? It's like we'd be the *Tattler*—"

"That's why we've been careful. We promised these women we wouldn't publish anything without their consent."

"But it's not a story if we don't get their name in the paper."

"Really? I mean, we quote people off the record all the time."

"If they accuse men of a crime like that, we have to be sure."

"But anyway there's so much more that's not supposedly salacious," she continued. "The police were ridiculously overwhelmed and unprepared for the scale of things, all the unchecked alcohol sales, even to minors. And some witnesses suggest that military police were slow to respond to disturbances. Nobody told the sailors to return to their ships.

They were just allowed to riot all day and night. And city government seems to have been entirely hands-off."

Mac leaned forward. "Do we have sources on all this?"

"Jane's working on it while Lambert works on the rape stories. I assume the others are too. But we need more. Some are off the record for now. And there's something else. I've got someone from the DA's office saying that Brown's rush to convene this grand jury might be politically motivated."

"Well of course it's politically motivated! Everything's politically motivated."

"Our source at the DA's office is concerned he's going to focus on what's easy to dispense with, the property damage, and ignore the rapes and the deaths, even."

"No surprise there. But systemic failures at every level—law enforcement, city government, military oversight . . ."

"That's why I wanted to be careful how we approached it. These women, Mac—they have to trust us. We can't just throw their stories out there without consideration. They trust us because I'm a woman and they believe I'll be responsible."

"Lambert's not a woman." Mac sank into the chair across from Sandy's desk, looking, and smelling, a mess. How long had it been since he'd showered? "Jesus. This is dangerous. I mean it's dicey putting details about rapes in the paper, plus blaming soldiers—"

"Sailors."

"Plus the police, the military, the city government." Mac stood abruptly, pacing the office. "And you didn't think to bring me in on this. I'm not some jerk, Sandy. I've been doing this forever. I need to be running this."

Sandy felt a flare of anger. "We've already discussed this. I said I was wrong. We're done with that, Mac. Besides, how did you help when I suggested we assign more women reporters to cover women's issues? And also, I'm good at this! I know things about what a story might be. I'm an actual reader, Mac!"

"Okay, but this is the kind of story that could break the paper. The board's going to have a fit when they hear about this."

Something in his tone made Sandy pause. "What about the board, Mac?"

A flicker of guilt crossed his face before he could hide it. "They . . . they've expressed some concerns about the direction of the paper lately."

"About me." Sandy felt as if the floor had dropped out from under her. "They've been talking to you about taking my job, haven't they?"

Mac's silence was answer enough. She'd wondered about the source of her distrust and there it was. She'd sensed he was underhanded.

She met Mac's gaze directly. "So while I've been working to save the paper, and then to uncover all this, you've been plotting to take my position. Is that it, Mac?"

He had the decency to look ashamed. "It's not like that, Sandy. I just . . . The board approached me. They're worried about the paper's future."

"As are we all. And do you think you could do a better job?" Sandy's voice was level ground, but with jagged rocks two steps ahead.

"I'm not smarter. Or even more intuitive. But I know how to navigate these waters."

Sandy answered, "I see. Well, let me make something clear, Mac. I'm not going anywhere. Edward believed in me. He trusted me. I'm going to see it through, with or without your support."

She'd known her position was precarious, but not how close she was to losing it all. But she didn't care. This was her paper. Hers! At least for now. And she would make the decisions. And she would announce that to anybody who doubted it, including Mac.

She looked up at him, assessing whether it would ever be possible to trust him. "I know I'm not the publisher you expected or wanted. I know you think *you* could be the publisher. I know I'm learning on the job, and I've made mistakes. But this story—it's not just about selling papers or making headlines. It's about uncovering the truth and holding people accountable. And it's about saving this paper. Making the *Prospect* what Edward wanted it to be. What I want it to be—a real paper."

Mac looked skeptical. "What happens if the board decides it's too risky?"

"Maybe they'll appreciate it if we actually start leading the other papers around here!"

"Not if all the advertisers pull out because we're ruffling the wrong feathers."

"Which advertiser is going to come out against putting rapists behind bars?"

"You might be surprised, if we're talking about sailors. You know it's not simple, Sandy. This was the end of the war. They want the celebration to be the point."

"But there are other points too!" She stood, lifting her chin. "Come on. We can face them together. This is the kind of story that defines a newspaper. It's why you're here. I know it is."

She could see the conflict playing out on his face—hunger for the story, worry about the consequences.

"I'll make you a deal, Mac. Back me on this. Help me navigate the politics, approach the guys who should have controlled the riot. If I'm wrong—if this blows up in our faces—I'll step down. I'll recommend you take over as publisher."

"Sandy, come on. If this blows up, I'll be out on the street too."

"It's a gamble, I know," she said. "But I believe in this story. I believe in what we can do. I'm willing to put my job on the line to prove it."

The silence stretched between them. Sandy could see the gears turning in Mac's head, judging risks and rewards.

Finally, he spoke. "Alright. But we do this my way too. I want to review everything before it goes to print. No sneaking, no rushing to scoop without considering all the parts."

Relief washed over Sandy. "Deal. Thank you, thank you, thank you."

"Don't thank me yet. I may be sitting on the other side of your desk before we're done. Now, let's see Jane's article."

She jumped up, rounded the desk, and hugged him hard before getting back to the story.

This wasn't perfect. But they understood each other. Maybe.

"Nice headline," Mac observed.

"What will the *Tattler* head be?"

He briefly considered and then had it. "First Comes the Party, Then Comes the Blame."

"Right. And the *Commerce Journal*: San Francisco Happy and Shopping Again."

"Exactly."

Mac pointed to one of Jane's paragraphs, frowning. "Here, we'll need another source."

Sandy made notes. "She needs to reach out to Chief Dullea about the police response, or lack thereof."

Mac considered this. "He'll be defensive. I don't know if Lady Bulldozer is the right one to call him."

Sandy couldn't resist the opening. "You know, if the guys gave her the respect she earned a long time ago she wouldn't have to fight for every morsel that just drops on their plates."

"Okay, okay," he said. "But you can't just let her loose on this story. She needs tempering. Do you plan to debate every point from now on? It's exhausting."

Sandy smiled. "You need to get some sleep so you can keep up."

They worked through the article, refining and strengthening it.

"Okay, let's get Jane in here," Mac said, leaning back in his chair.

Sandy called her.

"But Mac . . . what do we tell the board?"

His face turned somber. "For now, nothing. Let's just keep working. We'll figure it out."

The door opened and Jane entered, her eyes darting between Sandy and Mac. "So, we're doing this?"

Sandy and Mac exchanged a look, then Sandy nodded. "We're doing this."

CHAPTER TWENTY-FIVE

Doing Their Job

The pale blue weathered house sat nestled among similar pastel homes on a quiet street in Point Richmond. Paint peeled from its wooden siding, and the patch of lawn out front needed mowing, but bright pink begonias cheered up the porch.

Lambert knocked and, after a moment, they heard shuffling inside. The door opened to reveal a middle-aged woman with worry lines etched deeply around her mouth. "You're the reporters," she said. Sandy didn't correct her. "I'm Shirley, Renee's mother. Come in, I guess."

They stepped into a small, tidy living room, crowded with worn furniture, paperback novels, and family photos—prominent among them a big picture of a sailor. Renee sat on the couch, her hands clasped tightly in her lap. She nodded welcome as Sandy and Lambert entered.

"Is this Carl?" Lambert asked, tilting his head toward the picture.

"Yes. He'll be home from the hospital soon. Maybe another week." Renee's eyes darted nervously between the picture and her mother, who had settled stiffly into an armchair nearby, her face strained.

Sandy couldn't imagine the worry in her life, both of her children hospitalized in one week.

"I can't really say more about what happened," Renee began hesitantly. "I've been thinking about it. I'm not sure I can talk about it."

Sandy looked at Lambert. This was what they'd worried about, that the more time that went by, the less willing Renee would be to talk. And pressing her now could make her even more hesitant.

Keeping her voice steady, Sandy said, "Maybe if we talk about your concerns, we can figure out how to take them into account."

Renee's eyes welled with tears. After a moment, she said, "There's a guy in town, a sailor, who heard about it, and he's been telling people I was some 'good time girl' who regrets what she did and has started making things up. You know, we have to *live* here, talk to our neighbors . . ." She trailed off, looking miserable.

Her mother, who'd been looking out the window, now reached over to squeeze her daughter's hand. "Baby, you don't have to do or say anything you're not comfortable with. These two will understand if you change your mind." She looked at them both. "And it doesn't even matter if they don't understand."

Sandy saw that Shirley was discouraging Renee from talking, to protect her from neighborhood shame and judgment. Sandy felt a flame of resentment at Shirley, for not encouraging Renee to do what was right, what was brave. But then she doused it, knowing that was unfair. Shirley wasn't wrong. It would be terribly hard for Renee to go on with the life she'd led before if she told her story in the paper now. Shirley was focused on protecting her daughter against the world. Sandy saw there was bravery in that.

Lambert said, "Renee, I'm wondering how the sailor knew anything about this."

"I think because the police came by."

"They did?"

"One of the police is pals with the sailor I mentioned. I think he's the one who did the talking. But also, one of the guys in the group that raped me was from here. I don't know if he's talking too."

"Did the police say how they found you?"

Shirley said, "We were thinking you told them."

Oh God, that's why they don't trust us.

Lambert said, "It wasn't us. Or anyone at the paper."

But was it? Sandy worried.

"How were the police?" he asked. "Were they helpful?"

Renee looked away. Shirley laughed, bitterly. "Let's just say they didn't think anything good was going to come of our trying to press charges. Nobody knows who the boys are—there were thousands and thousands of those boys out there that night. The officers pointed out that these things usually don't go well for women who try to report them."

The police were scaring her off.

"They said rape was hard to prove, and that the newspapers would make it worse."

"No," Sandy interrupted. "I'm sorry, but no. I'm the publisher. I am absolutely not going to let the paper savage you. Absolutely not. You can trust me."

She saw Lambert's face, looking at her sadly, like he felt sorry for her. What was that?

Sandy leaned toward Renee. "We are serious about protecting you. We wouldn't publish anything that could identify you without your explicit permission. And we can be careful about details that might point to any specific individuals. This is not the same as taking those men to court. Though you could still choose that if you wish—and maybe you should consider it."

Sandy ached for Renee. But she knew the power this story could have, to help other women, maybe even to bring the rapists to justice. She hated being in this position. But she had to try.

"I can only imagine how difficult this is. What happened to you was wrong, terribly wrong, but your voice deserves to be heard, not silenced. Maybe start by telling us just a little bit, and see how it feels to talk? You don't have to accuse somebody."

Renee took a shaky breath.

Shirley got up and stood by the window.

Renee's fingers twisted the hem of her blouse. "We heard on the radio that Japan had surrendered. Everyone was calling it V-J Day. Me and my friend wanted to go celebrate with everybody else."

"It was quite an atmosphere," Sandy prompted gently.

"It was crazy," Renee continued, a hint of wistfulness in her tone. "The streets were packed. People were dancing, singing. We ended up near the Civic Center."

Lambert kept writing in his notebook. "What time did you get there?"

Renee's face scrunched in concentration. "It must've been around eight or nine. The sun had set, but the streets were full."

Her eyes grew distant. "It was . . . electric. Everyone was so happy, hugging, waving flags. There was music, people passing bottles . . ." She paused, looking apologetically at her mother. "That's where we met them."

Lambert leaned forward slightly, not too avidly. "Who do you mean, Renee?"

"The sailors," Renee said, her voice faltering slightly. "They were all in uniform. Like I said, one of them knew me from the neighborhood." She shook her head. "I didn't think anything about any of it at first. Everyone had been so friendly that night.

"But then I saw that I hadn't understood. You know—that feeling you get—that a guy is going to turn bad, that a night is going to turn bad, before anything even happens."

Sandy grasped her hands together.

"When they started surrounding me," Renee whispered, "I didn't see an opening. Then . . . there was the woman. She was in a WAC uniform. She tried to keep them away from me."

Renee's eyes widened. "She tried to fight them off, but there were too many. I saw her falling, and then . . . I feel so bad about her." She trailed off, unable to continue.

Sandy said softly, "That wasn't your fault. She's going to be alright."

"That's good," Renee said.

Shirley returned to her seat, pain crossing her face. Sandy glanced at her, then back to Renee.

"What happened next, Renee?" Sandy asked. "Take your time."

Renee's voice dropped to barely above a whisper. "Everything happened fast. When the WAC said to run, I ran. A couple of the guys caught up with me. I think a group of them were back with the WAC. Tasha wasn't anywhere near me anymore. The sailors started pushing me away from the crowd, into this alley near the Civic Center. Then the rest of them showed up."

The contents of Sandy's stomach churned. She clasped her hands over her belly.

Renee continued, "There were six, maybe seven. I couldn't . . . I couldn't get away." She paused, taking a shuddering breath. "They ripped my shirt, pulled down my pants. They took turns at me . . . up against the wall. But the one with red hair, he seemed different. Hesitant. I remember him saying, 'This ain't right, guys.' But the others just laughed. Their laughing was almost the worst part. Just laughing at what they were doing to me. That was the worst."

Sandy fought back a wave of nausea, trying to keep her face composed.

Renee's face was wet now. "I thought it would never end. Finally there was just one guy left. The others had taken off." She looked at her mother and sighed. "I wasn't a virgin. But still, they stole something from me."

Shirley got up and wrapped both arms around Renee's shoulders, not saying anything.

Sandy said, "Renee, this sheds light on not just what happened to you but to others that night. What you have to say is important."

Lambert muttered agreement. "Your story can help the others. They need to know this happened. Could happen. And that they aren't the only ones."

Renee's eyes welled. "I should have known," she whispered. "Even with all the excitement, I should have trusted my gut. That kind of celebration . . ."

Sandy reached out, touching Renee's hand. "Hindsight. You were just trying to celebrate with everyone else. You did nothing wrong. Those men are to blame."

Renee wiped at her eyes. "Yeah," she said, her voice shaky. "I built the ships for those guys to sail on. It wasn't right."

Lambert asked more questions to clarify things, Sandy remaining vigilant for any signs of Renee's distress.

Renee lifted her head, tears streaming down her face. "Why should I do this?" she asked brokenly. "Why does it matter? It won't change what happened."

Sandy felt a lump in her throat. She thought of all the women who'd stayed silent, all the perpetrators who'd never faced consequences. "It matters to others. Hearing your story might give them the courage to come forward. And the more who do, the harder it is for people to ignore them."

Lambert added, "But we won't publish a thing if you don't say yes."

"That's what you're claiming, but we don't know you. It's time you left," said Shirley.

Sandy and Lambert took their leave, unwelcome, untrusted.

CHAPTER TWENTY-SIX

Smoke-Filled Room

Afternoon sun burnished the cigarette and cigar smoke hovering just above head level at Breen's Irish Bar on Third, a favorite joint of the obvious crew of newsmen but also other in-the-know types with posh home addresses: those who liked to rub elbows in a dive where they might overhear something sensational to be traded later over drinks at the Pacific-Union, Bohemian, Olympic, University, or Commonwealth Clubs. The bar's allure had spread so that even visiting dignitaries often made a pilgrimage. Other than gossip, what were Breen's attractions? A twenty-four-inch jar of pickled pigs' feet sat at eye level on a dark wood bar as long as a football field. The alcohol was cheap. Also, it smelled like grease. It was the obvious watering hole for Mac and Jane, less so for Sandy, who preferred to keep her elbows off the sticky tabletop.

"First, what are we gonna call it?" Jane asked, after a swig of bourbon.

"Call what?" Sandy asked.

"The whole thing! Yesterday. Today. For the headlines."

"V-J Day Fray," said Mac.

"Surrender Skirmish?" tried Jane.

"Too cute," Sandy said. "How about peace riot?"

Jane said, "That's it."

"Simple and heinous. Perfect." Mac raised his martini, Jane her tumbler, and Sandy her champagne glass.

"To the peace riot," Mac toasted.

"Macabre, aren't we?" asked Sandy. "Not sure why we're toasting. We've likely lost our source on the rape."

"The depraved world of news. Gets nasty outside the corner office," said Mac. "I'm sorry about the source, but there's still a lot to put in the paper."

"I'm not giving up on that story. But the police acting like they did . . . the pressure against Renee, the fact that she doesn't trust us, all the stuff with the board, risking ad dollars by pushing the riot stories. Jehoshaphat." She drank her champagne in one swallow.

"Jeez, Sandy. How do ad dollars even belong in that list?" said Jane.

"So I guess you don't care about your weekly paycheck?"

Mac held up his nearly empty martini glass. "Here's to payday."

Jane and Sandy echoed, "To payday."

Still Sandy disliked the joke. She had to keep the paper running. Jane was in a position to pooh-pooh such matters—she wasn't responsible for the actual people on staff. Sandy was. She figured Mac saw both sides.

Mac leaned forward, his blue eyes twinkling. "Ladies, ladies. Let's focus on the positive. We got exclusive information, the other papers are behind us, and we've got options."

"At least we think we do," Sandy said.

"Who invited Killjoy?" Jane asked, flagging down the waiter.

The door to Breen's swung open, admitting a bright tunnel of light. Sandy glanced up to see her father-in-law stride in through the sun, followed by a group of well-suited men she didn't recognize.

Jane muttered, "Looks like the fun police have arrived."

Sandy watched as Wyatt pointed the group toward a private back room, which was no great shakes compared to any number of local alternatives. But it possessed a strange kind of gravitas because deals were made there. More deals led to even more deals.

As they walked by, she heard something about the United Nations.

"Giving another tour," Mac observed, his tone casual, eyes sharp.

"Has he been doing this often?"

"Often enough."

Sandy was glad of Wyatt's efforts to get UN headquarters for the city. It would be a coup. And honestly, she wanted to support him because she'd always longed for his approval, wanted to be welcomed into the rooms where he held court, more than Edward ever had. "He's working hard on that."

As the group passed their booth, Wyatt's eyes met Sandy's. She expected him to stop to say hello. But instead, he hesitated, an odd expression flitting across his face before he quickly ushered his companions into the back room.

Jane said, "That was weird. What's got him so jumpy?"

Sandy frowned. Not like him to avoid a social interaction, especially one that might conceivably interest his important guests. "Not really sure," she admitted.

Mac sat up straighter. "Maybe you should do a little rubbernecking, Jane. Ladies' room's near the room with all the suits."

"No, wait, Jane," Sandy said. On one hand, she didn't want to pry into Wyatt's business. On the other, her curiosity was piqued. "Let's focus on the main thing," she said. "Let's not get distracted by the suits."

Jane snorted. "Since when is following a lead a distraction? Isn't that my job?"

Before Sandy could respond, the door to the back room opened, and Wyatt reemerged. He puffed out his chest and approached their table.

"Sandy, Jane, Mac," he greeted them, his voice gruff but polite. "I didn't expect to see you here."

"It's a newsie bar," Jane answered.

Sandy smiled up at him, hoping to soften Jane's comment. "Just a quick drink, Wyatt. How are you? UN business?"

His eyes darted between the three of them and then he smiled. "Fine, fine. Yes, busy with the commission. The effort's going very well. Very. I'd say it's seventy percent likely at this point. And what are you three here to discuss that you couldn't discuss in the office?"

"We're planning a coup," Jane offered.

Sandy kicked Jane under the table. "We were catching up about the V-J Day unrest," Sandy answered.

Wyatt's expression tightened almost imperceptibly. "Nothing out of the ordinary, I expect. High spirits getting out of hand, I'm sure. Young men..."

Sandy watched Jane and Wyatt, her heart racing. She knew Jane was trying to gauge how much Wyatt knew about it. But she also saw the flicker of ... was it concern? Guilt? Something in Wyatt's eyes she couldn't quite place.

"We're working up some pieces," Mac said, his tone deceptively relaxed. "Any thoughts on how the city handled the celebrations?"

Wyatt's eyes squinted. "I'm sure the authorities did their best under challenging circumstances. Things such as this—world-changing historic events—are difficult to plan for. When you've been in a position to run such a vast ecosystem as city government, or any part of it, you understand its built-in complexity."

Sandy thought, Wyatt had never held such responsibility himself. But she supposed he knew a lot of men who had.

"Enjoy your champagne," Wyatt said to Sandy.

As he turned to leave, Sandy felt an urge to pull him back, to bridge the distance between them. He was Edward's father, after all. And her own father was gone. "Wyatt," she called softly. "Is everything alright?"

For a moment, his mouth opened, just a little. He looked at Sandy, and she thought she saw regret or worry in his eyes. But then it was gone, replaced by his usual certainty.

"Everything's fine, Sandy," he said firmly. "Please don't start bothering yourself about my concerns at this late date."

And he strode back to the private room.

"Owie," said Jane.

Sandy was rooted to her seat, her feelings hurt. She knew that, for too long, she'd sought his approval, tried to fit into the mold he'd created for her. But that role was waning now.

Mac asked, "What's he hiding?"

"We need to be careful," Sandy answered. "Whatever he's involved in, it's obviously sensitive. We can't just go charging in without considering consequences."

Jane leaned forward. "But we can't go soft just because Wyatt might pitch a fit. If there's something to know, we ought to find out."

Mac looked awkwardly at Sandy.

"Okay," she said. "Look into it, discreetly, Jane. See if you can figure out who those men are, where they flew or trained in from."

Jane grinned. "I'll know where they bought their tooth powder and buried their childhood dogs by breakfast."

Sandy got up to head home, leaving Mac and Jane ordering Hangtown fry, and at the exit nearly collided with Lambert, who was entering the bar.

"Well, well," he slurred. "If it isn't our lovely publisher." His eyes raked over Sandy in a way that made her skin crawl.

"Excuse me, Lambert," Sandy said stiffly, trying to move past him.

He reached out, grabbing Sandy's arm. "How about a drink? I've got some ideas about the women."

Sandy felt her face flush at his drunkenness. Before she could respond, Jane stepped between them, her voice threatening. "Hands off, Lambert. Now."

He raised his hands in mock surrender, but his leer remained. "Just bein' friendly. No need to get all worked up."

Sandy left with no comment to Jane, her cheeks burning with humiliation, furious with herself for thinking Lambert was someone she could easily manage. Really, for thinking anybody or anything was easily managed.

CHAPTER TWENTY-SEVEN

In the Dark

Sandy eyed two photographs. Her secretary, Ruby, hovered over her shoulder like a hummingbird trying to get its beak in the flower. The photos, meant for an article on how San Francisco would clean up and bounce back after V-J Day, couldn't have been more different.

The first showed overturned cars on Market Street, real attention-grabbing stuff that screamed "peace riot" loud and clear.

The second was quieter, city workers, men and women, young and old, cleaning up debris. Something about it stirred Sandy.

"What do you think?" Sandy asked, curious what Ruby would say.

Ruby hesitated, tapping her pencil. "The second one."

Sandy's eyebrow shot up. "How come?"

"Those flipped cars, sure they're shocking. But you've got a lot of the bad stuff, all over the paper." Ruby's words came faster now. "This one, with everyone pitching in? It shows hope. Grit. Isn't that what the city's all about? My San Francisco, anyway."

Sandy had been leaning that way herself. "You've got an eye."

Ruby straightened up, her cheeks going pink at the praise.

Sandy tapped Ruby's chosen photo. "The city isn't just one bad night. It's how we pull together the next morning." She added, almost to herself, "We're going to be hitting our readers with a lot. This one shows there's still light out there. That's true too."

Ruby glowed, proud at the validation.

Sandy scribbled notes for the caption. She thought maybe, just maybe, she was getting the hang of this paper.

A sharp knock interrupted her.

Mac stood in the doorway, looking like he'd swallowed a lemon. "We need to talk. Private-like."

Sandy froze at his tone, then followed him out her office door.

Instead of heading to his office like she figured, Mac led her up the spine at the building's core. She gripped the rail, following Mac to the barn-large third-floor composing room, past twelve operators who rode the keyboard seats of gawky mechanical beasts, the Linotype machines, seven feet tall and two tons heavy. She followed him all the way to the back corner, Darkroom 3.

"What?" Sandy asked.

Mac didn't answer, just pushed open the door to the red-lit room, the smell of rotten eggs and vinegar hitting like a bad picnic. A young photo guy was bent over a tray of liquid.

"Hey!" he yelled, before realizing who'd busted in.

"Take five, will you?" Mac said.

The guy scooted out without a further peep. As the door clicked shut, Mac turned to Sandy, half his face hidden in shadow.

"We got a problem. A big one."

Sandy's gut clenched. "Big enough to send us to the closet?"

He took a deep breath. "Cissy's gunning to buy us out."

"Cissy Patterson? The *Washington Times-Herald* Cissy Patterson?"

Mac nodded grimly. "The one and only."

"We're not for sale. I told her that."

"Word is, she's planning a takeover."

Sandy's mind flashed back to all the calls she'd had with Cissy, the older woman poking around about money, taking little digs at the paper, dropping invitations for a purchase, all of which Sandy had pooh-poohed, repeatedly.

"Where'd you hear about a takeover?" Sandy asked, seeking solid ground.

"Jane found the name of a guy who was with Wyatt in Breen's. Seems he works for Cissy in her business arm of things. The group had nothing to do with the UN bid. So I called a buddy at the *New York Daily News*—Cissy's brother runs it, you know. Anyway, word's getting out that she's looking to grow her empire west. We're in her sights."

Sandy leaned on a nearby table. "I told her no. Why us? Why now?"

Mac leaned against the darkroom counter, his usual energy subdued. "The board's spooked, Sandy. On top of everything else, they're worried we'll burn bridges with the peace riot coverage."

"How do they even know about it?"

"Come on, Sandy, they're our board! Charles asked and I told him!"

She understood his position, but still, it felt like a betrayal.

"Plus the advertisers are antsy, and word is City Hall isn't too pleased with us potentially airing their laundry about not managing things too well. But there's more. They don't think we're playing it safe like we always have, and that's making us look unpredictable. Cissy and her ilk, they see that as weakness. To them, we're a wild card, and that makes us ripe for the picking."

She got the picture.

Everything Sandy was aiming for pressed down on her. All the risks she wanted to take, the story she'd been pushing . . . She was doing the right thing. But was she just being selfish, trying to prove herself? Had her need to be seen as a leader, to make Edward proud, to show Wyatt she could do this job, left the paper and everyone who depended on it vulnerable?

The urge to fix everything, to make everyone happy, welled up. But how could she protect the paper, tell the truth, and keep the board satisfied all at once? She gripped the chair back, feeling like she'd missed a step on the stairway.

"Cissy sees a chance, and she takes it."

Cissy Patterson running the *Prospect*? The thought made her want to gag.

"We can't let it happen, Mac," Sandy said, sounding braver than she felt. "The *Prospect* isn't just a business. It matters to this city. We've got a job to do right here. Not from DC."

Some of the usual color came back to Mac's face. "How's she planning to pull this off? Cissy wouldn't try it if she didn't think it would work."

Sandy frowned, thinking back over the past few weeks. "So the board," she said slowly. "There have been gatherings I wasn't included in. Of course that's always been true, but now . . ."

"She's been sweet-talking them," Mac finished for her. "Of course I doubt it could have been all that sweet, considering the source." He paused. "It makes a twisted kind of sense," he said, his voice low. "Wyatt's got the old-money connections on the East Coast. He's tight with the kind of folks Cissy Patterson runs with. And ever since you took over, he's been making noise about how the paper needs experienced leadership."

Sandy pursed her lips. "He's been awfully chummy with Charles and Adam lately. All those lunches."

"Wyatt's's got a stake in this UN headquarters bid and the peace riot coverage could tank their chances." Looking embarrassed to say the obvious, Mac said, "Wyatt's never been shy about putting business before family."

"Obviously."

He went on. "Charles asked me to meet up for a drink and I did. He said to think about what this story could do to our ad revenue. Half the businesses downtown were involved in that mess, selling the alcohol that fueled it. They may pull their ads if we run this."

"We have a responsibility to report."

"Well, Charles thinks you have a responsibility to keep the paper afloat. He says Wyatt thinks Edward understood that. Though he wasn't very good at it."

She tossed a wadded-up paper at the trash can and a bitter laugh burst out. "Wyatt never supported Edward when he bought the paper. Called it a 'frivolous venture' and refused to invest a dime. When Edward put him on the board, he thought Wyatt would finally be behind him, but maybe Wyatt just saw it as the best way to control Edward. And he's always made it clear he thought I had no business in this job. That you—or anyone else—would do better."

Sandy's voice caught as she added, "It's like he's never been able to bear to see either Edward or me succeed."

"I'm sorry." Mac looked truly miserable.

"We need more to go on," Sandy said, pushing down the hurt. "We can't act without proof, not at Wyatt."

Mac said, "I'll dig. My guy at the *Daily News* might be able to get us more on Cissy's plans."

"I'll try to feel out the board, see if I can get any of them to reveal something. Or budge." She couldn't stand the thought of facing those men, of pretending everything was fine when they might all hold knives ready to plunge in her back.

"Watch yourself," Mac warned. "If Cissy catches wind we're onto her..."

"Keeping it under my hat."

They stepped out of the darkroom, blinking into the harsh light of the production staff's space—photo editors, graphic artists, engravers, proofreaders, and copy editors all hard at work, electrified by their shared goal. Sandy might have found it inspiring if she hadn't also felt like it was all about to crumble. Just minutes ago she'd been feeling sure of her place.

"We'll figure it out," Mac said, giving her shoulder a squeeze. She could hear the doubt in his voice.

As she walked back to her office, Sandy's mind trudged. How could she protect the paper, her people, everything Edward had built, from a threat she didn't know was there until now? She saw the *Bay City Times* headline: LADY PUBLISHER RUINS *PROSPECT*.

Back in her office, she saw Ruby bent over her desk studying those pictures.

"Everything okay, Mrs. Z?" Ruby asked, looking up, worried.

Sandy forced a smile. "Fine, Ruby. Just . . . just business stuff. What do you think for the caption?"

Ruby pointed at what she had typed: "San Franciscans pull together to rebuild."

CHAPTER TWENTY-EIGHT

Doing the Math

Sandy stood, gripping her telephone handset, willing Charles to answer. Rubber squeaked on old wood as Ruby wrestled with Sandy's chair behind her.

"Almost got it," Ruby grunted, yanking on a lever, risking her nylons, down there on the floor on one knee.

A commotion at the office door further interrupted Sandy's focus. Mrs. Connelly bustled in, looking flustered and holding a squirming Wilford in her arms.

"I'm sorry to intrude," Mrs. Connelly said, slightly out of breath. "Mr. Dumont's quit. He says he's had quite enough of Wilford's antics. He insists the dog can't stay at the house any longer. I told him I expected Wilford would be non-negotiable with you and so he quit."

Sandy hung up the telephone, sighing. "Never mind. You were right, Mrs. Connelly. I'll keep Wilford here with me. It'll make the office feel homier anyway."

Ruby raised her eyebrows. "Isn't Mr. Dumont your butler? Jeez."

Sandy caught Mrs. Connelly's doubtful expression and said, "Call the agency and set up interviews for Dumont's replacement. Say we're looking for someone competent but flexible. And it wouldn't hurt if he knows how to train a dog."

Mrs. Connelly set Wilford down. The pug immediately began sniffing around the office, his wrinkled face scrunching up at new smells.

Sandy glanced at Ruby, who was red-faced from exertion. "Ruby, the chair's fine."

"Your feet don't touch the ground," Ruby protested. "How can you run a newspaper dangling like that?"

Mrs. Connelly tilted her head in agreement.

A bang came from the hallway. Dick, the maintenance man, appeared in the door, hauling a beat-up oak desk. "Where do you want this, Mrs. Zimmer?"

Sandy stared at the monstrosity. "I don't want—"

"It's from storage," he huffed, somehow maneuvering the desk through her door, into her office. "Ruby said you needed something less imposing."

Sandy's eyes narrowed at Ruby. "Less imposing?"

"I meant smaller, Mrs. Z. More fitted to you. You're a good twelve inches shorter than he was. You wouldn't wear Mr. Z's overcoat, would you? Why should you keep using his desk?"

She wasn't wrong. But why hadn't Ruby done that math earlier, when Sandy was less busy?

Mrs. Connelly said, "I'm sure we have something in the penthouse that would be more to your liking, Mrs. Zimmer."

"Do we have to do any of this now?" Sandy asked, trying to keep the irritation out of her voice. "I'm in the middle of something here."

She turned back to her telephone, pointedly ignoring the shuffling and clanking behind her.

Since she hadn't been able to reach Charles—was he intentionally avoiding her?—Sandy asked the switchboard to call Adam Lowe, drumming her fingers on the wall.

"Mr. Lowe's office," a crisp voice answered.

"This is Sandy Zimmer. Is Adam available?"

"I'm sorry, Mrs. Zimmer. Mr. Lowe is at the Olympic Club."

Sandy's frustration mounted. "For crying out loud, why are they all, always, at the Olympic Club? Could you please have him call me as soon as he returns? It's urgent."

She hung up, then immediately picked up the receiver again, asking for the Olympic Club dining room rather than waiting for Adam's return call.

"Hallelujah!" Ruby's triumphant cry from the floor next to the chair made Sandy jump. "Try it now."

Covering the mouthpiece, she said, "In a minute, Ruby. I'm in the middle of—Yes, hello? This is Sandy Zimmer. I'm trying to reach Adam Lowe. I believe he's having lunch there?"

Sandy surveyed the chaos of her office. Dick was now on his hands and knees, tinkering with the drawers of the new desk. Ruby was removing Edward's photos from the wall. Mrs. Connelly's mouth hung open in shock.

"Wait! Ruby!" What was going on here?

"Mrs. Zimmer?" the maître d' said. "Mr. Lowe is in the cardroom."

"Playing poker? At noon?"

"Is this an emergency? Would you like me to ask the switchboard to get him there?"

"Yes."

After all that rearranging, Adam's impatient voice filled her ear. "What's the calamity?"

She straightened, focusing. "Adam, I need to discuss the paper. There have been some developments—"

"I figured you'd hear soon." His voice was not dismissive. "Here's my point of view. I see the risks you're taking with this riot coverage. Hell, I built my career on calculated risks. But you need to think bigger."

Sandy's anxiety mixed with hope. "Bigger?"

"The *Prospect* isn't just some small business. It ought to be huge in this city. What I've heard about your upcoming coverage plan itself—it's bold, it's probably necessary. But the reporting very well may tank the paper before you win the benefits. I'm not afraid of controversy, but I am concerned about going big enough, plan-wise, smart enough, so we all recoup our investment ultimately. You shouldn't be trying to weather a storm. You should be trying to ride the lightning all the way."

"You're not against our plan to really cover the riot?" Sandy asked.

"I just told you I'm not against the coverage, per se. But I don't see where it's heading. How are we going to turn this risk into opportunity? How do we use this to build something big and lasting? That's what I'm interested in, Sandy. Not just surviving, but thriving. If I don't believe you have a plan for that, I'm a no-go."

Sandy's grip tightened on the receiver. "Our readership's going up—I know it. And besides, we're supposed to tell the truth no matter what, even without a business plan. For a newspaper, the truth *is* the plan!"

"The truth is just a down payment. It's the foundation for what comes next, and that's what I want to know, what comes next?" Adam snapped. "And obviously I'm not the only one you'd need to persuade either. Charles has been going over the records, calculating every dime we might lose from advertisers pulling out if you blame downtown businessmen's alcohol sales for causing carnage, and if you argue that the police aren't up to protecting city streets. And of course Wyatt . . ."

"What's going on with Wyatt? Cissy isn't his type. I'm more his type than Cissy."

"Her money's his type. Listen, he thinks when he gets the UN headquarters, a properly sized gift will mean his name goes on the plaza, maybe even the building. You know how he is about the family name."

"Argh! Too bad he's not as strong on the people in the family as he is on their name."

"Be that as it may."

"What about Charles?"

Adam sighed. "Honestly? He's likely to go along with whatever Wyatt wants. Charles is a follower, not a leader. He figures Wyatt will throw him scraps, and Charles is in it for the scraps."

"That's it?" Sandy asked.

"There's just you, me, Charles, Wyatt, and Olive. I'm sorry, Sandy, but I can't support throwing good money after bad without a big vision. We can talk more tonight if you want, but now I've got to get back to the table."

The line went dead. Sandy stared at the telephone.

A plan. The details of the riot were terrible, but true. Publishing it *would* shake the city. But *not* publishing it . . . that would be a betrayal of everything she believed Edward had believed.

Sandy mentally tallied the votes: Wyatt and Olive each had 15 percent, she had 35 percent, Charles had 15 percent, and Adam 20 percent. With Wyatt obviously in the sell column and Charles following his lead, she needed Olive for a tie vote, or Adam for a win. Or maybe she could turn Charles? She was on the edge of losing it all.

"Mrs. Z?" Ruby's voice broke through. "Would you like to try the chair?"

Sandy saw the now bare wall, Edward's photos all in a box behind her new, scarred-up, right-sized desk. She went around the desk and sank into the newly adjusted seat. Her feet did touch the ground. But since the floor seemed to be falling beneath her, that wouldn't be true for long.

"This is just the beginning!" Ruby beamed. "We'll get this redecorated in no time!"

Mac burst into the office, his face bright red. Wilford, who had been quietly chewing on a chair leg, snarled, bared his teeth, and lunged at Mac.

Mac jumped back, startled. "What the hell is that?"

"Wilford," Sandy explained, scooping him up. "He's . . . adjusting to the office environment."

Mac scowled. "Well send him home!"

Mrs. Connelly quickly stepped forward. "I'll take him for a little walk, Mrs. Zimmer. He's probably overwhelmed by all the activity." She leashed him, snarling, and headed out of the office.

"What now?" Sandy asked Mac.

"It's confirmed. Wyatt approached Cissy."

She'd known this was true, but still. "I talked to Adam. Wyatt wants Cissy's money to get his name on the UN building. He really just wants an erection."

Mac spit up a little coffee. "You're getting coarser and coarser."

"It's the company I keep."

Then he leaned in. "Our reporting could tank the city's chances. Plus, word is, Cissy's going to keep Wyatt on the board. So he really has nothing to lose."

Fragments of memories flashed by. Wyatt's disapproval at board meetings. His recent closed-door sessions with Charles and Adam. The way he'd looked at her in Breen's, a mixture of guilt and resolve.

But still, she'd thought his resistance to her was because she was a woman. Cissy was a woman too.

She'd worked so hard with him, tried to be a good daughter-in-law, a good wife to his son, a real helpmate. She'd even served as Wyatt's aid in selling off the other pieces of the consortium.

She'd never—never—struggled so hard, so unsuccessfully, to please someone. And for that someone to be her virtual father. She was weary of thinking all that work wasn't good enough, she wasn't good enough.

"I don't understand why the UN would be so much more important to him than anything else," Sandy said.

"He may be rich, but that's family money. His father and grandfathers ran banks, but he doesn't have a job, Sandy. Even if you're an extremely wealthy man, to know that about yourself must make a guy feel kind of untethered. It's hard to be a man with no work."

Sandy tried to remember a time before she had a job. She'd started at fourteen—babysitter, waitress, tutor, secretary.

"He wants to feel power. He thinks getting the UN will prove it. He needs to be seen as some kind of institution here. His name on that building would do it."

"We can't make any more decisions just to bolster his ego," she said, though she knew she'd made plenty of decisions for that reason.

Mac sighed. "The vote's coming down in ten days. We're obviously low on board allies. If Adam's out . . ."

"He's not out exactly. He says he wants us to have a plan. Though I don't know anything about business plans."

"Don't look at me."

"There's no time, anyway. We just have to get Wyatt to scrap *his* plan."

Mac grunted.

"Maybe I can make him see the dishonor in what he's doing. He prides himself so much on family legacy, maybe I can show him how this will tarnish his name, Edward's memory..."

"You think you can make him back down?"

"I have to try. Edward trusted his father and he trusted me. Wyatt knows that. He won't really want to destroy everything his son worked so hard to build. I'll present the case to him for why the riot coverage will be good for business, and second, I'll remind him of the importance of his family's actual history and legacy." She was talking herself into this, she knew. "And we keep going on the riot reporting. That's a given. Lambert's trying to reach the other women, and returning to Renee, right?"

"Right."

After he left, Sandy slumped into her newly adjusted chair. She closed her eyes and saw Edward's face, his broad smile.

"I'm trying, I swear, I'm trying."

Edward didn't answer.

Mrs. Connelly returned with a now-calm Wilford and started tidying up.

Sandy sighed. "Mrs. Connelly, have you ever considered working outside of home service? Perhaps in an office setting? Like, here?"

Mrs. Connelly looked surprised, then she made a pooh-pooh face. "Oh, Mrs. Zimmer, I couldn't possibly. Mr. Connelly would never allow me to work in a place like this. Not very nice for a lady."

CHAPTER TWENTY-NINE

A Place for Gentlemen

Sandy sat in the Lincoln's back seat cupping two carved Cooper's hawk charms in her hand.

"These are lovely, Tommy. I can't believe it."

"Norm's good. One's for you, ma'am."

"I'll need it."

She put one charm in her pocket and the other in her purse, and exited the car in front of the Olympic Club. She'd been invited inside years ago on the arm of her unassailably welcome husband. She'd seen the club's grand dining room, well-stocked bar serving top-shelf liquors, and private meeting rooms where deals were struck and city politics shaped. So she knew the air would be thick with cigar smoke and the murmur of insider conversations, as members in bespoke suits lounged in leather armchairs or engaged in heated debates over brandy. But getting in with Edward was different than getting in on her own.

She rebuttoned her jacket and straightened her skirt.

As she approached the entry lectern, a tall uniformed man, his expression polite but firm, asked, "Your name, please."

"Sandy Zimmer."

He checked his binder. "I'm sorry, madam, but the Olympic Club is for members only."

Sandy lifted her chin. "I'm here to see my father-in-law, Wyatt Zimmer. It's urgent business regarding the *San Francisco Prospect*."

The doorman's face remained impassive. "I'm afraid that's not possible, madam. Mr. Zimmer has not left your name at the desk and the club has a strict policy."

So exhausting. Another reminder she didn't belong in this world of men and their deals. *Find another way.*

"Of course, I understand you're only enforcing their rules," Sandy said, forcing a smile. "I'm sure if it were in your power to let me in, you would." The look on his face said, *No, I wouldn't.*

"Oh well, always the optimist." And she exited the building.

Tommy jumped out of the Lincoln, around to her car door.

"I'm not finished here," she told him.

She marched down Sutter and turned right on Taylor, but didn't see what she was looking for, so she retraced her steps, passing the colonnaded entrance, to Mason, where she walked left until she found it, a gated entrance to a little alley leading to the service entrance. Outside the gates stood a young woman in serving clothes, black with a white collar, taking a cigarette break.

"Excuse me," Sandy said, approaching her. "I hate to bother you, but I have a situation. My father-in-law is in the library, and there's an emergency with our family business. I need to speak with him urgently, but they won't let me in."

The maid answered, "If your name's not on the list, you're out, ma'am. And I don't want to lose my job . . ."

Sandy reached into her purse, pulling out a crisp ten-dollar bill, an exorbitant bribe. "Please. It's a matter of saving our livelihood. I'll be in and out before anyone notices. I will never mention you, never." Sandy gave herself a little shiver recalling other promises she'd made.

The maid hesitated, judging Sandy's face, and then, whether or not she trusted Sandy, she did trust the ten-dollar bill, which she pocketed.

Sandy followed the maid through the locked gate, down the alley, to the service entrance and into a maze of back hallways. They ascended a staircase. The higher they went, the more she detected the scent of cigars and leather.

"The library's down that hall," the maid whispered, pointing.

Sandy remembered. That's where Edward had taken her for a drink as his guest. Sandy wondered if she should have tried to join this club on her own.

She shared her thanks and set off, her heels clicking on the polished floor. She winced at the noise, hoping it wouldn't draw attention. She navigated the hallways, passing ornate paintings and hushed conversations before rounding a corner and nearly colliding with a waiter carrying a tray of drinks. He stared at her in surprise, but she pushed past before he could raise an alarm.

Finally, she reached the library. Through the open door, she could see Wyatt sunk in a dark armchair, reading a newspaper. Sandy stepped inside, making a beeline to her father-in-law.

"Hello, Wyatt," she said, her voice steady despite her racing heart.

He looked up, his expression moving from surprise to annoyance. He looked left and right to see if anyone else saw her there in front of him. They were alone. "What in God's name are you doing here? How did you get in?"

"I'm learning all kinds of ways to get in where I don't belong," Sandy said, sitting in the chair across from him. "We need to talk about what you're planning with Cissy Patterson."

Wyatt's face hardened. "This is inappropriate, Sandy. Leave immediately."

"Not until we talk," Sandy insisted. "The riot coverage isn't just good journalism, Wyatt. It's good for the business of the paper, good for the city, and yes, even good for your precious UN bid."

Wyatt scoffed. "Don't be ridiculous. Your reckless reporting would jeopardize everything we've worked for. We've done a hundred necessary things to improve the likelihood of winning this bid. And you're trying to destroy all that effort."

"No," Sandy countered, her voice rising. "We're showing that San

Francisco is a real city, with real journalism. A sophisticated city, that deserves to host the United Nations."

"You're naive," Wyatt answered. "This isn't about truth or journalism. It's about stability, about presenting the right image to the world. It's about perception!"

Sandy felt her frustration mounting. "You want us to be a city that sweeps its problems under the rug? That pretends everything's perfect when it isn't?"

"You're missing it," Wyatt growled. "As usual. Do you have any idea what you're jeopardizing with this misguided crusade of yours? The UN bid could transform this city. Bring in thousands of jobs, for regular people. And you're willing to throw it all away for what? A few sensational headlines?"

"No, not for that!" Sandy changed tack. "What about your family legacy, Wyatt? What about everything your father built, everything your son worked for?"

"What do you think you're talking about?"

"Your grandfather," Sandy pressed. "A banker during the Gold Rush. He took risks, believed in this city when it was nothing but mud and shanties. The *Prospect* is part of that legacy. We can't just throw it away because things get a little uncomfortable."

Wyatt's jaw clenched. "Don't lecture me about my family's legacy. You married into this family. You don't understand the obligation that comes with the Zimmer name."

"I understand more than you think," Sandy shot back. "I saw what it did to Edward. He put you and Olive on the board though you never invested a penny, unlike Charles and Adam. You just clutched your bank book. Edward trusted me with this paper, trusted me to carry on what he started, what his grandfathers inspired. And I'm not going to let you ruin it because you didn't trust your own son."

"Edward made a mistake," Wyatt said, his voice cold. "More than one. He was always too idealistic for his own good. He insisted on buying a failing newspaper chain, and he chose to marry . . ."

He trailed off, but his implication was clear.

Sandy felt as if she'd been slapped. "Is that what you think? That your own son was a fool?"

"He was foolishly optimistic. And it led him to rash decisions, which could drag down our name. Your name. I think," Wyatt said, leaning closer, "you're in over your head. You're playing at being a publisher, Sandy, but you don't have what it takes. Not because you're a woman, but because you act like one. Emotional, impulsive, unable to see the big picture."

Sandy's hands clenched into fists. "I've kept this paper running. Now I'm going to increase our readership. I'm making sure we're telling stories that matter."

"You're telling stories that will destroy us," Wyatt countered, his face reddening and his voice rising slightly. "People don't want to read about sex on their front page. It's terrible. I won't let it happen."

"We're not writing about sex—we're writing about rape. That's not sex!" Sandy nearly yelled, "Besides, do you even know who Cissy Patterson is? She succeeds by plastering sex and violence, on every page, of every edition!"

Wyatt looked livid. "Keep your voice down. If you continue down this path, I'll use every bit of influence I have to discredit you. I'll make sure everyone knows what a disaster your leadership has been."

A chill ran down her spine. "You'd do that? To your daughter-in-law? To Edward's widow?"

"I told him not to marry you. 'She'll keep sleeping with you regardless,' I said. 'Find somebody suitable. Somebody who belongs. Not somebody who screwed her way to the corner office!' Would I discredit you to protect my family's interests? In a heartbeat."

Sandy wanted to spit at him.

"You are ruining your son's legacy!"

"My son was a disappointment! His ruination was built into every choice he made."

How could she reason with such a man? She thought of Renee, of Gloria, of all the women whose stories should be told. And she thought of Edward, of his belief in her. And she thought of herself, of how far she'd come, of the voice she'd found.

Who was he to judge her, to dismiss her accomplishments? She straightened her spine, meeting his gaze. "You're wrong," she said. "I didn't screw my way anywhere. I earned this position, and I'm doing what's right for the paper and for this city. If you can't see that, then maybe you're the one who doesn't belong."

Wyatt's face darkened. "You're making a grave mistake, Sandy. One you'll regret."

"The only thing I'd regret is failing to do what I know is right. Edward believed in me. I won't let him down."

"You have no idea. You didn't *begin* to know who your husband really was."

For a long moment, they stared at each other, mutual contempt poisoning the air. Then the sound of approaching footsteps broke the silence.

"Sir?" a voice called. "Is everything alright? I heard raised voices."

Wyatt's eyes narrowed. "We're done here. Get out, before I have you thrown out."

"I'll leave because I'm ready to leave. I am *choosing* to leave."

She followed the uniformed man out of the library, lifting her head high despite the weakness of her legs. He escorted her back to the service entrance, where she stepped out onto the sidewalk.

Then she heard it. The honking horns, the yelling of taxi drivers trying to make their way through traffic. She heard it and she felt it. The city, always alive, always busy, always moving, up the hills, down the hills. *This place is not for the faint of heart*, she thought.

CHAPTER THIRTY

Closed Doors

Jane poked her head into Sandy's office before Sandy had hung up her jacket and sat at her desk.

"Well?"

"Ugh. You have no idea. They practically barricade that place against the danger of an outsider entering. Unless she'll be serving them drinks."

"You don't say? What would I know about that? They let us tomato-picking Okie girls go wherever we want."

"Don't be defensive. I know I have it easier. I'm just saying it's almost impossible for any of us to earn our way into those rooms."

"Oh please. You're never gonna earn your way into their rooms, never! You've got to build your own rooms!"

"Fantastic, another item on my to-do list."

"You want to know what your problem is?"

"I assume you're going to tell me."

"Even after everything you've done, you still care whether they like you. Anybody in power, you want him to like you."

"I do not."

"You do! That's how you judge yourself. But your life won't be worth a plugged nickel if you care whether they let you in. Forget about that pat on the head. Claw your way to the top of the podium, girl. That's all that matters."

"That's what matters to you, not me. You were born with teeth. Maybe you'd be better off if you cared even a little about what other people think of you, rather than just how you can get what you want. I mean, how's Belva doing? Do you even know? When was the last time you spoke to her?"

Jane glowered. "Don't do that ever again."

Such matters were off-limits for Jane. To be fair, there were all kinds of practical reasons why Jane wouldn't want to talk about being head over heels in love with a woman. A Black woman. Who happened to be way over Jane, character-wise. The subject of Belva was definitely off-limits and Sandy knew it. But that was why she'd said it.

"I'm sorry."

"Okay. Me too. It's just, I think we're not all that different."

Sandy readjusted herself. "I'll take that as a compliment. You know how I feel."

She pushed two clippings in front of Jane, one from Lambert, the other from the *Tattler*. "I assume you've read these."

Jane took a look, first at the *Prospect*.

RAPE: SAILORS CELEBRATING PEACE WREAK HAVOC ON LOCAL GIRLS

By Reporter Derek Lambert

Six young women were seen by nurses and a doctor in the Central Emergency Hospital on the night of August 14, for injuries believed to have been caused by sexual attacks. Five of those women left the hospital without sharing their names, or indicating any interest in speaking with reporters or police. Just one victim was willing to speak about her experience, though she has asked to remain anonymous. She described to reporters what she can recall of the incident, involving approximately six sailors attacking her in an alley near the Civic Center. . . .

Then from the *Tattler*.

ALLEGED VICTIM SPILLS THE BEANS

By Reporter Reggie Jonas

An East Bay girl who traveled from the Lowe Shipyards to the city to join the party in celebration of V-J Day has met with police and *Prospect* reporters, suggesting she was attacked by multiple assailants following an evening of dancing and drinking with those sailors. . . .

"Ugh," said Jane. "Lambert did okay. This Jonas guy's awful—emphasis on the dancing and drinking, not the rape."

"It's what we expected."

Then Mac burst into Sandy's office without knocking.

"You look like death," Sandy said.

"Feel like it too. Cigarettes?"

Sandy tossed him the pack she kept in her top drawer. She didn't smoke much but kept them for sharing. As Mac lit up, she perched on the edge of her desk between Jane and Mac.

After his first deep inhale, Sandy asked, "I take it things didn't go well with our city's finest?"

Mac let out a bitter laugh. "I've been stonewalled. Every damn one of them."

This was what she'd been afraid of. "Talk," she said.

Mac launched into it. "First up was Naval Commandant Rear Admiral Francis Whiting Rockwell. I thought he might just want to set matters straight."

Sandy pictured all the drunken sailors running amok.

"I get to his office," Mac continued, "and it's like trying to talk to a brick wall draped in flags. Every question I asked he answered with a barrage of naval jargon and protocol."

He picked up his notepad, reading aloud. "'I'm afraid that information is classified under Naval Regulation blah-de-blah, subsection blah-de-blah. Any incidents involving naval personnel are subject to internal review as per the Naval Code of Conduct.' Like that."

Sandy frowned. "But he didn't deny anything happened?"

"Didn't confirm it either," Mac said. "Just kept hiding behind regulations. By the end, I wasn't sure if he was protecting his men or covering his own ass."

"Both," Sandy muttered. "What about Brown? Surely the DA had something to say?"

Mac's expression darkened. "Oh, Brown had plenty to say. All of it useless." He affected a pompous tone. "'Now, Mac, you know I can't comment on an ongoing investigation. The integrity of our grand jury process must be maintained.'"

Sandy rolled her eyes. "Lawyers."

"It gets better," Mac said. "He went on about how 'In these delicate times, we must be cautious about inflaming public sentiment.' As if the problem is public inflammation, and not rape on the streets."

"Delicate times, my dead mother," Jane snorted.

Mac raised his eyebrows. Jane's mother was very much alive.

"The war's over. What's he afraid of?"

Mac shrugged. "Your guess is as good as mine. But it's clear he's more interested in keeping the peace than pursuing justice."

"Did Chief Dullea say anything?" Sandy asked, though she knew the answer.

Mac's sneer said it all. "Dullea says a whole lot of nothing while pretending to say something. 'Rest assured, the San Francisco Police Department is conducting a thorough review of all incidents related to the V-J Day celebrations.'"

"And?" Sandy prompted.

"And nothing," Mac said. "When I pressed for details, he just kept repeating that they'd 'release a comprehensive statement at the appropriate time.' Whenever the hell appropriate is."

Sandy stood up, pacing the office. "So the navy's hiding behind regulations, the DA's worried about 'public sentiment,' and the police are just stalling. Fantastic."

"It gets better," Mac said. "Wait until you hear about my chat with our esteemed Mayor Lapham."

"I'm all ears."

Mac cleared his throat, once again adopting a mocking tone. "'Mac, my boy, you have to understand the delicate position we're in. San Francisco is on the cusp of greatness. We can't let a few . . . unfortunate incidents tarnish our reputation.'"

"A few unfortunate incidents?" Sandy repeated. "That's what he calls rape and manslaughter?"

"Gets worse," Mac said. "He went on about how 'in times of celebration, things can get out of hand.' He literally said, '*Boys will be boys*. But we must focus on the positive. On rebuilding. On our bright future.'"

"So that's it? Pretend it never happened?"

"That's the party line. From the navy all the way down to City Hall, they're closing ranks. Nobody wants to be the one to admit there's a problem."

Sandy sank back onto the desk. "It's a cover-up."

"We gotta get someone on record. Anonymous accusations and circumstantial evidence won't cut it. I don't know if we can survive the *Tattler* innuendo campaign."

Their story was slipping away with nobody willing to talk.

"We made promises."

Mac ran a hand over his face. "I know."

Not even two weeks after their first report, several advertisers had already pulled out, mentioning *Tattler* headlines about Sandy's investigation. But subscriptions were up 15 percent. People were hungry for real news, good or bad. Even if it involved a young widow publisher. No, especially if it involved her.

Sandy began to pace again, her thoughts racing. "Okay, so the brass won't talk. What now?"

"We go to the usual suspects, the people under them. We've already been knocking on those doors. Beat cops on duty that night, nurses at all the hospitals, bartenders and shopkeepers who saw what happened. It's always the people downstream who talk. It's never the brass."

"Some of them might be just as frustrated as we are. Maybe they *want* the truth to come out."

Mac drummed his fingers on the desk. Sandy could see the gears turning.

Finally, he said, "Alright. We'll take more guys off other stories—I've got an idea who—shift them to this for a couple days. I know for sure I'll get Shawn on the cops—they like him. See if he can get anybody to talk off the record. I can move Lambert off Renee and over to one of these other lines. That okay with you?"

Sandy sighed, ambivalent about Lambert and about giving up on Renee. "That's the right call. We need the unchecked alcohol sales, the slow response from law enforcement, the rush to sweep everything under the rug. It's all one thing."

"What one thing?" Mac asked.

"A city more concerned with its image than the safety of its citizens," Sandy said. "A leadership more interested in preserving their status than addressing real problems."

"That's a story."

"Something we can build on. A plan like Adam said, to cover a culture of negligence and deception that goes all the way to the top," said Sandy. "Maybe *this* is who we are—the paper that pulls the city's mask off."

As he rose to leave, Mac asked, "How'd it go with Wyatt?"

"Same. These guys may be the brass, but none of them have any balls."

"Good God, Sandy. We've ruined you. Though you do sound more like a publisher."

CHAPTER THIRTY-ONE

Railcar Revelations

Sandy dangled her high heels from her fingers, useless against the shifting terrain. Her nylon-clad feet sank into the cool sand as she and Mac approached Jane's railcar home on the edge of Ocean Beach. The roar of the Pacific grew louder with each step, drowning out the distant sounds of the road behind them. The narrow, metal-clad structure stood out against the darkening sky, a solitary sentinel on the sand.

"Quite a place," Mac muttered, eyeing the railcar skeptically.

As they drew closer, the wind picked up, carrying the salty tang of the sea and whipping Sandy's hair around her face.

Jane appeared in the doorway, her tall frame filling the entrance. "About time," she called out, her voice barely audible over crashing waves. "Get in here before you blow away, lightweights."

Lambert had beat them there. He sat on the floor, his legs extended, looking gloomy, with a bottle between his knees.

The railcar was even more cramped than Sandy remembered it. Jane had added to the space: a table with typewriter and papers, overfull bookshelves, mismatched lamps. It was no longer a monk's cell. Now it was more of a hamster's nest, every inch revealing Jane's interests, including a collection of bourbon bottles lined up on boards on blocks. A far cry from Sandy's own spacious penthouse, but she found something bracing about its specificity.

Sandy perched on the edge of a narrow bed, while Mac leaned against a wall covered in Jane's clippings.

Wind rattled the cracked windowpanes, creating a constant, unsettling backdrop.

"What's so urgent we had to meet here?" Mac asked.

Jane fixed them both with a serious look. "We've got a Renee problem. Plus I just didn't feel like going in."

Sandy rolled her eyes. "What now?"

"You tell 'em," Jane said to Lambert.

Lambert groaned. "Of course everybody in her neighborhood's figured out she's been talking to us. The *Tattler* made that clear. Remember, one of the sailors—the one she said she's known forever—was involved. Another local kid, also a sailor and his friend, is the talker. Everybody loves the first kid and so now they're coming down on Renee. You know, egging her house, that kind of thing."

"Dammit," Mac muttered. "Victor Reese at the *Tattler* is scum."

Jane added, "That's not the worst of it. Renee's shutting us out completely. She thinks we betrayed her, broke our promise to protect her."

Sandy stood up, forgetting how low the ceiling was with the cabinets above, and banged her head. She winced, rubbing the sore spot. "We didn't betray her. That article was careful. We protected her. It wasn't us that did it." Sandy could hear the strain in her own voice, trying to rationalize what had happened, though she expected the *Tattler* would never have found Renee if the *Prospect* hadn't.

"Come on, Sandy," Mac said. "We did the right thing, the right way, for a newspaper. But her mother was right too. Renee was *always* the one most at risk from our doing it."

That was true. Sandy thought of her own risk, of losing her job, and the paper, yet she knew Mac was right. Her own stakes were lower than Renee's.

"Doesn't matter," Jane said, shaking her head. "Even if we did everything the right way, she's spooked. Says she won't talk to anyone now, not Lambert, not even you. And I can't blame her."

The railcar suddenly felt even smaller, the walls pressing in on Sandy as the implications expanded. She began to pace, but found herself at the other end of the railcar in just three steps.

"This is all my fault," Sandy said, her voice barely audible over a particularly strong gust of wind that shook the entire structure. "I pushed too hard, too fast."

"No," Mac said, his face set in determination. "Hold on. We weren't wrong about what we're doing. We just didn't anticipate all the consequences, which is impossible to do."

"But the consequences are everything," Sandy shot back. "This is all too risky for too many people."

Jane sighed and leaned forward, her eyes intense. "That's why we have to keep going. I'm tired of this crap! What makes you always so afraid of rocking the boat?"

Sandy snapped, "I'm not afraid. But this is my boat. I can't let it sink. I can't let all the people who work there drown."

"No," Jane said. "You're afraid you'll lose something if you take a dang risk. Listen, I can see how far out on the limb you've gone, but now's not the time to stop."

"You're the one who called us here for this panic attack. And you're right. We promised Renee we'd protect her. How can we do that if we can't even keep her involvement a secret? On top of that—less important by far but still something—if we continue with this, we'll tank the UN bid. But if we *don't* do this, we're not really a newspaper. God . . ."

Sandy felt their gazes, heavy as the damp air blowing through gaps in the windowsills. She sank back down onto the bed, weighed down with dread. She understood that this required more from her. More personal risk.

"Maybe . . ." she began, then paused, gathering her thoughts. "Maybe we've been going about this wrong."

Mac raised an eyebrow. "What?"

Sandy stood again, careful this time of the cabinet. "What if we shift our focus away from the specifics of the rape until we hear from the grand jury? I mean, continue to investigate but hold back publishing. Meantime, let's move on, looking much more carefully at the bigger picture. We focus on the systemic issues that allowed this to happen in the first place."

The railcar fell silent, save for the constant roar of the ocean outside.

Lambert was the first to answer, his voice tired. "Nobody will read it without the personal stories. They care about the human element."

Sandy opened her mouth to argue, but Jane cut in. "Maybe we can get Martinez. Her story's good, if she'll tell it."

"Maybe," Sandy conceded. "But we can't count on it. We need more. What if . . ." She hesitated, then plunged ahead. "What if we use my experience from that night? What I witnessed? Without naming me."

Mac's eyes lit up. "Sandy, obviously you can see how much better it'd be if you're named? The publisher of the *Prospect*, out on the violent streets, witnessing the chaos firsthand?"

"That's too much."

Jane leaned forward, her eyes intense. "He's right, Zimmer. Your name gives the story credibility and drive. It would force people to take notice. I can see it."

"You gotta do it," said Lambert. "In the first person. Make it personal, what you in particular witnessed. I've read all your notes. It's great stuff. You can do this."

Sandy wondered again if she could trust Lambert or his instincts.

She closed her eyes, seeing so many consequences of such a decision. When she opened them, she saw Mac, Lambert, and Jane watching her expectantly, like she was preparing to strip in front of klieg lights and cameras, making herself completely vulnerable to scorn.

What about the paper? She knew this would sell copy, absolutely, every element of it—rich widow publisher down on the street, witnessing violent crime, the precursor to rape, all the human faces she saw there. It would sell newspapers.

What about the board? How would they react? She was sure this was the kind of thing Wyatt would see as tawdry conduct unbecoming of a publisher. So how would that play out on the board if it also led to increased readership? And if that led to increased ad dollars?

What would Edward think? Was this the kind of risk he'd want her to take? He'd taken risks, but he'd never exposed himself personally like this. Would he respect her? Would he be ashamed?

And what about her own feelings? Could writing this make her feel she'd done right by Renee and the others? Did she care if she was scorned as Renee had been by her community?

"Alright," she said with resignation, her voice barely above a whisper. "I'll write it, with my name."

Lambert repeated, "In first person."

She nodded.

Mac pointed at her. "It's the right move, Sandy."

Jane said, "It takes the light off Renee."

"And something else," Sandy said, her voice steady despite the butterflies in her stomach. "The UN bid."

"What?" Mac asked.

Sandy spoke slowly, working it out. "We frame our plan to the board not just as an exposé of the riot but as a demonstration of the city's commitment to justice and transparency, through *our* reporting," Sandy explained. "We can show that the people of this city aren't afraid to confront problems head-on. That's the kind of place the UN should want for its headquarters."

Mac said, "Optimistic. Maybe too optimistic. But if we pull it off..."

"A big *if*..." Sandy agreed.

"It's good, real good," said Lambert.

Jane closed her eyes, smiling, like she was picturing it all playing out.

As they continued to discuss the plan, the cramped space of the railcar expanded, filled with the energy of renewed purpose.

Finally, as the clock ticked past midnight, Sandy stood to leave. "We're doing the right thing," she said, as much to convince herself as them. "We may sink, but it's right."

Jane said, "Never thought I'd see Sandy Zimmer walk the gang plank."

"Hey, now," Sandy protested, but she was smiling too.

She stepped out onto the beach and the cold wind hit her face. She took a deep breath, tasting salt. The enormity of what she'd just agreed to stretched out before her, vast and dark. But for the first time in days, she felt equal to it.

"Get some sleep," Jane called from the doorway. "You'll need it."

Sandy, Mac, and Lambert made their way back across the beach to the parking lot, the sound of waves replaced by the hum of the highway. Sandy's nylons were ruined, clumped in damp sand, but she walked the edge of her world with conviction.

CHAPTER THIRTY-TWO

Shadows in the Park

Sandy tugged on Wilford's leash as the pug snuffled at yet another bush along the perimeter of Alta Plaza Park. The night air was cool against her face, a relief. Rereading her personal article in print had nearly given her an anxiety fever.

WITNESS TO CRIME: PUBLISHER SHARES FIRST-PERSON ACCOUNT OF ATTACK AT PEACE RIOT
By Sandy Zimmer

I'd been wandering downtown on the night of the fourteenth, V-J Day, for a couple of hours already.

I'd felt joyful when I saw a group of girls singing patriotic songs as they danced arm in arm down the middle of Market Street.

I'd felt alarm when I saw overzealous sailors overturn a streetcar.

I'd felt heartbreak when I saw a coroner's van carry off a newlywed young woman who'd been hit by a drunk driver.

But it was all nothing compared to the absolute fear I felt when I witnessed a half dozen sailors surrounding a young woman with a blonde ponytail, screaming for help.

I knew in my bones, this was it, the thing most women and girls—not just me—are afraid will happen to them if they dare to go out into the world, as a woman. This was going to be rape.

Before I could make myself move to say or do anything to protect her, a woman in a WAC uniform broke into that circle of sailors.

I got closer, though I was so afraid.

I saw that the ponytailed woman wore factory work clothes. It looked like she'd come straight from the shipyard. She was terrified, the way her head swiveled left and right, at the sailors surrounding her.

I heard her yell, "Let me go!"

I saw the surrounding crowd, not interfering with the sailors, just as I was not.

Then I heard the WAC yell, "Step away! Now!"

That's when the sailors turned on the WAC. I thought, she did it on purpose. To attract their attention. So the other girl could run away. And it worked, I thought, because the ponytailed woman ran.

The sailors surrounded the WAC. . . .

Even now she found the article painful to reread. There were also the other papers' headlines. From the *Tattler*, Zimmer Puts Herself on Page One. From the *Bay City Times*, Widow *Prospect* Publisher Alters Voice of Legacy Paper. And in a touching show of support, the *Pacific Commerce Journal* announced, Sources Say *Prospect* Faces Financial Scrutiny.

After all that, she'd read and reread the letters to the editor. Sure, there were the supportive comments: "You're so brave," "Shameful how those boys acted," "That's what happens when too much drink's involved," "Where were the police?" and "Thanks for telling the truth." She was grateful for those. They buoyed her. But the letters that screamed in her head were different, calling her a "stick-in-the-mud," "unpatriotic," "shrew," "liar," "out of touch," "man-hater." One said she had "tarnished our city." She'd needed to get out of the apartment, away from all those words.

"Come on, boy," she murmured to Wilford. "Just a quick one tonight."

The new butler, Mr. Ames, had indeed known how to train a dog, and he'd emphasized that Wilford needed three walks a day, so he wouldn't soil the rug but also so he got enough exercise and pleasure that he might willingly comply with Sandy's other expectations.

Mr. Ames took him for his morning walk as Sandy got ready for work. Wilford then rode with Sandy in the Lincoln to the *Prospect*, where he mostly lay under her desk as she took calls and had meetings, then followed along at her heels as she moved through the office. Ruby took him for his lunchtime walk through sidewalk throngs. They made sure to lay the front page of the *Tattler* on the floor in the corner of Sandy's office, in case he had an emergency. Everybody agreed that was the best use of the rag.

But the evening walk in the park was her time alone with Wilford. It had become important to her, a way to clear her mind. She was attached to the pug. He'd made her life better, more attached to something other than the vicissitudes of the *Prospect*. She hadn't known how much she'd needed his grumpy face.

As they rounded a corner, Sandy felt a pang of guilt, remembering the disappointment in Olive's voice during their telephone call that evening. "I always keep your best interest in mind, Sandy," Olive had said. "But Wyatt's furious."

"It's about the truth," Sandy had argued. "It's about justice for those women."

Olive's sigh was full of resignation. "You may not see just what you've done, I'm afraid."

She'd known there would be backlash, of course. Mac had warned her, his face creased with concern as they'd pored over the final draft. "You sure about this, Sandy? Describing the sailors?" he'd asked. "Once it's out there, there's no taking it back."

She'd been certain then, lifted by the conviction that she was doing the right thing.

A twig snapped behind her and Sandy turned, startled. In the dim light of the streetlamps, she caught a glimpse of a man's figure about twenty yards back. She quickened her pace, telling herself she was paranoid. This was Pacific Heights, after all. Her neighborhood. Safe.

But as she and Wilford continued their circuit of the park, Sandy couldn't shake the feeling. Every time she glanced over her shoulder, the man was there, maintaining his general distance but undeniably following her, slowly closing the gap between them.

Her heart raced. She tugged Wilford toward a different route, one that led deeper into the park to get her closer to the street on the other side. If she could just make it there . . .

Wilford let out a low growl, his stocky body tense at her side. Sandy's palms were sweating now, her grip on the leash tight enough to hurt. She thought of Edward, of how he would have handled this situation. Would he have confronted the man? Called for help?

Now he was upon her.

"Sandy Zimmer!" The man's voice cut through the night air. "That's you, isn't it?"

Sandy froze. Should she run? Scream? She was alone in the park, the surrounding houses dark and quiet. She turned and saw him, an ordinary-looking person, with a cap pulled low on his forehead, his hands shoved deep in his pockets.

"You're her, aren't you?" he said, his voice rough and plain. "The publisher. I've seen your picture in the society pages. You're the one who wrote that article about the riot."

Sandy straightened her spine, forcing herself to meet his gaze. "I am," she said, proud that her voice didn't shake. "Can I help you with something?"

The man let out a bitter laugh. "Help me? That's rich, coming from you." He gestured around at the manicured lawns and stately homes surrounding them. "Living up here, looking down on the rest of us."

"I'm not looking down on—"

"That's what it looks like to me, talking about those boys celebrating not having to go to war."

"I was there," Sandy said, her voice low but firm. "I saw what happened."

"I guess you saw what you wanted to see," the man answered. "But did you stop to think about those boys? What they've been through? The things they've seen and done for this country?"

Sandy felt a flicker of doubt. "Of course, I—well, those boys had never shipped out."

"You couldn't understand. You're a woman who's never seen a day of real hardship. And now your paper is trying to tear down the fellas who fought to keep you safe. Like my boy." His voice cracked.

The accusation stung—it was inaccurate! Sandy held her ground. "That's not what I was trying to do. I was reporting the truth—"

"The truth?" The man's voice rose, and Wilford let out another growl. "I'll bet your paper made a fortune off of war stories. And now you're turning on the soldiers for what? A few broken windows? Some high spirits that got out of hand?"

Sandy felt her cheeks flush with anger. "It was more than that. There were assaults, rapes—"

"Sure," he answered. "Then where are the charges?"

"No," she said, her voice steady and clear. "I'm not doing this to sell papers or make a name for myself. I'm doing it because those women deserve to be heard. Because our city deserves better than leaders who turn a blind eye to violence and assault."

The man looked away, disgusted.

"You talk about the sacrifices those sailors made," Sandy continued, gaining momentum. "And you're right, they deserve our respect and gratitude. But that doesn't give any of them the right to hurt innocent women. It doesn't excuse what some of them did that night."

She took a deep breath, meeting the man's gaze square on. "I'm not trying to tear anyone down. I'm trying to make sure everybody—soldiers, civilians, women, men—is held to the same standard of decency and respect. That's what I'm trying to do."

He stared at her for a long moment. "You believe that, don't you?"

Sandy straightened her spine. "I do."

He shook his head. "Be careful out here, lady. Not everybody's as reasonable as me."

Sandy opened her mouth to respond, but the words wouldn't come. Fueled by anger, the man had shaken her more than she wanted to admit.

Wilford let out a belated bark, placing himself between Sandy and the stranger.

"Why don't you stick to the society pages."

With that, he turned and stalked away, leaving Sandy rooted to the spot, her heart pounding.

She sank onto a nearby bench, Wilford jumping up onto her lap. She stroked his fur, trying to calm her racing heart. The man's anger, his accusations, reinforced the importance of what she was doing.

She whispered to the pug, "No matter how hard it gets, we have to see this through."

People needed to be held accountable for their actions, regardless of the circumstances.

She thought back to the chaos of that night—the overturned streetcar, the shattered windows, the terrified face of Renee trying to escape the mob. It had been real, and someone needed to answer for it. The sailors who had assaulted women, the police who had failed to maintain order, the city officials who had allowed the situation to spiral out of control—all of them should face consequences for their actions or inactions.

But the man's words nagged at her. Had she been overzealous? Had she failed to consider the complexities of the situation, the traumas and tensions that had led to that night's events?

She closed her eyes, remembering the promises she'd made, that individual stories could help ensure that those responsible would face justice. But now, faced with the backlash, she wondered if that promise had been too naive.

Still, if the riot was brushed under the rug, dismissed as high spirits gone awry, what would prevent similar incidents in the future? How could the city heal and move forward without acknowledging and addressing what had happened?

"We'll do better," she whispered to Wilford, which was like whispering to herself. "We have to. But it's going to be uncomfortable."

Then they made their way back to her building, where the leafy shadows of the park still cast a pall on her thoughts.

CHAPTER THIRTY-THREE

A Grand Jury

Sandy approached the steps of City Hall. The windows she'd broken the night of the riot had been replaced; the bench she'd moved to climb inside was back in its normal location, giving rest to tourists and government workers, as if Sandy had never moved it, like it was all a dream of her own daring.

The grand jury's findings would be announced today, and anxiety fired through her veins.

Inside, the marble halls echoed with the sound of hurried heels as reporters and city officials made their way to the Board Chamber, which had been loaned out to the DA for his announcement. Sandy nodded to a few familiar faces, noting the tense set of their shoulders, the worried furrow of their brows. They all knew the importance of what was about to unfold—whether there would be charges of any kind, more newspaper attention to the riot, or whether they might all return to normal, a better normal.

Sandy spotted Mac near the front, next to Jane. He caught her eye and gave her a dismal nod.

Sandy found a spot near the back.

At precisely 2 p.m., forty-year-old District Attorney Pat Brown stepped up to the podium. His face was a mask of professional neutrality, but Sandy thought she detected a hint of tension in the skin above his brows. It was easy to miss, what with his robust, broad-shouldered stance. Brown was generally an avid man, with bright, engaging eyes. But today, Sandy saw the shadow of worry on his face. For someone whose future turned on political popularity, his handling of this moment mattered.

"Ladies and gentlemen," Brown began, his voice carrying through the hushed room. "I'm here today to present the findings of the grand jury investigation into the events of August fourteenth and fifteenth, what some have called the 'peace riot.'" He paused, his gaze sweeping the room, collecting attention. "I'd like to introduce Mr. J. Leslie Vogel, the grand jury's chairman, who will deliver the report."

The crowd vibrated like bees in the hive.

Vogel stepped up to the microphone, clearing his throat. There was something in his demeanor, a casualness that seemed at odds with the gravity of the situation, that immediately set Sandy on defense.

He smiled warmly at the DA, like a spaniel, she thought.

"After a thorough two-week investigation," Vogel began, "the grand jury has concluded that the riot of August fourteenth and fifteenth can be primarily attributed to a large number of servicemen who didn't want to be in the service and who suddenly realized that the surrender announcement meant they might not have to be in service for much longer."

Sandy blinked. *Yes, obviously.* The rampage *was* born of their understandable relief. But that led to their over-drinking the cheap alcohol sold by businessmen up and down the street, and to their celebrating en masse, and to the military thinking they couldn't possibly rein them in. And that led to rape and manslaughter.

Vogel continued, "It's the jury's opinion that the riot could have been broken up with tear gas bombs and other forceful methods, but the situation would have been made worse by that."

So the police just decided not to intervene for good, solid reasons? Intervention would have made things worse? What about the military? Was it good decision-making that they'd not called the sailors back to their bunks? And why has nobody truly investigated, discouraging Renee or any rape victim from saying what happened?

But Vogel wasn't finished. "After careful consideration and a thorough investigation, the grand jury is not recommending that charges be brought against any individuals in this matter. It was just boys letting off a lot of steam, and couldn't be helped." His tone shifted, from proudly official to almost jovial. "Now, I'd like to take a moment to commend several individuals for their exemplary conduct during this challenging time."

Commend?

Next followed a flood of such commendations. He praised Police Chief Dullea for "the fine manner in which he handled himself and his staff." The head of the state Board of Equalization was lauded for taking "every precaution to circumvent citywide drunkenness." Even the press was thanked for their reporting on the riot.

Vogel finished speaking. Sandy looked around the room, in shock and disbelief. No one would be held accountable for any of it. DA Brown thanked Mr. Vogel and took no questions.

This was a whitewash, pure and simple. Sure, there was no current proof of who had done what. But wasn't it the job of government officials to dig for the proof? Was there only the newspaper to do this?

She knew the *Tattler*'s headline would be something like THANKS, DA BROWN! LET'S GET BACK TO NORMAL. The *Pacific Commerce Journal*? Her guess was THE REAL PROBLEM? HOW TO PAY FOR DAMAGED STOREFRONTS AND BUSES. It was enraging.

She pushed through the crowd toward DA Brown, catching up to him just as he was about to exit the room.

"Mr. Brown," she called out, her voice higher than she wished it were. "May I have a word, please?"

Brown turned, his expression guarded as he recognized her. "Mrs. Zimmer. I'm afraid I don't have time for an interview right now."

"This isn't for an interview," Sandy said, lowering her voice.

Brown looked over his shoulder for help, and Una Tyler appeared at his side.

"Mr. Brown," Una said, and looked briefly at Sandy.

"We need a room for five minutes," said the DA.

Una turned around, briskly leading the way.

As Sandy followed them both into an adjacent space, she felt the rise of a familiar urge to soften her approach, to find a way to make this conversation more comfortable for both of them, an instinct honed over a lifetime. Smile, don't ruffle feathers, keep everyone comfortable. That had been her way for so long.

Una left them alone.

As Brown began immediately to defend the grand jury's findings, Sandy looked at her lifetime of pleasing authority figures, of putting their emotional safety before her own convictions. It felt ridiculous in the face of such blatant injustice.

"Mr. Brown," she interrupted, her voice sharp. "You can't possibly believe that this report represents a thorough investigation of what happened during the riot."

Brown's face hardened. "The grand jury has spoken, Mrs. Zimmer. Their findings are a matter of public record now."

"There's no substance to those findings," Sandy pressed. "No real explanation for the violence, no accountability for not managing the crowds or investigating assaults, even the property damage. You're letting everyone off the hook."

"We're maintaining order," Brown countered, his voice low but intense. "Do you have any idea what kind of chaos could ensue if we started pointing fingers? Accusing servicemen, on the day of our victory, for which they've contributed more than any of the rest of us?"

"What kind of chaos happens when men aren't held accountable for rape? You want to pretend it never happened? Ignore the victims, the damage done to this city? Accept that it'll happen again and again?"

"We move forward," Brown said firmly. "We focus on rebuilding, on San Francisco's bright future. Dwelling on one night of . . . excessive celebration . . . serves no one. Especially when no woman comes forward to press charges. If they had the courage of their convictions, then a different chain of events might follow."

Sandy nearly hyperventilated. "Are you saying this is the fault of the victims? For not being brave enough to go up against cynical, bullying men in power who would undoubtedly shame them publicly? How brave do they have to be to earn justice? One of the women survived a multi-assailant military rape. Another woman, a WAC, was almost killed by the same sailors for trying to save the woman they raped. Is that not enough courage to deserve justice?"

Brown was very still, very quiet, his eyes narrowing. "Be careful, Mrs. Zimmer. You're running into a briar patch."

"I've *been* in the briar patch. I'm telling you the truth," Sandy shot back. "Something you conveniently led your grand jury to avoid."

Brown laughed, but there was no humor in it. "The truth is messy. It doesn't fit right into a newspaper column or a courtroom testimony. We did what needed to be done to preserve the peace, to keep the city moving forward."

Sandy shook her head, disgusted. "You did what was politically expedient. You protected the powerful at the expense of the vulnerable. You protected *yourself*. And everybody like you. That's not peace, Mr. Brown. That's cowardice."

The words hung in the air between them, irretrievable. Brown's face flushed red, his hands shoved in his pockets.

"I think we're done here, Mrs. Zimmer," he said. "I'd advise you to think very carefully about your next move. The *Prospect* isn't the only paper in town, and I'd hate to see it lose its standing, whatever that currently is, over one lady's misguided crusade."

Misguided crusade. That was Wyatt's phrase.

"Is that a threat, Mr. Brown?"

"It's friendly advice," he replied. "From one public servant to another. Don't make enemies you can't afford, if you aim to stick around."

Sandy didn't care about Brown's friendship, or his warnings, or the potential consequences of crossing him. She cared about the promises she'd made.

"Thank you for your time, Mr. Brown," she said. "I'll be sure to consider your 'friendly advice' as the *Prospect* covers your office in the future."

As she left, the consequence of what she'd done—the powerful enemy she'd made—wrapped her shoulders like a blanket on fire.

Outside City Hall, she spotted Mac and Jane waiting for her at the bottom of the steps.

"She's alive," said Mac.

Sandy grunted. "I told him it was a whitewash. They're not holding anyone accountable. Not the sailors, not the police, not the city officials. No one."

She filled them in on her confrontation with Brown as they walked.

"Jesus, Sandy," Mac said when she finished. "You're leading with your chin."

"My doggone hero!" Jane said.

"What if . . . Could we lose the paper over this?" she asked.

Mac's face paled. "Brown has connections everywhere. Our advertisers, the board . . . he can ruin us if he wants to, even if it's in many small stabs."

Sandy thought of the people who depended on the paper for their livelihoods, of her own reputation, of Edward's legacy.

"We'll figure it out," Mac said.

"What if I've gone too far? What if—"

"Stop," Jane interrupted. "No more second-guessing. I can't stand to listen to it."

But Sandy couldn't help herself. Her mind replayed every mistake, every misstep that had led her to this moment.

What if she was wrong? What if, in her zeal, she'd blinded herself to the bigger picture? Maybe Brown was right. Maybe the city did need to move on, to focus on rebuilding rather than dwelling on one or two nights of violence.

Sandy pictured City Hall in the distance, a mocking symbol of the power and influence arrayed against her.

As they entered the *Prospect* building, she felt none of the determination, none of the anger that had fueled her earlier. She was hollow, drained, overwhelmed.

CHAPTER THIRTY-FOUR

The Ledger of Loss

The clock on Sandy's office wall ticked past midnight, its rhythm a contrast to the chaos in her mind. She sat at her desk, surrounded by stacks of newspapers and reports, the detritus of weeks spent chasing the peace riot story. The office was dark save for the small pool of light from her desk lamp.

She rubbed her eyes, exhausted. Her confrontation with DA Brown repeated in her head, each replay bringing a fresh wave of doubt and fear.

With a sigh, she reached for the pile of magazines on the corner of her desk to take her mind off the mess she'd created. As she flipped through the pages of *Time*, a familiar name caught her eye: Cissy Patterson.

The article was a profile detailing Cissy's rise to power and her iron-fisted control of the *Washington Times-Herald*. Sandy frowned as she read about Cissy's latest triumphs and scandals.

> . . . widely considered the most powerful woman in American journalism . . .

> . . . known for her unapologetic approach to news and her willingness to ruffle feathers . . .

> . . . her papers consistently outsell the competition, despite—or perhaps because of—their sensationalist bent . . .

AN UNLIKELY PROSPECT | 173

Here was a woman who had faced challenge, who had stood up to the old boys' club and come out on top. But at what cost? The article didn't shy away from criticizing Cissy's methods, her ruthlessness, her disregard for ethics when it suited her purposes.

As she reached the end of the article, Sandy's eyes fell on a quote from Cissy herself:

```
In this business, you can't afford to be liked. You
have to be respected, even if that respect comes
with a healthy dose of fear.
```

Sandy set the magazine down, her hands shaking slightly. Was that what it took? To be feared rather than liked? She thought of her confrontation with Brown, of the satisfaction she'd felt in standing up to him. But that satisfaction had been short-lived, quickly replaced by the reality that she might have made everything worse.

Almost without realizing it, Sandy found herself standing at the large chalkboard that dominated one wall of her office.

She picked up a piece of chalk, which grounded her somewhat. At the top of the board, she wrote in large letters, "STAY OR SELL?"

Beneath this, she drew three columns:

REASONS TO SELL
REASONS TO FIGHT
PEOPLE AFFECTED

Sandy stared at the empty columns for a moment, the chalk hovering. Then, with a deep breath, she began to write.

Under "REASONS TO SELL," she listed:

Financial stability
Escape from pressure

No battles with board
Escape backlash
Best for Prospect?

Her hand moved almost of its own accord, giving form to the fears and doubts that had been plaguing her. As she wrote, she could almost feel her hand lighten. How easy it would be to just walk away, to leave it to Cissy. Someone who wouldn't be fazed by threats from the DA or worried about ruffling feathers.

But as she moved to the next column, "REASONS TO FIGHT," other thoughts surfaced:

Edward's legacy
Responsibility to victims
Integrity of Prospect
Me (ambition)

Sandy paused, the chalk tapping against the board as she considered these points.

The final column, "PEOPLE AFFECTED," proved most difficult. Sandy's hand trembled slightly as she wrote:

Staff (jobs at risk)
Victims (privacy, safety)
Readers (right to know)
Board members
Advertisers
Me (reputation, future, relationships)

As she wrote each line, faces flashed through her mind. The reporters who had worked tirelessly on this story, risking their careers. The women who'd whispered their traumatic experiences. The readers who relied on the *Prospect* for honest news.

She stepped back, staring at that last point. For the first time, she grasped how isolated she'd become. In her newfound willingness to stand up to power, she'd alienated nearly all the powers around her.

She returned to her desk, picking up the photo of Edward. "I used to be good at making people happy."

But that skill, that desire to please, had withered. She'd stood up to DA Brown, challenged the grand jury's findings, and pushed her reporters to dig deeper despite the risks. And in doing so, she'd shed the comfortable skin of the agreeable, accommodating Sandy Zimmer.

She set the photo down, a wave of loneliness washing over her. Who was in her corner now? Mac somewhat, certainly Jane, maybe Lambert. Wilford definitely. She laughed at that thought. But beyond that? She'd made more enemies than friends in recent weeks.

Sandy turned back to the chalkboard, adding a new column: "CONSEQUENCES OF CHANGE." Under it, she wrote:

No more being liked
Feeling vulnerable
Who to trust

Yes, she felt exposed, vulnerable, unsure of her footing in this new terrain. But she also had to admit a strange sense of freedom in it. She was acting purely on her own convictions now, not on what others expected of her.

Sandy sank into her chair, reached into the bottom desk drawer, and pulled out a bottle of bourbon, Edward's stash, which had become her own. She poured a generous measure, the amber liquid catching the light from her desk lamp.

As she sipped, its warmth spreading through her chest, Sandy's gaze drifted between the chalkboard and the pile of notes on her desk.

She thought of what Cissy might do with the peace riot story if she owned the *Prospect*. Would she pursue it sensationally, damn the consequences? Would she bury it to curry favor with the money men? Neither option sat right with Sandy.

The bourbon softened the edges of her anxiety but did nothing to clarify her path. She stood, feeling looser, and made her way to the window. The city sprawled out before her, lights and shadows. Somewhere out there were the rapists, and the officials who were helping them hide.

She pressed her forehead against the cool glass, staring at her close-up reflection. She barely recognized the woman she saw—tired, conflicted, a far cry from the woman she'd imagined herself becoming.

She returned to her desk, picked up the telephone handset. One call to Cissy could end all this, setting her free from this burden.

But images flashed through her mind. Renee's tear-stained face as she recounted her assault. Gloria's determination as she fought to protect others despite her own injuries. The face of Lambert, surprisingly moved to be working on such an important story.

With a shaky exhale, she lowered the telephone back into its cradle. Not tonight. She couldn't make this decision tonight.

Selling to Cissy would be the easy way out. But at what cost?

Sandy leaned back in her chair, her eyes drawn once again to her lists. No easy answers. Each option came with its own set of consequences, its own potential for regret.

She thought about erasing the board, as if removing the words could somehow simplify the choice. But she couldn't bring herself to do it. Erasing the words wouldn't erase her reality.

"What am I going to do?" she whispered to the empty office.

Only silence in response.

Sandy flicked off her desk lamp, plunging the office into a darkness broken only by the faint glow of the city lights outside. As she closed the door behind her, she felt as if she were leaving part of herself behind—the part that had been so briefly sure of her path, so certain of her ability to navigate the waters of her world.

Tomorrow she would have to face these questions again, to decide whether to fight or flee, to stand by her convictions or retreat to the safety of being liked and accepted. Tomorrow she would have to figure out how to move forward in a world where she could no longer rely on charm and agreeability to smooth her path.

But for now, in the quiet of the night, she allowed herself uncertainty, fear, doubt. For now, she would go home, pour another drink, and try to find some peace in the midst of the storm she'd created, alone.

CHAPTER THIRTY-FIVE

Courage

Late morning sun filtered through the heavy curtains of Sandy's bedroom, casting a muted glow over rumpled bedsheets. Sandy lay motionless, her head pounding with the aftermath of last night's bourbon. The events of the previous day—the grand jury's whitewash, her confrontation with DA Brown, her late-night soul-searching—each brought a fresh wave of nausea and regret.

Wilford nuzzled up against her, snoring and drooling on her cheek.

She pulled the covers over her head, shutting out the light and the dog breath. Maybe if she lay here long enough, everything would sort itself out. Maybe she'd wake up to find this had all been a terrible dream, that she was still Edward's adorable wife, not the controversial publisher who had managed to alienate half the city in her irrational pursuits.

A knock at the door shattered her illusion of escape.

"Mrs. Zimmer?" Mr. Ames's voice was muffled through the heavy wood. "I'm sorry to disturb you, but you have a visitor. From the military."

Sandy's stomach clenched. *What now?* Had her article somehow jeopardized national security? Were they here to interrogate her? She wasn't thinking clearly.

"Tell them I'm indisposed," Sandy called out, her voice hoarse.

"I'm afraid they're quite insistent, madam," Ames replied. "They say it's urgent."

Sandy groaned, forcing herself to sit up. The room spun slightly, and she took a deep breath, willing the nausea to subside. "Give me a few minutes."

She dragged herself out of bed, catching sight of her reflection in the mirror. Her hair was a mess, her eyes bloodshot, her complexion pale. She looked every bit as awful as she felt. With a sigh, she splashed water on her face, brushed her teeth, and ran a brush through her hair. She pulled on a navy skirt and a lightweight floral cotton blouse, and slipped into the loafers she'd worn in the riot. Not her usual fashionable self but respectable enough for a visit from the authorities come to scold her. She added a string of pearls as extra protection.

Sandy made her way to the living room, steeling herself for whatever new calamity awaited. But as she entered, she stopped short, surprised to see a familiar face.

"Corporal Martinez?"

Gloria stood in an at ease posture—her feet apart, hands clasped behind her lower back, head up, looking straight ahead, face neutral. She wore civilian clothes, a nondescript dark blouse and khaki skirt.

"Mrs. Zimmer," she said, nodding formally. "I'm sorry to intrude without warning."

Sandy waved off the apology, gesturing for Gloria to sit. "No, no, it's fine. I just . . . wasn't expecting you. Is everything alright?"

Gloria's face tightened, and Sandy noticed the dark circles under her eyes, the tension in her jaw. "Not exactly alright," she said.

Sandy sank into a chair opposite Gloria, trying to ignore her hangover. "What happened?"

Gloria took a deep breath. "I've been reprimanded," she said, her words clipped and controlled. "Reassigned to a desk job. Punished. Managed."

"What?"

"Official reason?" Gloria's voice was bitter. "Because of 'conduct unbecoming' and 'unauthorized intervention in civilian matters.' Real reason? They saw the WAC described in the paper and obviously figured out it was me. They don't want me stirring up trouble, especially not now that everyone's supposed to be celebrating the end of the war. Especially after I did what I did."

My fault again. "I'm so sorry. I never meant for you to be hurt. I've messed everything up, haven't I? The story, the paper, your career . . ." She trailed off. She was destroying the career of one of the true heroes of that night.

"Sandy." Gloria's voice cut through Sandy's self-recrimination.

Sandy raised her eyes, meeting Gloria's steady gaze.

"You didn't do this," Gloria said firmly. "They did. The men who assaulted us. The officials who are covering it up. The system that won't face the truth. Not you. Not me. Not Renee. You're doing the right thing."

Sandy cleared her throat, trying to clear everything.

Gloria leaned forward, her eyes almost frightening. "I'll go on the record. Maybe that will make a difference."

"Gloria, really? Are you sure?"

"I thought I could protect myself by staying quiet. But I couldn't. Why the hell shouldn't I talk now?"

Sandy straightened. "What about your job?"

"Is the *Prospect* hiring?"

Sandy jumped up and hugged Gloria. "Whenever you're ready, we'll find a spot for you. Or I'll help you find something better."

Gloria smiled. "I'm kidding. Stop, really. But something else I want to say. When I was trying to help Renee, I saw this man in the crowd. He was an officer."

Sandy's eyes widened. "An officer? Was he involved in the fight or the rape?"

Gloria said, "Not the fight. I don't know but I doubt the rape. I don't recall his interacting with any of them. But he was there, he saw, and he didn't do anything on my behalf or hers. Most men aren't like him. Most sailors aren't. But I know the kind of man who's used to getting away with things, who thinks he has the right. I want to talk because I hate that kind of guy who has the opportunity to help but chooses not to, because helping women might mean hurting other men."

The fog of Sandy's hangover was clearing. "If we can prove an officer was involved..."

"No, don't. I don't know if he did anything. I'm not saying that. I'm just saying he was there. He witnessed it. The whole system is made of men like him, the military, the police, the government—they all close ranks when one of their own is threatened. I'm just done with that."

"It's a culture of impunity."

"I just want you to know why this is important to me, why I'm making this decision to let you use my name."

She took both of Gloria's hands. "I can't promise to protect you."

"I'm already losing the career I wanted. But I haven't lost myself."

"You are very much yourself." Gratitude washed over Sandy. "I wish I had what you have. And I'm sorry you have to have it."

"You do," she said firmly. "I've seen it."

"What if we fail?"

"We'll fail fighting," Gloria said. "We'll know we didn't stay quiet when we should have spoken up."

That was something.

Gloria said, "I can't be as involved as I'd like, not with this reassignment hanging over my head. But you've got my name to add to your story," she suggested. "We don't have to solve everything today."

Sandy was grateful for the advice even if she wasn't sure how to implement it. As Gloria rose to leave, Sandy opened her purse and pulled something out, which she set in Gloria's hand.

Gloria's mouth dropped open. "Where did you get this?"

"My driver Tommy knows someone who works with wood."

Gloria hugged Sandy and put the Cooper's hawk charm in her pocket. "Just what I need." And she left with a smile on her face.

Mr. Ames entered the parlor. "Excuse me, Mrs. Zimmer. Your mother-in-law called. She requests that you see her at her home this morning."

I've been summoned, she thought, certain that Olive had been enlisted by Wyatt to deliver the coup de grâce.

"I'll need coffee, Ames. Dry toast and three aspirins too, please."

CHAPTER THIRTY-SIX

Unexpected Allies

Sandy approached the imposing gates of the Zimmer Broadway mansion to answer Olive's call. What did she want? After everything that had happened in the past couple weeks, she couldn't imagine the impromptu meeting would bode well for her or the paper.

Sandy walked through the gate, up the path, to the door, each step bringing her closer to another confrontation, another reminder of her precarious position.

The butler met her at the door, his face still. "Mrs. Zimmer is in the garden, madam," he intoned, gesturing toward the back of the house.

Sandy swallowed hard as she made her way through the dark hallway, feeling like a prodigal daughter, if there were such a thing. Framed on the walls on both sides of the hall were artifacts of Wyatt's great grandfather's place in California history as founder of a bank that kept Gold Rush merchants afloat. Railroad ties, gold miner tools, photographs, even a framed gold nugget. The hall was like a narrow museum. Yet, she noted, it was a museum dedicated solely to the Zimmer forebears. Nothing on display honoring Wyatt or Olive or Edward.

As she stepped out onto the terrace overlooking Olive's stunning garden, Sandy froze, momentarily confused by the sight before her. Olive Zimmer, always the picture of elegance and propriety, was crouched in the dirt, in overalls, a small metal can in one hand.

"Olive?" Sandy called out hesitantly.

She looked up, a faint smile crossing her face. "Ah, Sandy. There you are. Come, join me down here."

Sandy made her way down the stone steps to where Olive was working. As she got closer, she tried to understand what her mother-in-law was doing.

"Are those snails?" Sandy asked.

Olive chuckled, a sound Sandy couldn't remember ever hearing before. "Nasty little creatures, always after my hostas. The beer cans lure them in, you see—much more humane than crushing them underfoot. Though that's kind of fun too."

Sandy tried to reconcile this earthy, practical Olive with the genteel society matron she'd known for years. "You wanted to see me?"

Olive stood, brushing dirt from her knees. "I did. Let's sit, shall we?"

Sandy followed her to a small wrought-iron table nestled among a cluster of rosebushes. As they sat, Sandy noticed for the first time how tired Olive looked, the lines around her eyes deeper than she remembered.

"Of course, as you know, I've been studying your peace riot stories," Olive began without preamble.

Sandy tensed, bracing herself for reproach. But Olive's next words caught her completely off guard.

"It's good work, Sandy. Especially your personal one. Important work. The kind Edward always dreamed of."

Sandy blinked, sure she must have misheard. "I . . . Thank you," she managed. "But I thought . . . I mean, given Wyatt's point of view on the board . . ."

Olive sighed, her gaze drifting to the carefully manicured garden around them. "Wyatt and I don't always see eye to eye—maybe that surprises you. Especially when it comes to the paper. Or Edward."

She fell silent for a moment, lost in thought. When she spoke again, her voice was tinged with regret. "Did Edward ever tell you about the summer he turned eighteen? When he first informed his father he wanted to be a journalist?"

Sandy shook her head, leaning in despite herself. She'd heard bits and pieces of Edward's youth from him over the years, but never this story, she thought.

Olive's eyes took on a faraway look. "Wyatt was furious. He'd always assumed Edward would follow in his footsteps, watching over the family's financial interests. They argued for days. I can still hear Wyatt's voice booming through the house, calling journalism a 'frivolous pursuit, for dreamers and rabble-rousers.'"

A shadow crossed her face. "Edward came to me one night, after a particularly heated argument. He was so passionate, so sure of his path. He begged me to talk to his father, to make him understand. And do you know what I did?"

Sandy shook her head, though she had a feeling.

"Nothing," Olive said, her voice barely above a whisper. "I told him to be patient, to give his father time. I was so afraid of causing a rift, of disturbing the peace of our home. I thought if I just stayed neutral, things would work themselves out quietly."

She looked directly at Sandy then, her eyes shining. "But they didn't, did they? Edward left for college, and things were never the same between him and Wyatt. I've carried that guilt ever since."

Sandy sat in silence, trying to process this unexpected glimpse into the dynamics of the Zimmer family.

"When Edward started buying up those newspapers," Olive continued, "I saw that same passion in him. And when things started going wrong, or rather, when he needed help to save the consortium . . . I stayed silent again. I let Wyatt make the decisions, let him tell Edward he was on his own. Even back when Edward put us both on the board, without our contributing a penny. By all rights, Wyatt should have begged off. But he wanted his hand in things, without contributing. And so I said yes, too, thinking maybe I could help just by being there."

She reached across the table, grasping Sandy's hand. "I failed my son, Sandy. I failed him when he was a boy with a dream, and I failed him when he was a man fighting to keep that dream alive. It makes me disgusted. I'm worse than Wyatt because I disagreed with what we were doing and yet I didn't speak up. I didn't act. I won't make that mistake anymore."

Sandy's mind reeled. This was so far from what she'd expected. "I don't know what to say," she admitted.

Olive squeezed her hand. "I want you to know that I see what you're doing with the paper, with this peace riot story. I see Edward in you, in your determination to uncover the truth. And this time, I won't quietly stand by."

Hope, fragile and tentative, bloomed in Sandy's chest. "What are you saying, Olive?"

"I want to help," Olive replied, her voice firm. "In whatever way I can. It's time I started honoring Edward's memory by supporting the things he believed in, not just paying lip service to them at society functions."

Sandy thought of the possibilities this support could open up. But years of caution in dealing with the Zimmers made her hesitate. "And Wyatt? What will he think of this?"

Olive looked a little sad. "Wyatt's had his way for a very long time."

They sat in silence for a moment.

Sandy decided to take the risk. "Olive," she began, "when you say you want to help . . . does that extend to the boardroom?"

Olive's eyebrows rose slightly.

Sandy pressed on. "The vote is coming up. On whether to sell the paper. I know Wyatt's position, but . . . would your desire to help include voting with me rather than Wyatt?"

The question hung heavy between them. Sandy held her breath, aware she might have overstepped, might have asked for too much too soon.

Olive's face was unreadable as she considered the question. The seconds stretched into eternity, the only sound the buzz of bees in the rose garden.

Just as Sandy was about to backtrack, apologize for her presumption, Olive spoke.

"I've spent my entire married life avoiding conflict, always deferring to Wyatt's judgment. It cost me my son's trust, and now, potentially, his legacy." She paused, her eyes meeting Sandy's. "I think it's time I started making some of my own decisions, don't you?"

Sandy's heart leapt, but she forced herself to remain calm. "Does that mean . . . ?"

Olive's lips curved into a small, determined smile. "It means, my dear, that you've given me a lot to think about. I look forward to hearing what you have to say to the board. Wyatt may find himself quite surprised at our next meeting."

It wasn't a definitive yes, but it was far more than Sandy had dared to hope for when she'd arrived at the mansion. With Olive's support, even just her potential support, Sandy's fights no longer seemed insurmountable.

As she stood to leave, Olive caught her hand once more. "Edward would be proud of you. I hope you know that."

Tears pricked at Sandy's eyes, but she blinked them back, nodding her thanks.

She wasn't out of the woods, but this was progress.

CHAPTER THIRTY-SEVEN

Olive's Organizing

Sandy fumbled with her rarely used Women's Athletic Club membership card. Edward had encouraged her to join, just as he belonged to the Olympic Club. His mother, of course, was also a member here. It didn't matter that neither Sandy nor Olive were athletic. Sport was just the club's original organizing principle, as was true of the Olympic Club. It was much more than sports by the time Sandy had been recruited, interviewed, and joined. And though she rarely attended, she did recognize its use. The club had hosted the wives of the delegates during the establishment of the UN last spring. They'd even extended dining privileges to women working in the Red Cross Motor Corps through the war. So it wasn't as if it embarrassed Sandy to belong. She just hadn't felt she fit in. Maybe because she thought of it as Olive's place. Now that didn't sound so bad.

The young receptionist's eyes widened in recognition—or perhaps surprise—as she welcomed Sandy and directed her to the Sutter Room, an elaborately wallpapered room with overstuffed sofas and chairs, a library, tables arranged just where a person might want to set down her teacup. It was so comfortably female, or at least geared for a particular sort of female, looking for a space of her own, quiet and comfortable.

Sandy paused at the entrance, smoothing her skirt nervously.

"Sandy, dear!" said Olive. "Come join us. We've been waiting."

Sandy was surprised to see a familiar, tired face. "Dr. Bayer? What a treat."

Dr. Bayer stood, extending her hand. "It's good to see you again. All cleaned up this time."

Olive smiled, looking pleased with herself. "I arranged this meeting, inspired by all I've learned in the *Prospect*. I thought it was time to do something concrete about the situation you described."

Sandy's eyebrows rose. Olive was full of surprises lately.

"As I told you before, your personal article was quite compelling," Olive continued. "But so was Derek Lambert's description of Dr. Bayer's work. It started me thinking about how I and this club might help. It turns out that many of the members read your piece and were moved by it, and by Dr. Bayer, of course. Women here may look to you like the world is perfectly made for them, but you might be surprised how many of them can relate to some of the stories, some of the experiences, you wrote about. No matter our wealth, we are still women. We have stories of our own."

Dr. Bayer nodded. "Mrs. Zimmer, I mean Olive, has some intriguing ideas about how the Women's Athletic Club could support us in caring for women."

Sandy was caught off guard. "Please, tell me more."

Olive leaned forward, her eyes bright with purpose. "After reading about the victims' needs—medical care, psychological support, legal advice—I realized we have a unique opportunity here. This club has resources, connections, and, just as important, awareness of the need for discretion. At least that's true for the members whom we would involve."

"That's right," Dr. Bayer added. "Olive suggested we could use the club members' support to create a safe space for victims of rape and abuse, a place where they could receive complete care without fear of exposure."

Sandy felt a surge of emotion, gratitude, hope, and respect for her mother-in-law. "Olive, this is . . . incredible. I never imagined this. But, what do you mean by *complete* care?"

Dr. Bayer said, "We haven't worked out the details," cutting off Sandy's question. Would abortion be part of the care rape victims could receive? Did Olive see that? Would she approve that? Sandy hoped so. But she understood Dr. Bayer's desire not to talk about it just now.

Olive broke in. "Your words moved me, Sandy. I realized I couldn't stand by and do nothing."

"Will you need my help?" Sandy asked.

"I believe we can handle the nuts and bolts," Dr. Bayer said, and Sandy was relieved.

As they delved into the details, each woman contributed her perspective. Olive outlined how she could quietly rally financial support among the club members. Dr. Bayer explained how they could set up a discreet clinic downtown. Sandy promised she would personally contribute to the cause.

The conversation flowed with only a few bumps.

"We need to be careful about publicity," Olive cautioned. "If word gets out about our location, or the people involved, it could scare women away."

"If we don't raise awareness, how will they know where to turn?" Sandy countered.

Dr. Bayer intervened. "Perhaps we can find a middle ground. Sandy, could your paper write about the service without revealing its location?"

Sandy pondered this for a moment. "We could . . . Let me explore that, how to share the information but not put anyone at risk. This is something I can handle."

Olive nodded approvingly. "And I can spread the word through trusted channels. We can create a whisper network."

This was so much more than she'd hoped for when she'd entered the club.

Olive said proudly, "We make quite a team."

"I can't thank you enough for putting this together, Olive."

She answered, "I've been a member here for three decades. I've poured tea, organized galas, gossiped about neighbors. And in all that time, I'm not sure I've ever done anything that truly mattered much to me here. I'm not saying no one else has. Just me. I haven't."

She straightened her shoulders, smoothing down her impeccably ironed dress. "It's time for that to change."

Dr. Bayer left and Sandy turned to Olive. "Can we talk about the board meeting?"

"I imagine you mean the vote?" Discomfort flickered across her features.

"Your vote combined with mine would give us fifty percent. We would still need to persuade at least one more board member to stop the sale."

Olive tensed in thought. "Charles might be swayed, but he's always been more interested in the bottom line than ideology. If we can convince him the paper will be profitable under your leadership, I suppose that's a possibility. And of course Adam is a wild card. I've given up ever knowing in advance what route he will take to any destination. But either of them is possible, don't you think? Let's just figure this out."

Sandy would have to change someone's mind. Yet as she had recently learned, change could come from unexpected places.

CHAPTER THIRTY-EIGHT

The Meeting

Sandy stood outside the double closed doors to the *Prospect*'s boardroom, her heart hammering against her ribs. She checked her watch. Two minutes to 4 p.m. *Cutting it close. My choice. No time for Wyatt to rattle me.* She smoothed her hair and took a deep breath. *Showtime.*

The boardroom's dark paneling absorbed what little sunlight filtered through heavy curtains, and the portraits of the past publishers stared down from the walls with painted disapproval. All except Edward. The crinkly lines around his eyes actually made him the only amused man on the wall.

The four other board members fell silent as Sandy found her spot. She made brief eye contact with each of them as she took her seat at the table opposite Wyatt.

Wyatt was still, his fingers stretched wide on polished mahogany. Olive sat beside him, appearing detached. Charles, next to Sandy, smiled, twitchy as a fat rat. And Adam, at the far end of the table, leaned back in his chair, his muscles taut. *He's enjoying this.*

"Good afternoon," she said, her voice steady. "Shall we begin?"

Wyatt didn't waste a breath. "I move that we accept Cissy Patterson's offer to purchase the *San Francisco Prospect* and incorporate it into her expanding news consortium."

His words hung sulfurous in the air. Sandy had obviously known this was coming, but hearing it stated so baldly made her nauseous. *My own father-in-law.*

Charles cleared his throat. "I second the motion."

There he is.

Olive recorded that, as board secretary.

Sandy let her face betray nothing. "Very well. Wyatt, would you elaborate on your reasons for accepting this proposal?"

Wyatt leaned forward onto his forearms, grasping his hands. "Let's be frank, the *Prospect* has been struggling for years. Edward's idealistic approach left us in a precarious financial position. Mrs. Patterson's offer would provide the paper with stability, resources, and the backing of a larger organization. It's the sensible choice. The numbers don't lie."

He paused, his gaze sweeping the room before settling on Sandy. "Moreover, recent events have made it clear that our current leadership is, shall we say, out of step with the realities of running a newspaper business in these times. Mrs. Patterson has the experience and the connections to guide the *Prospect* back to respectability and profitability."

He'd rather give it all to another woman than leave it in my hands.

Wyatt continued, "We have a fiduciary duty to manage this paper as we would a financial portfolio. A responsible board sees the need for steady, reliable returns over risky investments. The world is risky enough as it is without our joining the fray with reckless reporting. Our job is to stabilize, not to rock the boat. We're here as custodians of a legacy, not as crusaders tilting at every wild story that dashes by."

Every wild story? She kept her voice level. "Does anyone else care to speak before I respond?"

Silence. All eyes were on her now.

Sandy stood, pushing back her shoulders to feel taller. She'd rehearsed this speech fifteen times, but now she discarded her prepared words.

"Gentlemen, and Olive, I won't deny the *Prospect*'s challenges. Yes, we've struggled some as we've taken these risks that so worry Wyatt. But the risks are paying off."

She pulled out a sheet of paper from her portfolio. "Our readership is up fifteen percent through our coverage of the peace riot and its aftermath. Our ad revenue has temporarily decreased in the same period. But we're not just surviving—"

"We know the numbers, Sandy," Wyatt said.

Shaken at the interruption, she quickly recovered.

"Excuse me," Sandy said. "It's my turn."

Wyatt's nostrils flared. "I don't care if you feel it's your turn. Things don't work that—"

She raised her voice over his. "This isn't just about money, Wyatt. The *Prospect* has a unique place in San Francisco journalism. We're not afraid to ask hard questions, to challenge the status quo. That's not a liability—it's our greatest asset. And it *will* make us money. If we give it time. This *will* pencil out."

She turned to Wyatt, meeting his gaze—*Look at me*. "You often speak of respectability, but I would argue there's nothing more respectable for a newspaper than pursuing the truth, no matter where it leads. That's what Edward believed in. That's what I believe in. And I think that's what San Franciscans—"

Wyatt cut her off. "Pretty words, Sandy. But sentiment doesn't pay the—"

Not again. She returned the favor. "If we sell to Cissy Patterson, we become just another cog in her machine. *Her* machine. We lose our independence, our local focus, our ability to serve this city we all love. She and her people on the other coast take over. We lose control over our product. Our readers and our advertisers will find us less useful or informative. Is that what we want? I don't think so. I think what we want, what we need, is a newspaper dedicated to telling the stories of *our* city, staffed and published by dedicated reporters and owners who live in this city, and who love this city, and who want to tell the truth about this city, warts and all. Owning a newspaper is more than a business. It is an obligation. To our readers, and to the truth, despite the consequences. That is the true bottom line of this business, Wyatt."

She looked at each of them and then she sat down, her heart racing. For a moment, the room was silent. She had nothing more to add.

Wyatt reacted, his voice precise as a dealer's shuffle. "The truth is just an abstraction, Sandy. Let's look at something concrete. Your obsession with this riot story is jeopardizing everything. The UN bid, the city's reputation, the paper's relationships with advertisers and city officials. Is that what you want? To knock it all down? Nickel by dime?"

"No," Sandy shot back. "What I want is to run a newspaper that matters. And to succeed as a business as a result. Because readers—our customers—want a newspaper they can trust to tell them what's really happening."

"Edward," Wyatt said, "at least pretended to understand the balance between idealism and practicality. You're just a toddler in a china shop. Enough talk. It has been moved and seconded that we sell. I vote yes, obviously."

The first entry in the yes column, Wyatt—15 percent.

All eyes turned to Sandy. "I obviously vote no," she said, moving the tally to 15 percent yes, 35 percent no. The count was on.

Now it was Olive's turn. Sandy held her breath.

Olive sat very still, her eyes downcast. When she finally spoke, her voice was barely above a whisper. "I vote no."

She did it!

Wyatt's head snapped around fast.

"Olive!" he sputtered. "What are you doing?"

She raised her chin, meeting her husband's stare. "I'm honoring our son, Wyatt. He was the publisher; it's his vision we're talking about. As a board member, I want to empower his vision. We . . . I didn't support him enough when he was alive. I won't fail him again in death."

So much nerve to do that. One more courageous woman. It was 15 percent yes, 50 percent no. What would happen if it came to 50–50? She hadn't gotten that far.

Charles cleared his throat. "While I appreciate Sandy's . . . passion, I have to think of the paper's best financial interests. Recent events have put us at odds with city leadership, which is untenable for a business that relies on access to important news sources through long-term relationships. This newspaper has always had the trust and partnership of city government. In the newspaper business, Sandy, it's about ad revenue, but it's also about alliances. I vote yes."

Of course it was about alliances for Charles—he depends on Wyatt.

The vote was 30–50 percent.

It now came to Adam, a 20 percent shareholder. Sandy held her breath.

"Well," Adam said, drawing out the word as he stood. "On one hand, Wyatt's hand, we've got concern over harming our ad dollars. On the other, Sandy's hand, we've got a desire to invest in important reporting right now, regardless."

He walked around the table to a chalkboard, where he proceeded to draw a very rough picture as he spoke. It looked like a boat.

"As you can imagine, I learned a few things building Liberty ships these past few years."

Liberty ships? Sandy thought.

"The government told us we had to build 'em good and we had to build 'em fast. Figuring out how to do that was not simple until we decided to decouple the deck plating installation from the hull assembly."

For crying out loud, what does this have to do with anything?

"That seemed wrong at first. We thought it might slow us down. But by separating these processes, we actually sped up production and improved quality because we were able to address two critical components of construction at one time."

Wyatt stared at Adam, both confused and furious. But Adam didn't seem to notice. He looked back at the table, urgently pleased with his explanation.

"Don't you see? We've got to do the same thing here. Let's not hang on to a false choice. Let's separate our short-term concern over ad revenue from our long-term goal of building a stronger, more profitable newspaper. Let's do both of these things, because we can."

Sandy was almost panting.

"Investing in more and better reporting on significant stories others are afraid of might decrease our ad dollars right now, but it'll lead to a more robust, trusted newspaper, which will attract more readers and advertisers in the long run. Then we can expand to radio and then television—really! We've got to give Sandy's goal the attention it needs, right now. I'm in this—in the *Prospect*—for the big picture, over time. I'm not looking for a short-term return on my investment. If I wanted to make my money fast and be safe at the same time, I would never have invested in a newspaper. I'd have become a banker."

Adam stopped behind Sandy's chair. "I vote no. We're thirty-seventy. The motion does not pass."

Tears filled Sandy's eyes. Wyatt leapt to his feet, his face mottled with rage. "You can't be serious! This is reckless! We'll go under."

Charles shook his head, muttering. Olive sat very still, looking down.

Sandy felt lightheaded. *We've done it! We've actually done it!*

Adam raised his hands, calling for attention. "Strong reporting is going to lead in the long run to strong ad sales. I think it's a solid plan. Invest in what your business is designed to do." He turned to Sandy. "Now go get it."

She found her voice. "Thank you so much, Adam. Thank you."

He frowned. "This isn't generosity. I'm a businessman. I started a construction company at the beginning of the New Deal, a shipbuilding company just before a world war. Now I'm working on insurance and health care. Sure, like you, I do the math, but I also keep my ear to the ground. I'll tell you what, I think information is going to be critical in our future. Getting people information, clearly, accurately, quickly. The equation has changed. America is moving from tangibles to intangibles, from needing to own, to needing to know." He looked around the table. "The *Prospect*'s onto something. San Francisco is onto something too. I can feel it. And I want to be part of it."

Wyatt slumped back into his chair. "This is a mistake," he muttered. "We'll regret this."

Sandy stood, straightening her shoulders. "Thank you for your thoughtfulness, everyone. I know this wasn't easy. But I promise you, I'll do everything in my power to make the *Prospect* the best paper in San Francisco. And the most successful."

Wyatt's glare promised continued conflict, and she knew Charles would be a dangerous board member at best. *But now I've got a chance.*

As she gathered her things, Adam said, "You've bought yourself time, but now you've got to deliver. Don't just report the news. Make it. Show me I was right to believe in you."

She looked around at the portraits on the wall. For the first time, she didn't feel intimidated by their stares. Instead, she felt weirdly connected.

We're still in the game.

She caught her own reflection in the window—confident and determined, and admittedly exhausted. The job was making something new of her.

CHAPTER THIRTY-NINE

Legacy's Shadow

Tension lingered like marine fog. Charles and Adam made their way out, their heated discussion muffled by the thick oak door. Olive had left immediately after the vote, her eyes shining with unshed tears—of relief or regret, Sandy couldn't tell.

She let out a long breath, feeling the adrenaline of the past hour begin to ebb. She looked back to see Wyatt still seated across the table from her.

"Quite a performance," he said, his voice calm now. "Stay a moment?"

Every instinct told her to leave, not to give him any room to undermine her hard-won victory. But curiosity—and if she was honest, a hint of pride—made her nod. "Of course."

She settled back into her chair, noticing for the first time how the sun cast its rays across the room from behind Wyatt, whose face was mostly in darkness, his full expression unreadable.

"I apparently underestimated you. We all did."

What's his angle now?

"Thank you," she said flatly.

Wyatt leaned forward, his eyes glinting in the fading light. "You're certainly better at vote gathering than Edward ever was, if today is an example. I admire that skill."

The left-handed compliment—he was surprised she could count to a hundred—left Sandy momentarily speechless. Wyatt pressed on, his voice taking an almost paternal tone.

"Edward was a dreamer, always chasing something ineffable. But you—you've apparently got some kind of head for business, how to balance ideals with practicality. You do the math, as Adam said. At the very least, the basic math, but more than that, the metaphorical math. It's . . . surprising."

Sandy felt a wave of guilt. She shouldn't let herself enjoy even a jot of Wyatt's approval, not when it came at Edward's expense. "Edward built this paper," she said. "Everything I'm doing is because of the foundation he laid."

Wyatt held up a hand, placating. "Of course, of course. But you've taken what he built and run with it." He paused, his expression growing serious. "Which is why I hate to bear bad news."

Here it was. "What?"

Wyatt sighed, as if heavy with regret. "Someone's been combing through Edward's old business dealings. Specifically, from the time when he was struggling to keep the paper afloat, before you and I sold the other editions."

Something thrummed in the air between them. She tried to piece together what Wyatt was hinting at. "What dealings?"

"The kind that respectable newspaper publishers don't engage in," Wyatt said, his voice low. "The kind that, if they came to light, could tarnish not just Edward's personal legacy but the reputation of the *Prospect* itself."

The floor dropped out from under her, as she remembered the dark days not so long ago, when Edward had grown increasingly desperate to save the paper. He'd been secretive, working late into the night, holding hushed telephone conversations that stopped the moment she entered the room. At the time, she'd attributed it to stress. Now, a colder, darker possibility presented itself.

"Exactly what are you saying?" she managed to ask, her throat dry.

"Two things have been shared with me. First, financial fraud. Edward misrepresented the paper's financial situation to secure a rather large loan. That was obviously illegal. And stupid. Second, he's reported to have suppressed a news story that would have negatively impacted an important advertiser, who then did not drop their advertising plans. There is apparently a record of their communications. Records."

No, no, no! She knew the stress of running this paper, the impossible decisions to make every day, the compromises and accommodations. She knew what a bad place they'd been in. Her heart went out to him. *But Edward, no! How could he?*

"It's gossip."

"Whispers have a way of getting loud."

Wyatt himself may have made those arrangements he was blaming Edward for, she thought. Or maybe he was making this up to frighten her.

He leaned back in his chair, regarding Sandy with what almost looked like sympathy. "I can try to make this go away, to ensure these rumors never see the light of day."

"Then do it!"

He didn't respond.

"Are you actually trying to make a deal with me over this?"

Wyatt's smile was a razor. "Smart girl. You're right, of course. There is a condition." He paused, letting the moment stretch. "Drop the peace riot investigation. Let sleeping dogs lie."

"You can't be serious," she said, her voice barely above a whisper.

"Deadly," Wyatt replied. "You've made your point. You've shown the board, shown the city you're a force to be reckoned with. You're in charge. But pursuing this story further is both reckless and selfish."

Sandy wanted to hit him. "Selfish? How is seeking truth selfish?"

Wyatt's eyes hardened. "Because you're not just risking your own reputation anymore. You're gambling with Edward's legacy. With the future of this paper. With the good name of everyone associated with it. With the paychecks of everyone who works here. With the future of the whole city." He leaned forward, his voice intense. "Is that a price you're willing to pay?"

"And you're gambling with your own son's legacy! Why don't you make this gossip go away without trying to extort me? Why don't you want to protect your own name without leveraging that for anything in return?"

"Because that's not how it works, Sandy. We all make transactions."

"You just want this UN win! This is all about your power, your pride!"

The walls were closing in. She stood, needing to move, to think. "What do they say he did?" she demanded. "Exactly what? I have a right to know."

Wyatt shook his head. "The less you know, the better. Plausible deniability, Sandy. But I can assure you, if this comes out, it won't just be embarrassing. It could be ruinous."

Sandy paced the length of the boardroom, her mind whirling. Everything she'd fought for, everything she believed in, now stood in opposition to protecting Edward's memory. It was impossible!

"I have to think," she said finally, her voice sounding strange to her own ears.

Wyatt stood slowly. "Of course. But don't take too long. Secrets have a way of escaping, no matter how tightly we hold them."

He moved to the door, pausing with his hand on the knob. "You've proved yourself a formidable woman, Sandy. You've achieved something impressive today. Don't throw it away."

Then he was gone, leaving Sandy alone in the boardroom. She sank into a chair.

The past publishers stared at her accusingly. What would they think of Edward? What would they think of her, if she abandoned the search for truth to protect his lie?

Sandy's eyes fell on her husband's portrait, his beaming smile forever frozen in time. "Oh, Edward," she whispered. "What have you done?" She needed to get to the bottom of it, so she would know what to do. She had to talk to Jane. Uncovering other people's secrets was her specialty.

As the room grew darker, she remained at the table, motionless. The triumph of the board meeting was distant. Now, she faced a choice that would define not just her future but the legacy of the man she had loved and the newspaper they cherished. The *Prospect* was safe, for the moment. What price was she willing to pay to keep it that way?

She gathered her things slowly, her movements mechanical. She had decisions to make, hard ones. But not here, not in this room thick with history and expectation.

She took one last look at Edward's portrait before closing the door behind her. The man smiling back now seemed like a stranger.

CHAPTER FORTY

The Mechanics of It

Reeling from Wyatt's revelation, Sandy wandered through the *Prospect* building, almost without realizing it, finding herself at the door to the basement press room. She hesitated, her hand on the cool metal of the doorknob. This wasn't her usual haunt. The noisy, inky, oily heart of the paper's operations had always been Edward's domain. But tonight, she felt drawn to it.

The cavernous space was dominated by massive, gleaming printing presses, intricate mechanisms stretching from floor to ceiling. The air was thick with the chemical smell of ink and the musty scent of newsprint. A symphony of clanks, whirs, and thuds filled the space.

Men in ink-stained overalls bustled about, shouting instructions as they monitored the presses, adjusted settings, and maneuvered large rolls of paper into place. The floor vibrated with the rhythmic pounding of the machines; long sheets of freshly printed newspapers cascaded down, to be cut, folded, and bundled at dizzying speeds.

Overhead, a network of pipes and electrical conduits crisscrossed the ceiling, while banks of windows high on the walls let in natural light that mixed with the harsh glow of industrial lamps. It was organized chaos, man and machine working in concert to produce a newspaper.

It was really something, she thought. She ran her hand along the nearest machine, her fingers coming away smudged with oil. How many stories had these machines told? How many truths—and lies—had they spread across San Francisco?

On her first day as Edward's secretary, he'd brought her down here. "This is where the magic happens, Miss Abbott," he'd said with pride. She'd been overwhelmed then, intimidated by the noise and complexity. Now she felt strange comfort.

As she moved deeper into the room, something caught her eye. A framed newspaper hung on the far wall, yellowed with age but still legible. It was one of Edward's favorite stories—an exposé on corruption in the dock workers' union that had earned him both accolades and death threats.

She remembered the night the *Prospect* had broken the story, how alive Edward had been with the thrill of it. He'd swept her into his arms, twirling her around his penthouse.

"This is why we do it," he'd said. "This is why we matter."

Now that memory was tainted by Wyatt's insinuations. Had Edward compromised his integrity to save the paper? Had the man who'd preached the value of journalistic ethics stooped to shady deals and backroom bargains?

Sandy sank onto a nearby stool, suddenly exhausted. She'd spent her whole life trying to please the men around her—her father, Edward, Wyatt. Always smiling, always accommodating, always putting their needs before her own. It had seemed so natural, so right. After all, wasn't that what a good daughter, a good wife, a good woman was supposed to do?

Dammit. She was furious. At Edward, for whatever compromises he'd made. At Wyatt, for using those compromises against her and the paper. But most of all, at herself for always trying to do what someone else needed her to do—meeting their expectations, not her own.

"No more," she whispered, her voice echoing in the empty room. She stood, approaching the nearest control panel, remembering how Edward had explained each button, each lever.

Sandy thought of the UN bid, of all the hopes for San Francisco pinned on it. But she also thought of Renee, of Gloria, of all the women whose stories she wanted to fill this newsprint. The truth matters. But had Edward lied?

She flipped a switch. A nearby machine rumbled to life, the familiar whir and clank filling the air. She felt a rush. And then she flipped it off.

It's time, she thought.

A long-buried memory surfaced, sharp and painful. She saw herself sitting by her father's bedside, his once-robust frame now gaunt and frail. The doctor had just left, his bleak prognosis repeating in her ears. "A few months at most. He needs to get his affairs in order."

When her father had asked, his voice weak but hopeful, "It's not so bad, is it?" Sandy had forced a smile and nodded.

"Of course, Daddy," she'd said, patting his hand. "The doctor says you need more rest. You'll be fine."

Relief shone in his eyes, and Sandy had felt glad at having eased his worries. But now, the memory filled her with regret.

Her father had slipped away just weeks later, without ever saying goodbye to his siblings, without settling old debts and grievances, without giving Sandy the chance to tell him how much she loved him one last time. Because she'd been too afraid, too eager to please, to tell him the truth. She'd been too afraid of losing him, like she'd lost her mother. She couldn't afford to upset him.

Tears pricked at her eyes, but she blinked them away. She wouldn't make that mistake again. No more ingratiating half-truths, no matter how uncomfortable reality might be.

Sandy stood abruptly, pacing the press room. Her heels clicked against the concrete floor, the rhythm matching her racing thoughts. Where had her need for approval gotten her? Here, alone in a darkened press room, faced with an impossible choice between protecting Edward's legacy and upholding the very principles he'd claimed to cherish.

She thought of Wyatt's offer—his promise to make the rumors disappear if she dropped the peace riot investigation. It would be easy to say yes. To preserve Edward's reputation, to keep the paper safe, to win Wyatt's approval. The thought was tempting, seductive even.

But then she imagined having to look Renee in the eye, having to tell Gloria that her sacrifice had been for nothing. She thought of all the other victims, their stories silenced, their pain ignored. Could she turn her back on them?

Sandy paused in front of another framed article—this one Jane's, about women in the workforce and their contributions to the war effort. It hadn't been as explosive as Edward's exposés, but it had mattered. It had given voice to women whose service often went unrecognized.

Sandy felt a flicker of something she hadn't experienced in a long time—pride. Not in pleasing others or living up to their expectations but in doing something that mattered, something true to herself.

She'd been so focused on being what others wanted that she'd lost sight of who she was. Of what she believed in.

Sandy returned to Edward's framed article, studying those words with new eyes. "Oh, Edward," she whispered, her fingers tracing his name on the masthead. "What a mess."

She would forgive him for what he might have done. Not because it was right but because holding on to anger and disappointment wouldn't change the past. It would only poison the future.

But that didn't mean forgetting. It didn't mean compromising her own integrity. Edward had made his choices, for better or worse. Now it was her turn to make choices.

No more lies, no more evasions. Not even kind ones.

She'd restructure the investigative team, bring in fresh voices. They would reach out to their sources again, reassure them of the paper's commitment to protecting their identities. And they'd prepare the board for the potential fallout. Wyatt would fight her every step of the way. The board might turn against her again. Advertisers might pull out. But she was sure she was doing the right thing.

She placed her palm flat against cool metal. This machine, this newspaper, they were more than just Edward's legacy. They were a trust. And Sandy was done letting others dictate how she should fulfill that trust.

"I'm sorry, Edward," she said softly. "But I have to do this my way now."

As if in response, more lights flickered on, more motors whirred, and the massive rolls of paper began to spin. Sandy jumped back, startled, before realizing a press man had flipped more switches, preparing for the next edition.

She watched in awe as the papers moved through the press. Blank newsprint entered the machine, making a roundabout trip, emerging on the other side filled with words, with stories, with truth, a reminder of why she'd fallen in love with this paper in the first place. They were making something useful.

Sandy walked to the end of the machine and picked up one of the freshly printed papers, the ink still wet on her fingers. Tomorrow's headline stared back at her: CITY HALL STONEWALLS PEACE RIOT INVESTIGATION.

She left the press room, feeling light. She would call Jane with a new assignment—to find out exactly what Edward had done. And fast.

CHAPTER FORTY-ONE

A Publisher's Gambit

Sandy stood again at the *Prospect*'s boardroom table, her pulse thrumming with this Hail Mary pass, a gamble so audacious it bordered on lunacy. She glanced at the clock: 9:55 a.m. In five minutes, the most powerful publishers in San Francisco would walk through that door, and she'd attempt the impossible—collegial consensus.

She silently recited the pep talk she'd given herself that morning. *You have nothing to lose. The Prospect's already on the brink. If it fails, we'll be no worse off than we are now. But if it works . . .*

Sandy caught herself, surprised by the steel in her own thoughts. Just months ago, she would have been paralyzed by self-doubt, seeking approval from Wyatt or deferring to Mac's judgment. Now, here she was, taking the biggest risk of her career. *Edward would hardly recognize me.*

The door opened and Harrison Wells of the *Bay City Times* entered first, his imposing frame filling the doorway. At sixty-five, he was the elder statesman of San Francisco journalism, his silver hair and patrician bearing a testament to decades at the top of the newspaper food chain. He was a member of all the same clubs as Wyatt, had even been chosen for Skull and Bones with him at Yale. Though he'd never treated Sandy with discernible disrespect at the society galas where they nodded and raised glasses, she suspected he extended that grace due mainly to his connection with her father-in-law and Edward. Since she'd become publisher, his treatment of her had evolved from public sympathy at her widowhood to dubious amusement at her elevation.

Next came Victor Reese of the *Golden Gate Tattler*, a wiry man in his forties with piercing blue eyes and a permanent smirk that illustrated his attitude about the scandalous stories he'd always trafficked in, including his paper's recent work exposing Renee to the scorn of her neighborhood. Victor knew what his readers expected to find in his pages and he gave it to them, except when he'd made prior arrangements with powerful people who expressly did not want to appear in his paper. Sandy, of course, had found herself there, particularly when she was Edward's unmarried secretary, appearing on his arm at all the right and wrong places.

Robert Cavendish of the *Pacific Commerce Journal* followed, his round body and ruddy complexion suggesting a man more comfortable with balance sheets than city streets. She suspected Robert would never have wrestled with the questions she'd agonized over recently. His beat was clear—covering and supporting the views of downtown business. She was sure he found the *Prospect*'s recent coverage annoying from a business perspective.

Harrison approached her, his face unreadable. "Bold move, Sandy, your personal essay. Risky, but bold."

"Thank you, Harrison," Sandy replied, intentionally using his first name. "Sometimes the truth is worth the risk."

"Often," he observed. "Other times it isn't. It's key to know the difference."

"Welcome, gentlemen," Sandy said, gesturing to the chairs around the table. "Please, make yourselves comfortable." Her voice betrayed none of the tumult in her head.

As they settled, Sandy couldn't help but see the *Prospect* through their eyes. The boardroom, once Edward's pride and joy, now seemed shabby compared to what she imagined their opulent offices must be like. She pushed that thought aside. *We're not here about decor.*

"Thank you all for coming," she began. "I know it's unusual for us to meet like this—"

"Unheard of," Harrison butted in.

"But I believe we're facing a situation that affects us all."

Harrison leaned back in his chair, his expression skeptical. "And what situation is that, Sandy? Your ad numbers dropping below four digits?"

The others laughed.

Arrogant snob. But Sandy pressed on as if she hadn't noticed. "This is about more than just the *Prospect*, Harrison. It's about the integrity of journalism in San Francisco. Powerful forces in this city are attempting to suppress a story of vital public interest. They're using threats and extortion to keep the truth from coming out."

The room fell silent. Sandy could see the mix of curiosity and disbelief on their faces. She'd gotten their attention. *Don't lose your nerve.*

"Reporting on the peace riot," Sandy continued, her voice growing stronger, "the *Prospect* has uncovered evidence of widespread failures by city officials, the police, and the military in handling the situation. These groups appear to be covering up their failures. But it goes further than that. Not only are the police discouraging rape victims from coming forward, but we also have reason to believe a naval officer was present at the scene of one of the assaults and did nothing to step in."

The men erupted. Harrison shook like a wet retriever. "Do you have *any* idea what an unfounded accusation of rape does to a man?"

"I do," she answered. "This is not unfounded. And I also have an idea what an actual rape does to a woman. And how official refusal to acknowledge it repeats the crime. But back to the point of our discussion. I have a source ready to go on the record, though powerful people are trying to bury all of it. They're using the UN headquarters bid as leverage."

Robert Cavendish leaned forward, his eyes narrowing. "How does the UN factor in?"

"City officials are worried that if this story keeps growing, it could jeopardize our chance of winning the bid. They're pressuring us to keep quiet about anything untoward, using the promise of economic prosperity as a carrot and the threat of ruin as a stick."

She looked each man in the eye, one by one, knowing her next words could make or break her plan. Harrison's face was stony. "I'm here to propose that we work together on this. Divide up the reporting, ensure that the full, accurate story gets told, from all the relevant angles, no matter who tries to stop it. And that we don't let up, or give up early, or stay too shallow. This isn't just about one night of violence. It's about permanent accountability."

Sandy steeled herself. She expected resistance. Now it was time to show she could handle it. "By working together, we can create a comprehensive narrative that no single paper could achieve alone. Each of us will do well. Isn't that worth stepping out of our comfort zones?"

Harrison looked at her with steely eyes. "You're trying to save your job."

"I'm trying to make sure no one stops the story."

She saw greater support in other sets of eyes.

She pressed on, outlining her vision for how the collaboration could work—each paper continuing to focus on its own domains, sharing information while maintaining individual editorial control. As she spoke, she could almost see the story taking shape, a mosaic coming together to reveal a complex picture.

Victor Reese leaned back, a smirk spreading over his face. At once it occurred to her that he literally looked like a weasel, a rare case when she might best judge the book by its cover.

"Interesting proposition, Sandy. But the *Tattler*'s not in the business of collaboration. We prefer to uncover things on our own." There was something in his tone, a hint that made Sandy's blood run cold. *He's got Edward's story. That's where Wyatt heard it.*

"What are you saying, Victor?" Sandy asked, keeping her voice steady.

His eyes glittered. "Just that there are always multiple sides to a story. We've heard some interesting whispers about the late Mr. Zimmer's business dealings. It might make for a juicy exposé. Might make sense for us to plan our upcoming headlines about that."

I should have expected this. She took a deep breath.

Jane hadn't gotten her the answers about this yet. She didn't know what hung out there about Edward, what Victor knew, what was the truth. But she had to say something, with or without those answers.

"Whatever you *think* you know about Edward, I can assure you that you don't have the full story. I suggest you fully investigate it before you risk going out on a limb that may lead to retractions and legal trouble. But of course you know that. And that's not why we're here today."

She leaned forward, meeting Victor's gaze squarely. She was surprised that he didn't look at her as if about to attack, but as if he was interested in what might come next.

"You say the *Tattler* uncovers things. Well, here's your chance to continue to uncover something big and important. Something that affects every person in this city. Isn't that worth more than chasing unvalidated rumors?"

His smirk faded slightly and his eyes lit up. "Go on."

"Work with us on this," Sandy pressed, sensing movement. "You'll have exclusive access to parts of the story no one else has. Think of the headlines. WE SMELL A RAT: WHO'S BEHIND THE FAILURE TO FIND FAULT—THE MAYOR, THE POLICE CHIEF, THE NAVY? Is that titillating enough for you?"

For a long moment, Victor said nothing, his snaky eyes studying Sandy. The pause was painful. Finally, he said, "I won't throw out the story I alluded to. I'm not making any deal about that. We're looking into it. If it's real and it's good, it's fair game. Understood?"

Resigned, Sandy nodded. "Yes."

"But on the WE SMELL A RAT? The *Tattler's* interested."

Relief washed over her. "Understood, Victor. Thank you. But you have to really dig in, accurately, and not let up. We all have to do that with our share of the story."

"Okay, Sandy, I get it. Stop talking before you insult me beyond repair."

She turned to Robert Cavendish. "And the *Commerce Journal*?"

He shifted in his seat. "I'm not sure, Sandy. This kind of story . . . we were preparing to drop it. It's riling up the business people, our readers, our advertisers . . ."

Sandy leaned forward. "Think about the economic implications. The riot's affected—no, is affecting—businesses all over the city. And it will continue to do so."

"If the cover-up goes public, it could impact investor confidence, maybe even the UN bid," he argued.

"But you're not a government official. You're an economic newspaper. Isn't that exactly the kind of financial news your readers need to make their own decisions?"

She saw a flinch in his face. She continued, "Think of the exclusive angle you'd have. While everyone else is focusing on the social and political aspects, you'd be the one digging into the financial side of things. This would definitely attract national attention. You'd be providing an essential service to your readers. They don't want to be coddled or lied to. They want information they can act on. Come on, picture your headline—BUSINESSES WANT TO GET BACK TO BUSINESS—REAL LAW-AND-ORDER HELP."

"But the risk..."

"Is shared," she interrupted. "We're all in this together. Strength in numbers, Robert. We are diffusing the risk. What do you say?"

Finally, he came around. "We'll cover the financial aspects. Though this is dangerous for us."

"I respect that. I know. We all understand."

She was persuading them, leading them. Maybe not all of them. Yet.

Harrison stood. "I cannot join in. I stand on the side of editorial independence. Coordinating coverage with all of you would compromise our journalistic integrity. I will take no part in the kind of collusion that could put our paper and its board in legal jeopardy."

Sandy didn't give up. "Harrison, you know this isn't collusion. There's no price fixing going on here. It's just an agreement to support one another in fully covering this news. The story is too big for any one paper to cover it all."

"You have my answer. I will not collude. Though I will *continue* to encourage my reporters to investigate, as they already are, and to report it if they find anything worthy."

The way Harrison left the room, so full of certainty, reminded her of Wyatt, which made sense, as she knew their connection at least partly steered his response. *You might even call it collusion.* She saw his headline: GRAND JURY VERDICT DISSATISFIES CRITICS.

No matter. Against all odds, she'd convinced two of the three publishers to join her cause. It wasn't a complete victory, but it was more than she had reason to expect. Besides, she expected that Harrison and the *Bay City Times* would come around. They'd have to cover the biggest story in town if every other paper in town was covering it. She saw that clear as day, even if it was less clear to Harrison at this moment.

As the three remaining publishers hashed out details of their collaboration, Sandy felt a mix of emotions wash over her. Pride in what she'd accomplished, worry about the challenges ahead, and a new sense of responsibility. She wasn't just fighting for the *Prospect* anymore. She was leading a coalition.

They agreed on a framework: The *Prospect* would focus on the personal crime stories and the overarching narrative, the *Tattler* would dig into the political double-doings behind any cover-up, and the *Commerce Journal* would investigate the business and economic impact. They'd share relevant information, with each paper maintaining control over their own stories.

Sure, she still might lose everything—the paper, her reputation, and possibly face legal consequences. But the potential was worth the risk.

When Victor and Robert finally left, Sandy sank into her chair, exhilarated. The *Prospect* might still be the scrappy underdog, but it was no longer alone in its fight.

As she gathered her notes, Sandy's eyes fell on the old consortium map still hanging on the wall. The pins marking their former papers in Cincinnati, Charleston, Springfield, and Dallas, a reminder of what they'd lost. But now she saw them differently. Those losses had forced the *Prospect* to adapt. Forced her to adapt.

Ruby knocked on the door and poked her head in. "You've got a call, Mrs. Z."

Sandy was tempted to let Ruby take a message, but something made her pick up.

"This is Sandy."

"Well, hello there," a raspy voice came through the line. "If it isn't San Francisco's publishing powerhouse."

Sandy's grip tightened on the receiver. "This is unexpected."

Cissy Patterson's throaty laugh filled her ear. "I bet it is, kiddo. I couldn't resist calling to congratulate you. Keeping the *Prospect*, breaking that riot story wide open . . . you're running quite a noisy circus over there."

"Thank you, I think," Sandy said cautiously, unsure where this was going. "Sorry about your failed manifest destiny or whatever."

"I'm annoyed as hell," Cissy chuckled. "But I appreciate a good play. You outmaneuvered me, Sandy. Not many do."

"I hope you're not preparing to have me rubbed out?"

"Good Lord, I don't have those connections. Yet. Anyhow, I think we may have more in common than I realized before. You may actually be a publisher."

"I am."

"Well, if you ever need somebody to bounce ideas around with . . . I fly out West on occasion, and I expect you'll be making trips to DC if your paper keeps kicking up dirt in government business. Let me know if you'd like to meet to talk. Who knows? Maybe we can find a way to work together someday."

And then, in her usual abrupt fashion, Cissy hung up before saying goodbye.

Sandy sat back in her chair, stunned. There was so much to process.

CHAPTER FORTY-TWO

---◆---

The Dirt

"Wanna start with the lurid bits?"

Jane slurped black coffee in a chunky mug at the back corner table of the South O'Slot Diner, its long counter full of singles hunched over eggs, sausage, biscuits, and newspapers.

"Keep your voice down, dummy," Sandy said, feeling nauseous at the sight of grease on Jane's plate. Sandy didn't have the stomach this morning for any of it. And she wanted to avoid stains on her work clothes.

Jane set her mug down and began. "So I found the link between Edward's supposedly suppressed story and a *Prospect* advertiser, featuring Frank Rendell, son of Lawrence Rendell."

"Not so loud." Sandy looked around at the other customers—longshoremen, policemen, artists, mostly men, none of whom seemed to be listening to them. People had tipped their hats and waved at Jane when they entered. She was a regular. They were all regulars. Sandy was the oddity, in her expensive mint suit and good calf shoes, less girly than she'd been in the beginning but still several levels above Jane's uniform of dark slacks and silk blouse, with a napkin tucked into the neck.

"So Lawrence Rendell of Rendell Department Store?"

Jane leaned in, her elbows on the table. "The one and only. Looks like his son Frank was catting around with a young lady in the glove department.

Turns out she was seventeen. Frank got her drunk at the Pied Piper—at least he took her someplace swank for her trouble—and they continued the evening upstairs in a room he regularly keeps at the Palace."

"More coffee?" the husky-voiced waitress leaned over to ask Jane, who smiled.

"I ordered some tea, also," Sandy reminded her.

The waitress walked away without answering.

"So that's where her father found her the next morning," Jane continued. "In Rendell's suite at the Palace, not in the best condition. Bellman tipped daddy off. Couple months down the line? The girl made an all-expenses-paid trip to the Western Addition, to our friend Inez Burns for a top-notch society abortion. Everybody's problem solved. No story in the *Prospect*, of course. It never even crossed my desk."

"Ugh. Why not?"

"Apparently the senior Rendell doubled his ad dollars for six months afterward."

"Well that's all pretty unsavory."

"Honestly? If the story had crossed my desk? No way would I run it in the gossip column. Girl was seventeen, a kid. And you know how I feel about Inez Burns and that topic generally, and not so generally. More specifically, in fact."

"I know. I know. Everybody ought to mind their own business." She thought of Olive and Dr. Bayer and their secret arrangements.

"I mean, if it wouldn't go in the gossip column why would it go anywhere else in the paper?"

"Though it might go in the *Tattler*," Sandy said, looking around for the waitress with her tea.

"That's the thing. It didn't get into the *Tattler* either. Then, anyway."

"But why didn't it?" Sandy asked. "I mean this kind of story is their stock in trade."

"So maybe they didn't run it because they were paid not to run it. But I can't find a thing about that—anybody paying to kill a story."

"It could have been Rendell himself."

"Or it could have been Edward, using a bit of the increased ad dollars to do it for Rendell."

"But there's no proof that's true, right?"

"Correct."

"Jehoshaphat."

"Whatever that means, yes."

"If there's nothing about Edward paying Victor to stop the story at the *Tattler*, and if it's more admirable that the *Prospect* didn't run the story, then the only question is about the ad dollars?"

"And who cares about that?"

Sandy sighed, relieved. "How about the banking part?"

The waitress set down Sandy's mug of tea, letting it slosh on the table. Sandy pulled the napkin out of Jane's collar and used it to sop up the mess—the waitress hadn't brought Sandy one.

"This is where it gets bad. Edward took out a $250,000 loan at First Embarcadero. He was going to use this loan to upgrade the printing press, expand distribution, and do some aggressive marketing."

Sandy recalled, "When he had that new press brought in, he was walking on air. Preparing for the postwar growth and change he expected whenever the soldiers got home and the economy shifted." It was starting to come together for her. "He saw big things ahead."

"I guess he had his reasons." Jane had never been Edward's biggest fan. "Well, I talked to the secretary of the banker who signed off on the loan. Apparently Edward misrepresented himself on the paper's application, said he'd arranged for someone to offer a guarantee on the $250,000, and that's why the loan went through. But now it seems nobody can find any record of a letter of credit like that, or any record of any type of guarantee at all. Nothing. Edward just took the risk. He let the paper take the risk. And the bank missed it."

"He said he had a backer, but there was no backer? And that's why we got the loan?" Sandy's heart sank at this, first because it was wrong, and second because he'd put her in a compromised situation.

Jane explained, "I guess maybe he had a backer but they can't find the letter? Even so, that's fraud. I mean, we're paying off the loan just fine. And it would make the banker look bad to have made that mistake, so it isn't their idea to let this get out. The banker doesn't want the government involved. So this must be the *Tattler* instigating, not the bank."

"I don't know. It could be Harrison Wells and the *Bay City Times*. Along with Wyatt," Sandy said.

"Why?"

"I just think so. Harrison's aligned with Wyatt."

"Lordy. Wyatt's not the ideal board chair."

"Or father-in-law."

"Or father. What are you going to do?"

"I think we have to cut Wyatt off. Let's not give him the time he needs to exploit the story. We'll figure it out on the way back to the office."

As Jane wiped her mouth and rose to go, Sandy fished change out of her handbag, dropping forty-five cents for breakfast, and then another ten for tip.

"Jeez, Sandy. You think you can win her over with a big tip?"

"Oh, be quiet. I don't know why everybody likes you."

CHAPTER FORTY-THREE

Guarantee

Wyatt and Olive were the last to arrive for Sandy's emergency meeting. Settling in his usual chair, Wyatt used his pocket square to wipe the section of conference table in front of him before resting his forearms there. "Well, what is the purpose of this gathering? It couldn't wait until the next board meeting?"

"Let's consider it a subcommittee."

"With every board member present?"

She looked around the room at a small circle of nervous faces.

"Yes. A very important subcommittee. Let me catch you up. After our previous board meeting, Wyatt informed me of some gossip—"

"I do not share gossip."

"Wyatt shared some dangerous scuttlebutt he'd heard, which I now need to share with the rest of you, so that you can meet your fiduciary responsibilities as members of this board."

Wyatt's face went dark at Sandy's grabbing the reins.

"Of course, I knew, Wyatt, that you would want the entire board to be informed."

"What's going on here, Sandy?" Adam asked.

"Wyatt heard some rumors, which I then had Miss Benjamin investigate. I've asked her to join us today, in case you have questions for her."

The group rustled as they turned to look at a grinning Jane, sitting cheerfully next to Adam.

"First, a spoiled son of a prominent local business family got his father's employee pregnant, and then his father paid for the abortion of the young employee."

Olive gasped. Charles shifted in his chair. Adam and Wyatt remained quite still.

"The young woman is healthy, everyone's alright, and no police activity ensued. Properly, the *Prospect* did not report on this matter, as gossip or otherwise. Then the man's family business increased their advertising for six months afterward."

Olive asked, "How old was the girl?"

"Seventeen. It was obviously terrible behavior on the part of this wealthy adult man. Of course, I suspect if we decide to regularly report on such bad behavior on the part of wealthy adult men, we'll have to add a new section to the paper."

Wyatt glowered.

Olive said, "It seems to me that choosing not to publish such a story does not imply indiscretion but the reverse. Edward was demonstrating relevant discretion."

Adam jumped in. "Any evidence of quid pro quo? Anything in writing or whatever where we traded an agreement not to report for an agreement to increase ad dollars?"

"No."

"So can we adjourn this meeting? I have actual work to do." Adam looked impatient.

"That's not all," Wyatt interrupted. "Sandy, are you planning to tell them what else Edward has done?"

Olive looked in Wyatt's direction, hurt in her eyes.

"Yes, Wyatt. Edward apparently acquired a loan for $250,000 from First Embarcadero, which I am sure you were all aware of, for a new printing press and other necessary things."

Charles said, "I am well aware of the loan, obviously. It is one reason I am so concerned about our income, or lack thereof."

"Yes. Well, it appears that Edward claimed to have a guarantee for that loan, but there is apparently no record of such a guarantee. The bank would not like to turn over this rock, as we've been making regular payments on this loan, and they don't like the way it looks that they did not do their due diligence. They'd just like to move right along. But someone has now stirred this up, making trouble for us and for the bank." Though it was her plan to deliver this straight, just the facts, she could not stop her cheeks from reddening from worry and resentment at her husband and his father.

Wyatt broke in. "Perhaps you don't understand that to commit bank fraud is an enormous matter, business-wise, and legally, which leaves us, individually, and the paper, generally, at risk."

Olive said, "Wyatt, are you the one stirring all this up?"

Her husband's face went white. "Do not intervene in matters you don't understand."

Olive's lips quivered slightly. "I certainly do understand that it is shocking you would do such a thing to the paper and to our son."

Wyatt said, "I am protecting our whole family's legacy and the city's legacy and its future. If we can win the UN bid, our future is set."

"Not to mention your reputation," Olive growled, "which I expect is your real consideration."

"Seems to me the UN bid's dead in the water anyway," added Jane.

Even the tips of Wyatt's ears turned red. "What would someone like you—"

"Someone like me? Yes, I'm an outsider." Jane looked meaningfully at Wyatt. "So I'm capable of seeing what's right in front of my face, which somehow gets blurry for insiders. New York makes a whole lot more sense, geographically, than San Francisco, since every player in Europe can get there faster than they can get here. Besides, there's no way Nelson Rockefeller is going to let us get the UN instead of New York. He'll give all the money and property they need to win. And let's face it. None of our bigwigs, you included, can win a money fight with him. It isn't a *Prospect* story that's gonna derail that UN dream—it's the puny size of our money bags."

Wyatt gagged with rage. "The Rockefellers be damned! We will win this headquarters battle fair and square!"

"So none of this is worth the trouble," said Olive. "Neither the bank nor the government is prone to bringing out this fraud question."

Wyatt spoke up again. "We are seriously at risk of competitor newspapers doing so."

"And whom do we have to thank for that situation?" asked Sandy.

"What are you saying?" Though he knew what she was saying.

"Listen, none of this matters if we locate the guarantee," said Jane.

"Correct," said Sandy. "If we can find the letter guaranteeing that loan, which we are already reliably paying off every month, and which we are fully capable of continuing to pay off every month, and which has purchased our excellent new press, improving the quality of our paper, none of this makes a whit of difference. Am I right?"

"That's right," said Jane, looking straight at Adam.

He tilted his head to the left, pursed his lips, and crossed his arms. Then his gaze ping-ponged between Jane and Sandy.

Sandy said, "It's very hard for me to believe that Edward did not plan to file that guarantee letter. He cared so much for the future of this paper. He was so certain that success was just around the corner, as we all are." She continued staring at Adam.

Wyatt jumped. "You are sickeningly naive. Do you begin to know just how much money we are talking about? Only a handful of people could guarantee they would pay off the loan if the *Prospect* failed to do so. I for one would not endanger my family, such as it is, by doing so. That's why there's no letter. Edward lied knowing he couldn't do what he promised, and was not willing to back down."

Edward asked Wyatt for that letter, she thought.

The table was quiet for just a moment, before Adam cleared his throat.

"Well, this is embarrassing," he said, spreading his hands apologetically before the group.

Sandy literally gulped.

"Edward did ask me to provide that letter in support of his plan for the loan. I wrote it, I sent it, but apparently it was lost. I can't believe Edward didn't tell me about this problem. I'll forward the carbon copy tomorrow. My apologies to all of you for causing so much worry."

Wyatt exploded. "Are you claiming to have made that arrangement then and not now?"

"Yes, I am," said Adam. "I will get you and the bank that letter tomorrow."

"This is not at all believable. I do not believe you."

"What does it matter, Wyatt, if I give the bank the letter tomorrow? You'll have a carbon copy in your hands. No need to believe me at all."

Jane radiated giddiness. *No poker face at all*, Sandy thought.

Sandy answered, "That's what I suspected, Adam. I appreciate your forwarding the letter tomorrow. Wyatt, I assume that resolves your concerns?" She felt both queasy at the lie and relieved at its result. And very glad if it meant the paper would survive this chapter and go on to do more good work.

"I hardly..."

"Excellent," said Olive. "Then we're all done here. I have a meeting at the Women's Athletic Club. Wyatt, I will see you at home." She rose with an upright posture that made her seem much taller than usual. "Come to think of it, my dear, this might be one of those nights when it's best to stay over at your club." And Olive exited like a queen.

"Thank you, everyone, for coming so quickly," Sandy said. "I appreciate your willingness to resolve this matter. And Adam, I'd like to speak with you after."

Wyatt huffed out the door, followed by Charles, who was mumbling to his patron.

Adam stood and turned to Sandy and Jane. "I've got a full schedule. I trust you'll draft that letter and forward it to me to prepare and sign tomorrow?"

"We will. Thank you so much," said Sandy.

He added, "Let's aim to have no more snafus for a few weeks, okay?"

"We'll try," said Sandy.

"Listen, Adam," said Jane. "What would you think about cosigning a loan for a nice little place on Telegraph Hill for me? I was thinking—"

"Good afternoon, ladies."

CHAPTER FORTY-FOUR

Mending Fences

The steps to the narrow Victorian seemed to stretch endlessly, a daunting climb to a conversation Sandy both dreaded and considered necessary. In her hand, she clutched a folder of information, her knuckles white with tension.

As she approached the door, she revisited their last interaction. She cringed inwardly at the memory of her persistence, her singular focus on getting the story. How blind she'd been to the pain she caused.

Her knock echoed in the quiet afternoon. For a long moment, there was no response. Sandy was about to turn away when the door creaked open, revealing Renee's wary face.

"Mrs. Zimmer," Renee said, her voice flat. "I didn't expect to see you again."

Sandy swallowed hard. "Hello, Renee. I . . . I was hoping we could talk. May I come in?"

Renee hesitated, then nodded curtly, stepping back to allow Sandy entry. The tidy living room smelled of lemon oil, and a jelly jar of zinnias brightened the coffee table. Sandy perched on the edge of an armchair, while Renee sat across from her, arms crossed defensively.

"I owe you an apology," Sandy began, her voice soft but steady. "I was so caught up in uncovering the truth about what happened that night that I lost sight of the most important truth—the impact it could have on you. I pressured you when I should have been fully supporting you. I'm so sorry, Renee. Your mother was right to protect your privacy."

Renee's posture relaxed slightly, surprise spreading across her face. "I . . . Thank you for saying that. It's hard to know if staying quiet helps or hurts. I don't know. I think I don't want to talk about it with an audience, though. That hurts."

Sandy leaned forward, her eyes earnest. "Dr. Leona Bayer has set up a support system for the victims from that night, and from other nights. She's set up counseling, medical care, and legal advice if needed—all confidential, and at no cost to you—with no audience, only trained women, in privacy."

Renee's eyebrows rose. "Why should I trust anything associated with you again?"

Sandy winced. It was a fair question, one she had anticipated. "Dr. Bayer is operating independently. And the funding . . . well, that's coming from the Women's Athletic Club. They want to help, no strings attached. They have secured a private space—no signs at all—where you and other women can go for help. No one will know. I don't know who is there or where it is, nor will the *Prospect* ever divulge any information."

Sandy watched as Renee processed this information, conflict clearly playing across her face. "It's been hard since that night. I can barely sleep, I jump at every sound." She touched a yellow bruise on her arm. "I feel like the marks should be gone by now. The idea of talking about it again, that might kill me . . ."

"I understand," Sandy said gently. "Everything about this is your choice. But I want you to know that help is available to you and the others, if you want it."

Renee was quiet for a long moment, her fingers twisting in her lap. "Why are you doing this?" she asked finally. "Really?"

Sandy took a deep breath. "Telling the story wasn't enough. I want to help. You deserve support and care, Renee. All of you do. But it's not just me. Other women, lots of them, want to help too."

Something in Renee's expression softened. "And Dr. Bayer . . . she understands? About what happened?"

"She treated you at the hospital. She's been working with rape victims for years. She knows how to help, and more importantly, she knows how to listen. She'll direct things and train others how to do the daily work."

Renee's shoulders slumped. "I'm very alone," she whispered. "No one else can understand."

"You are not alone," Sandy said firmly.

She handed Renee the folder she'd brought. "Here's all the information about the program. Dr. Bayer's contact details are in there, her private phone number and a post office box where you can send a letter. If you're interested, she'll give you information about how to get their help. You can use as much or as little of it as you're comfortable with."

Renee took the folder, her hands shaking slightly. "I'll read it."

Sandy left and walked back to her car. Thinking it over, there were better ways to have handled that. There was more to do later, more to arrange. There was always more to do.

She slid behind the wheel of her Lincoln, having given Tommy the day off. Wilford placed both paws in her lap, then she started the engine and headed back to the city.

CHAPTER FORTY-FIVE

Prospects

Late for dinner, Sandy rushed down Ellis Street, Wilford's short legs working hard to keep up. No time to bark or snarl at Union Square's other rushers-by.

There it was—John's Grill, a boozy, white-cloth headquarters for those who currently ran the city and the politicians, cops, entertainers, lawyers and business men who conspired to run it.

She entered the warm vestibule and was greeted by Arnold, the maître d'. "Good evening, Mrs. Zimmer. Miss Benjamin is waiting at the bar. We'll have your table ready in just a moment, right under your photo."

She laughed. They'd only just hung a picture of her, standing with the chef, on the wall of the locally famous. It was silly, but she sheepishly liked being on that wall and assigned her own table. She'd somewhat consciously dressed like what she wore in the photo—black and white glen plaid jacket, with a subtle thread of gray running throughout, sharply tailored with strong, padded shoulders. Cut to hit just below the hip, with three covered buttons and deep, functional pockets, trimmed in black silk that caught the light as she moved.

Arnold handed Wilford a doggy treat, asking him, "Who's the ugliest boy?" in a thick French accent. Then he stood and looked away, apparently embarrassed at how besotted he was by the dog. Technically speaking, no pets were allowed in the restaurant. But this was Wilford, who was also in the picture on the wall, tucked under Sandy's arm, looking fairly arrogant for a smoosh-faced mutt.

"Thank you, Arnold," she said, picking up the pug and heading to the tiny, dark-panelled bar tucked into the restaurant's corner.

"Jeez, Sandy, I've been through two Manhattans already. I almost gave away your stool."

"It's like Valley Forge, the sacrifices you make," answered Sandy. "I'll have the same as last time, Jim, the Veuve Clicquot." She might have chosen the Dom Pérignon, but the Veuve was made by the widow Clicquot, and naturally Sandy preferred to send a few dollars overseas to a lady owner.

She turned on her stool to assess the bustling crowd and to note anybody interesting. She smiled and returned the waves of a city supervisor at one table and the fire chief at another.

Arnold arrived with menus to deliver Sandy, Jane and Wilford to their table, as promised, right under Sandy's picture. Taking her seat, and tucking Wilford under the table on a cushion Arnold had provided, she released the sigh of a hungry and happy person having arrived at the place where her needs will be met.

With the tinkle of glasses and murmur of conversation a comforting backdrop all around them, Jane raised her Manhattan in a toast. "We pulled it off."

Sandy clinked her glass against Jane's. "Well, some of it. I feel sick that nobody will be prosecuted. That breaks my heart. But I suppose we got enough of what we wanted to keep at it, right? We might get there yet. In a few years. Maybe?"

"Maybe."

Sandy's eyes then drifted across the room, pausing on a corner table whose occupants nearly caused her to choke on her champagne. There sat Wyatt and Olive. She had zero desire to see or talk to Wyatt in public. Absolutely not. She made a practice of avoiding him at every opportunity.

"What's wrong?" Jane asked, following Sandy's gaze. "Oh, brother. Count Dracula."

Sandy shifted uncomfortably. "You think we should go? I mean, I don't want him to ruin our meal."

"Don't be ridiculous," Jane scoffed. "We were here first."

"No, we weren't."

"Okay, well his back is to us. You won't have to look in his zombie eyes."

They went ahead and ordered the oysters Wellington and lobster bisque. Jane added the chicken Jerusalem and Sandy the lambchop. As Sandy would be paying, Jane was freed up to get everything she wanted, so she ordered a bottle of Sancerre, with no trouble pronouncing it. There would definitely be dessert.

As they waited for the entrées, Sandy found herself stealing glances at her in-laws' table. Something seemed off. Wyatt, usually so commanding, looked a little shrunken, his shoulders curving inward.

She watched as Olive reached across the table, covering his hand with her own, her eyes wide and generous, listening to him talk. The tenderness of the gesture and the look on Olive's face startled Sandy. She didn't know what she might have expected, after the difficulty of their boardroom clashes, but she certainly didn't expect to see that delicacy. It wasn't diminishing, what she saw on Olive's face. It was kindness. Could it be love? She thought of Edward, how she'd loved him and also the trouble he'd caused her.

"I need to use the powder room," Sandy announced, standing abruptly.

Jane frowned and looked at the Zimmer table, which was en route to the bathroom. "Oh boy, here we go."

Sandy made her way across the restaurant, her heart pounding as she approached Wyatt and Olive's table. Wyatt's back was to her, and she walked right behind him without his seeing her. But, as she intended, Olive did look up in surprise at her daughter-in-law.

Sandy exhaled as she pushed open the bathroom door. She reapplied her red lipstick, close to the mirror. She was washing her hands when the bathroom door opened. In the mirror, she saw Olive enter.

"Hello, Sandy," Olive said. Sandy turned and they hugged lightly.

Sandy smelled Olive's rose fragrance rustling up from the light crepe of her lavender blouse.

"How have you been? I was worried you might be suffering the consequences of our boardroom fights."

Olive's smile was thoughtful. "No, I'm fine. It's good to see you, dear. How are you?"

The genuine care in Olive's voice disarmed Sandy.

"I'm . . . I'm doing well. But really, how are you and Wyatt?"

Olive's expression softened. "We have our challenges. We've always had them." She pushed a tendril off her cheek. "But it's honestly easier now that I've decided to be more truthful with him. And Wyatt's struggling with some health issues. We're managing."

Sandy nodded, unsure what to say. It didn't seem like Olive wanted to share the details of Wyatt's health. She was protecting him.

Olive continued, "There's something I've been meaning to tell you."

Sandy met her gaze in the mirror. They were thirty years apart, but Sandy thought Olive looked younger than she had before. Or was it that Sandy was reading her as younger now? Maybe she'd always misread her before.

"My son wasn't perfect," Olive said plainly. "I know that. No one is perfect. None of us. But you were very good for him, Sandy. You brought out the best in him. You made him want to be his best. Don't doubt any of that."

Sandy didn't try to stop the tears that immediately wet her eyes, didn't wipe them off her cheeks.

"But you're still young," Olive continued. "There may be love in your future again. There may even be a baby."

Sandy choked back a sob.

"I hope there is. But when that time comes, don't lose yourself in that new love. You've truly become yourself. That doesn't mean you have to be alone to be who you are. But be careful who you choose. Listen to what he tells you he wants. And tell him honestly what you want."

Sandy blinked through her tears as Olive lifted her chin. "It's possible to love a flawed person, and to choose to stay with them," Olive said. "I've loved Wyatt all these years, despite his imperfections. That was my choice. You've never seen the whole of our marriage, just the surface. There has been good in it. But loving someone doesn't mean you should make yourself small. I did that for too long."

Her gray eyes looked urgent. "The right person will love you for who you are, not who they want you to be. Even if it takes time to become the person you're meant to be, to accomplish what you're meant to accomplish. They should trust your belief in yourself."

Sandy nodded, overwhelmed, and wiped away her tears with a handkerchief. In the mirror, they almost looked like mother and daughter, not their specific features or coloring, but the openness of their faces. She thought about coming to California, half believing she would find her real mother here. Maybe she had, in a way.

Olive squeezed her hand. "You're a remarkable woman, Sandy. I'm proud of you. And you're not done yet."

Then Sandy stood at the bathroom door and watched Olive return to Wyatt, sit, sip her wine, and smile sweetly at her husband.

Sandy made her way back to Jane, passing Olive's table, her eyes straight ahead.

"Everything okay?" Jane asked.

"I think it is."

"What did she say?"

The restaurant's front door swung open and Sandy looked out at the crowded sidewalk with so many people, of all kinds, and at the cabs and buses and sedans passing, headlights and horns blaring, so much noise and energy. She took it all in, and smiled.

"She thinks I have prospects."

DISCUSSION QUESTIONS

1. Sandy is still grieving her husband Edward three years after he died. How do her memories of Edward both help and hinder her growth? Is her memory accurate? Are her interpretations accurate? Can any of us fully know anyone else?

2. What are the gender expectations in the novel? How do they affect Sandy's journey, and how does she challenge or conform to these expectations? Is this familiar to you?

3. How does the peace riot affect both the plot and Sandy's personal transformation? Can you understand how it happened the way it did?

4. How does the novel portray the tension between journalistic integrity and journalistic business interests? Do you think Sandy strikes the right or wrong balance? How does this relate to today's media landscape?

5. Discuss the Cooper's hawk charm in the story. In your experience, does luck play a role in life?

6. The novel explores various forms of power—political, social, and economic. How does Sandy navigate these worlds? What does she have to offer that other powerful people in the story do not?

7. How does Sandy's relationship with Olive evolve, and what does this reveal about both characters' understanding of their own power, family, and independence?

8. The story touches on the aftermath of World War II and its impact on society. Where do you see suggestions of what would follow in the decades to come?

9. By the end of the novel, how has Sandy's definition of success changed? Do you think she's achieved it?

10. Throughout the novel, Sandy struggles with the concept of truth—both personal and journalistic. How does her understanding of truth evolve from the beginning to the end of the story? Consider specific moments where she must choose between comfortable lies and difficult truths.

11. The novel features several mentor-mentee relationships (Sandy-Jane, Sandy-Olive, Gloria-Sandy). How do these relationships differ from each other, and how do they contribute to characters' growth?

12. Wilford the pug appears at key moments in the story. How does his presence affect Sandy's development, and what might he show about her journey from Edward's widow to independent woman?

13. How do different female characters (Sandy, Jane, Gloria, Renee, Olive) respond to and navigate male-dominated power structures? What does this reveal about different strategies for survival and success?

14. The novel explores various kinds of silence—institutional, personal, and societal. How do different characters break or maintain silence, and what are the consequences?

15. Many characters in the novel struggle to trust others. Where do you see this? Why is the question of trust so powerful?

AUTHOR'S NOTE

When Sandy Zimmer first appeared as a side character in my earlier Jane Benjamin novels, I had no idea she would eventually demand her own story. But some characters refuse to remain in the background, and Sandy—with her evolving determination to succeed in a male-dominated industry and her commitment to truth—proved impossible to ignore.

The decision to elevate Sandy to publisher was inspired by a photograph that has stayed with me for years: Katharine Graham, publisher of the *Washington Post*, sitting in the *Post*'s boardroom wearing a bright blue suit, the only woman at an enormous table surrounded by men in gray and brown. Graham's memoir, *Personal History*, offers an essential account of what it meant to be a woman in power decades after Sandy's time, and reading it helped me understand the daily courage required of many women who dared to lead.

The character of Cissy Patterson, who appears alongside Sandy in these pages, draws from the real newspaper publisher of the same name. Patterson was a formidable figure in American journalism of Sandy's era, known for both her aggressive business tactics and controversial editorial decisions. (You can read more about her in Amanda Smith's excellent *Newspaper Titan: The Infamous Life and Monumental Times of Cissy Patterson*.)

These two women—Graham and Patterson—helped me understand the complex landscape Sandy would have navigated in 1945.

While the *San Francisco Prospect* is a fictional newspaper, the events that inspired this novel are tragically real. On August 14, 1945, as President Harry Truman announced Japan's surrender and the end of World War II, San Francisco erupted into what local papers euphemistically called a "peace riot." Over three nights, the celebration devolved into violence, primarily involving young navy enlistees who had not yet served overseas.

The official toll was devastating: thirteen deaths, at least six reported rapes, over a thousand injuries, and widespread property damage throughout the city.

The horror of those nights was matched only by the official response—or lack thereof. Despite witness accounts of police and Navy Shore Patrol inaction, no officials were held accountable. The San Francisco Junior Chamber of Commerce worked to minimize the incident to maintain good relations with the navy. Police never filed a single rape report. A grand jury, convened by District Attorney (and future governor) Edmund G. "Pat" Brown, completed its investigation in just two weeks, offering commendations rather than criticisms or indictments.

My research into these events led me down countless paths. I discovered that while the grand jury reports from the years before and after 1945 were preserved, the report from this crucial moment had vanished. This gap in the historical record—this silence—helped shape my novel's central conflict. In particular, creating the character of Renee, I sought to give voice to the unnamed women who were attacked during those nights, whose stories were buried beneath official indifference.

The novel weaves other historical threads as well. The Women's Army Corps (WAC), in which Gloria Martinez serves, saw over 150,000 women supporting the war effort, though their contributions were often minimized or ignored. And San Francisco's bid to house the United Nations headquarters—which serves as a plot point in the novel—was a real ambition in 1945–46, though the city ultimately lost out to New York, when Nelson Rockefeller apparently donated the land and considerable money in support of that bid.

I started my research by reading a brief passage about the riots in *City by the Bay: A History of Modern San Francisco, 1945–Present*, by Charles Fracchia. I found more in reporter Gary Kamiya's "Portals of the Past" columns in the *San Francisco Chronicle*.

I benefited from the generous assistance of numerous institutions and individuals. I am particularly grateful to Kris Kasianovitz and Paul King at the Institute of Governmental Studies Library at the University of

California, Berkeley; the San Francisco History Center; the clerk office at the San Francisco Superior Court; James Scott, the chief archivist of the Sacramento Library system; and Angelina Illueca at the Witkin State Law Library. Their diligent investigation helped me piece together what I could of a complex historical moment.

This novel would not exist without the support and guidance of my beloved She Writes Press team, Brooke Warner, Julie Metz, Shannon Green, Addison Gallegos, and Katherine Caruana; indie editors Anne Hawley, Louise Hare, and Carol Strickland; and my invaluable critique group, authors Gretchen Cherington, Ashley E. Sweeney, and Debra Thomas. Special thanks to Reed Rahlmann for a brilliant driving tour of San Francisco that brought the city's history to life.

For additional historical details, photographs, and discussion of the events portrayed in this novel, as well as information about upcoming works, please visit www.shelleyblantonstroud.com.

ABOUT THE AUTHOR

Photo credit: Anita Scharf

SHELLEY BLANTON-STROUD grew up in California's Central Valley, the daughter of Dust Bowl immigrants who made good on their ambition to get out of the field. She recently retired from teaching writing at Sacramento State University and still consults with writers in the energy industry. She has served as President of the Board of 916 Ink, an arts-based creative writing nonprofit for children, and continues to serve on the Board of Advisors for the Gould Center for Humanistic Studies at Claremont McKenna College. She previously co-directed Stories on Stage Sacramento, where actors perform the stories of established and emerging authors.

Shelley sets her historical mystery Jane Benjamin novels—*Copy Boy*, *Tomboy*, and *Poster Girl*—in 1930s and '40s Northern California, where a cross-dressing, tomato-picking, San Francisco gossip columnist spends her off hours investigating crime stories that never make the front page.

Her writing has won a gold medal in the Readers' Favorite Awards for historical mystery and she has been a finalist in the Sarton Book Awards, IBPA Benjamin Franklin Award, Killer Nashville's Silver Falchion Award, the American Fiction Awards, the IPPY Awards, and the National Indie Excellence Awards. She and her husband live in Sacramento, California.

Shelley is a member of the Authors Guild, the Historical Novel Society, Sisters in Crime, PEN America, and International Thriller Writers.

Looking for your next great read?

We can help!

Visit www.shewritespress.com/next-read
or scan the QR code below for a list
of our recommended titles.

She Writes Press is an award-winning
independent publishing company founded to
serve women writers everywhere.